Vivian Chastain is an transitioning to civilian li.. ... .amento, California. She settles into a new routine while she finishes up college and works as a bartender, covering up her intense anxiety with fake bravado and swagger. All Vivian wants is peace and quiet, but her whole trajectory changes when she stumbles upon a heinous crime in progress and has to fight for her life to get away.

While recovering from the fight, she falls in love with someone who is tall in stature but short on emotional intelligence, and this toxic union provides Vivian the relationship that she thinks she needs. Given Vivian's insecurities and traumatic past, she clings to the relationship even while it destroys her.

Vivian's relationships are strained to their breaking points as she continues to seek balance. She turns to her best friend for support, only to be left empty handed and alone until she finds comradery and care from the last person she would have thought.

CANOPY

Vivian Chastain, Book One

Liz Faraim

A NineStar Press Publication

www.ninestarpress.com

Canopy

Printed in the USA

Print ISBN: 978-1-64890-122-5

First Edition, October, 2020

Also available in eBook, ISBN: 978-1-64890-121-8

WARNING:
This book contains sexually explicit content, which may
only be suitable for mature readers, graphic violence,
self-harm, abuse of a child by a parent, abuse by a
sibling, alcohol abuse, and depictions of PTSD.

Chapter One

JANUARY 2004
Paso Robles, California
Elevation: 14,000 feet AGL

Scott shouted into my ear over the deafening roar of wild, whipping wind and prop engines.

"Okay, Vivian. On the count of three, I want you to take a big step forward and jump!"

Sucking in my breath, I held it as churning wind buffeted my body. Scott's goatee tickled my ear as he leaned into me again and shouted, "One! Two! Three!"

Just as I began to step forward, Scott's full body weight pushed against my back and together we teetered on the edge before tipping out of the side door of the tiny Cessna.

In the moment I stepped out of the plane, my vision and hearing stopped. And just as quickly, it all came rushing back. I took in the reality that I was plummeting toward Earth. My training kicking in, I briskly checked the altimeter strapped to my wrist before folding my arms across my chest.

*

Even in the shade of an enormous maple tree, I had a film of grimy sweat on my forehead, arms, and neck. I lay on my belly in the crunchy dead grass of Mom's backyard. Sweat pooled on my lower back. I rolled over and peered up at the broad canopy of the tree. Branches crisscrossed; the leaves hanging perfectly still in the hot summer air, the blue sky visible though the gaps.

I concentrated on the speckled sunlight as it danced on the backs of my eyelids and then flopped my arm across my eyes, listening to trucks rumbling in the distance on Highway 113. Dishes clinked in a sink. The back door of the house opened and closed with a rattle, followed by my brother's familiar tread.

I tensed and moved my forearm slightly down, so it covered the bridge of my nose. My other arm covered my abdomen. Otherwise I kept my eyes closed and stayed still.

His footsteps stopped near my head. I waited. Sweat dripped from my armpit and was wicked away by my well-worn T-shirt. The seconds drew out as he stood over me, likely considering his options. Another big rig rolled by on the freeway, its trailers rattling loudly. Grass tickled my ear.

"Vivi, where's Mom?"

My tongue was stuck to the roof of my mouth. The heat was too much, and I was incredibly thirsty.

"Viv-iiiii...where's Mom?"

"Just running errands. Should be back soon." I turned my head toward him and opened my eyes. His brown hair was tousled, the bangs hanging past his eyebrows. He scuffed the toe of his shoe in the scrubby grass. Joey was bored, and Mom wasn't home, which meant trouble wasn't far behind.

Closing my eyes, I turned my face back toward the sky. Sweat gathered between the crease inside my elbow *and the spot where it rested on my nose. Cautiously, I took my arm away from my face and let it flop into the grass.*

"Hey, give me the comics," Joey demanded. The newspaper I had been reading rustled as he snatched it up. His footsteps crunched away, and I heard wood creak as he climbed up the ladder that was leaning against the house.

Thirsty, I stood up. Stars dazzled in front of my eyes and my head and hands tingled. Once the dizziness had passed, I trotted across the small yard toward the back door. My worn-out sneaker slapped onto the concrete of the shady back porch when Joey called out. I froze, one foot on the porch, the other on the old brick walkway. Standing there in silence, I waited.

"Viv, come up here." Joey's voice was syrupy, traveling down to me from the roof.

"No, thanks. I got stuff to do," I said, still not moving.

"Viiiiivv, up here. Now." His voice took on a sharp edge.

I clenched my jaw as my temper started to rise.

"Joey! I got stuff to do. I'm goin' inside." I stepped up onto the porch and strode resolutely to the sliding glass door.

"Vivian," Joey said, taunting. "Come up here now, or I'll tell Mom it was you who broke the piano bench."

Joey had hit the nail on the head. He knew I would do anything not to get into trouble with Mom. My hand slipped off the cool metal handle of the sliding glass door. I spun on my heel and marched to the ladder. It was huge and weathered, the white paint peeling to reveal graying wood below. I nimbly climbed up and made the scary transition from the ladder to the roof, swinging my leg over the top rung.

The sun was brighter up there, and I squinted as I walked to Joey.

"What!" I balled my hands up into little fists, my mouth set.

Joey pointed to the tops of some trees growing over the far side of the house.

"Go over there and pick me some loquats." He fanned himself with the comics and fixed his muddy-brown eyes on mine.

I didn't move and didn't respond, glaring at him. Joey stood up, walked straight up to me, and punched my upper arm as hard as he could. I staggered, trying to keep my balance on the steeply pitched roof. Tears instantly welled up, and I bit back a yelp of pain. My arm throbbed deeply, but I wasn't going to give him the satisfaction of making me cry.

The heat from the roof radiated through the soles of my sneakers as I willed the tears not to fall. Breaking eye contact with him, I walked carefully up and over the peak of the roof. The trees were planted close to the house, so the branches hung low over the gutters, heavy with ripe fruit. Holding the hem of my T-shirt out, I created a pouch and began picking loquats until I had gotten the closest ones. Inching closer to the edge, the toe of my shoe over the gutter, I stretched my short arms up to pick a few more.

When the pouch of my shirt was full, I squatted down in the shade of the tree and chose a fat, golden loquat. Biting into it, I was thrilled with how sweet and juicy it was. Carefully, I ate around the large seeds and then tossed them into the side yard. I wiped my sticky fingers on my shorts.

Standing up, ready to face Joey again, I heard a heavy wooden thunk. Walking back up and over the peak of the roof, I didn't see Joey. I scurried over to where the ladder had been. Joey stood in the yard, looking up at me. He barked out a malicious laugh that instantly piqued my anger. With my sore right arm tucked into my side, still holding the hem of my shirt, I grabbed a ripe loquat and threw it at Joey as hard as I could. I missed. The loquat bounced across the dead grass. Joey's laughter immediately stopped. I threw another, this time hitting him in the gut. The overripe fruit left a smear of juice on his raggedy, striped, hand-me-down polo shirt. I threw two more. Both fell short.

Recalibrating, I continued angrily throwing until all of the fruit was gone. I dropped my hands to my sides, the sun beating down. Joey gaped at me. A long pause followed while he decided what to do. He finally blinked and spoke.

"Look at you up there. Stuck like a stupid stray cat. With your stupid black hair and stupid blue eyes. You don't even look like anybody in the family. You're not a real Chastain."

My bottom lip trembled, but I held in the tears. "Good! Maybe I don't wanna be a Chastain. You're all terrible people!"

His eyes narrowed as he turned and walked toward the back door. "Good luck getting off the roof, Vivi," he said over his shoulder.

"Joey! Joey! Joey! Bring back the ladder!" I screamed as hard and loud as I could. "Joey! Joey! Come onnnn!"

Trying to stay calm, I looked around the backyard. The wooden ladder lay useless in the dirt, surrounded by smears of loquat. I peered over the edge, trying to judge how high up I was. It was a straight drop to hard packed dirt. I walked back over to the loquat trees.

"Joey! Come onnn!" I shouted again, as I tested the branches. I was too heavy to shimmy down the branches to the trunk. Dishes clinked at the neighbor's house, and I looked across the side yard. Old Mrs. Hadler was standing at her sink looking out of the window at me. She shook her head with a disapproving glare and then went back to washing her dishes. Embarrassed, I stopped shouting and walked around to the front of the house. It was still high up, but there was nice green grass below. Mom always watered the front yard and made sure the planters on the porch had flowers in them; meanwhile, she let the backyard die.

Sweat dripped down my face and neck. It was the hottest point of the day, and the street hummed with the sound of air conditioners working hard. Nobody was out except for Gail, who lived half a block away. She pedaled by on her bicycle, dressed in her usual hospital scrubs, and looked at me with concern.

Anger coursed through me and frustrated tears started to well up again. I let a few silently roll down my grimy cheeks. The salty tears hung on my jaw before dripping down onto the roof, where they evaporated. I wiped my face with the front of my shirt, clenched my jaw, and stepped off the roof.

*

The wind blasted past my ears like a freight train. Behind goggles, I looked at the vineyards and ag land below, and then out toward the coastal mountains on the horizon. The beauty of it all brought a smile to my face. I opened my mouth to give a shout of victory, but the wind immediately sucked away all the moisture from my lips and tongue. I didn't even need to breathe because the air forced itself into my nose and mouth, inflating my lungs.

Scott hooted with excitement behind me and extended his arm around me as he checked his altimeter. Grabbing my forehead, he pulled my head back against his shoulder, and yanked the ripcord. My whole body racked hard against the harness straps as the parachute deployed and stopped our freefall. Instantly the roaring wind was gone, and we were surrounded by a serene silence as we floated over the valley, descending slowly.

I licked my impossibly dry lips and scanned the flat ground below, taking in the lay of the land and the sheer, raw, unapologetic realness of it. Green grasses, dark-brown tilled earth, narrow country roads.

I let out a whoop. Scott took that as his cue and began narrating to me what his next steps would be as he prepared to land us on the airfield.

I could see my best friend Jared standing in the landing zone far below, head tilted back, hand across his brow shielding his eyes from the sun. He tugged at the collar of his jumpsuit.

As we got closer Jared walked off the landing zone and stood by the jump school's van. Scott pulled down hard on both toggles just before we landed. My feet hit the ground, and I tried to gauge how fast I needed to run. It was similar to getting on a treadmill that had already started.

My feet skimmed and skipped along before a gust of wind caught our parachute and yanked us abruptly backward. Scott steadied us and quickly began unbuckling all the clasps that secured the back of my harness to the front of his.

I pulled off my goggles, wiped my eyes, and tried to find some words. Scott patted me on the back. I turned around and hugged him. Although a total stranger, I had just entrusted my life to him.

Jared was nervously bouncing from one foot to the other.

"How was it?" he asked, grinning, his chipped front tooth gleaming.

"Ahhh, pffft, I can't even describe it. Nothing like the static line jumps we did in the Army. Jared. Get up there!" I pointed skyward.

Jared stepped in close and hugged me, his bristly jaw scraping against my cheek before he marched off toward the tarmac. I stood in the landing zone amid short cropped brown grass and ground squirrel holes. In that moment I was totally at peace. My mind was blissfully quiet inside the cloud of adrenaline pumping through my veins. I focused on the sound of a flag flapping sharply in the distance.

Rather than riding in the van back to the hanger, I decided to stay out on the field to watch Jared's jump. To absorb the sun on my skin and enjoy the absence of the sounds of the city. Eyes closed, I took it all in, through every pore, relishing the moment, telling myself to hold fast. To save that feeling for the dark days.

Once Jared had landed, full of hoots and hollers and frantic leftover energy, I refocused and joined him in his celebratory jumping around. After returning the rental gear and saying our goodbyes, the two of us piled into his ancient Audi. The seats were well-worn leather, the old springs in them nearly flattened. The car smelled of mildewed floor mats, Jared's gym bag, and something else I couldn't quite pinpoint.

Jared expertly navigated the twists of Highway 46 and Old Creek Road, heading back to Morro Bay. He shifted between gears smoothly and handled the steering wheel like it was an extension of his body. He played Van Morrison and Kenny Rogers cassettes while speaking in his low, baritone voice.

That jump was different than the static line jumps I had done while in the Army. I hadn't been jumping into the unknown, armed to protect, but also to kill. On that day I was jumping for the thrill of it, no goal or mission after I hit the ground. My mind flitted around memories of past jumps, and I started to tense up.

I rolled the window down, hung my hand outside, and focused on the sensation of the cool breeze flowing across my fingertips. The adrenaline from the freefall began to recede but those old thoughts persisted, leaving behind a fatigue that threatened to consume me. I interrupted Jared midsentence.

"Hey. I'm super hungry all of a sudden. Can we grab something on the way back to your house?"

Suddenly screaming for calories, my entire body began shaking uncontrollably. Muscles in my thighs and lower back thrummed and my hands shook. I grabbed my water bottle off the floorboard and downed every last drop.

Jared cut over to Highway 1 and the Pacific Ocean burst into view.

I looked at Jared and saw a sparkle in his eyes. I knew how incredulous he was about living so close to the ocean.

"I never get over the fact that I live here! Pinch me!" There was a touch of awe in his voice. I punched his upper arm. He yelped in mock pain, and we both laughed.

"Damn, Viv. I need to remember not to tempt you."

"I think we're both punchy from those free falls. Fucking feed me already!"

Jared cruised the car down Highway 1, sandwiched between the coastal mountains and the ocean. I watched Morro Rock get larger and larger as we approached town.

Soon enough, we were drinking beers and scarfing down black beans, rice, tacos, and tamales. I didn't taste any of it. I was more concerned with getting calories into my body as quickly as possible before I passed out. The shakes and muscle spasms finally subsided as I sat back from the empty plates.

The patio of the restaurant was mostly deserted as I drained my water glass. Jared slid his water toward me.

"Wow, I've never seen such a performance," he said, looking at my empty plate, water glasses, and beer bottles.

"That jump totally depleted me. It's the weirdest thing. I feel like I could sleep for a week." I stifled a burp.

Jared drove us the three final blocks to his house. As soon as we arrived, I meticulously brushed and flossed my teeth, peed, and changed into boxers and a tank top. Laying down on the futon in Jared's spare room, I pulled a blanket up to my chin and finally allowed the tidal wave of fatigue to take over.

Sleep was intermittent as I wrestled my demons and ground my teeth mercilessly. At one point, I woke and saw Jared standing in the doorway, checking on me. The dying light of the day cast an orange and red light over him. Later, I woke to hear Jared washing dishes, Pink Floyd on the record player. At another point, a full-body flinch jerked me to the surface. My hands were clenched into fists, protecting my face. My arms and legs tangled up in the light blanket. Jared poked his head around the corner of the doorframe, concern on his face. He took a deep breath, his barrel chest and broad shoulders expanding as he did so. He let out the breath, rubbing his palm along the top of his high and tight haircut. I closed my eyes and heard Jared step out, gently closing the door. That was followed by the sound of Jared flipping light switches, closing windows, and locking the front door. I knew from when I had been his roommate before that he couldn't sleep until he knew the house was secure. I drifted off knowing that, as always, Jared had my back.

Chapter Two

The sun was just beginning to rise over the hills behind the house and fatigue hung heavy on my body, but it was chased away by a glimmer of excitement sparked by having a bit more time on the coast with Jared before having to head home to Sacramento.

After a few minutes of contemplating Bruce Lee's abs on a poster that was thumbtacked to the wall, I got up and straightened out the blanket on the futon before opening the sliding glass door leading from the guest room to a small wooden balcony. The air was brisk and still as I stepped out onto weathered wood. The sound of waves breaking on the distant shore came clearly to me. I looked past Highway 1 at the vast horizon and the Pacific Ocean laid out before me, interrupted only by Morro Rock. Watery blue sky met choppy gray water. Massive cargo ships and oil drilling platforms were mere specks in the distance.

Drawing in a deep breath, I caught the scent of the tide and eucalyptus trees. Slowly and methodically, I stretched my cold, stiff muscles by running through the routine I had done countless times in PT formation in the Army. I was at ease in that moment. The sun had risen over the mountains enough to glint off the water.

Body and mind alert, I went back inside and stripped out of my boxers and tank top and slid into some running gear: slippery two-ply running socks, compression shorts, a sports bra, an old T-shirt, and some lightweight running shorts. Sitting on the floor, I laced up my well-worn shoes. They still had a few miles left in them.

I glided across the hall to the bathroom and closed the door without a sound. Moving around silently was something I had mastered, that movement affectionately deemed "the creep" by soldiers in my old unit.

Once in the bathroom, I peed, washed my hands, brushed my hair and teeth, and then pulled my jet-black hair back into a tight, flawless bun. Anxiety started to well up in my abdomen, its tendrils wrapping around my organs, and ever so gently squeezing. I looked at myself in the large mirror over the sink, taking inventory. Checking in. I wasn't happy with the weakness I thought I saw creeping in around my eyes.

I stepped back from the sink and raised my hands up. Drawing in a short breath, I slapped myself fiercely across the fronts of my thighs. The sound was incredibly loud in the small bathroom. I bit the inside of my cheek as my hands and quads instantly lit up with the sudden pain from the slaps. Red, hand-shaped welts immediately rose up on the flesh of each of my legs. I stood there for a moment, taking in the burning sting that followed. It wasn't enough. I held my hands up and viciously slapped myself again. My thighs were on fire and my breath caught in my throat. I stood silently, jaw clenched, lungs tight, and waited until the burn subsided.

I quietly exited the bathroom but found that trying to use the creep was pointless. Jared was in the living room, the pale light of the rising sun filtering in. He was dressed in running gear and stood facing me. The curious look on his face showed clearly that he had heard the slaps. He scanned me as I stood in the doorway. Spotting the welts, he locked eyes with me, a small crease of concern around his mouth.

"Let's go," I said, and headed for the door.

We jogged west down San Jacinto Street and crossed Highway 1, and then continued along San Jacinto until it petered out to the beach access at the end of Azure Street. At the damp sand along the shoreline, we finally headed south toward Morro Rock and the three enormous smokestacks at Morro Bay Mutual Water Company.

We ran in silence. The only sounds were our feet pounding the wet sand, the waves breaking, and our breathing as it became heavier. I kept my eyes focused on Morro Rock as we fell into a comfortable pace, running in step side by side. My thoughts drifted. I tried to force myself back to focus on the act of running, but the rhythmic movement allowed my mind to slip. We had run together so many times that Jared knew I tended to drift.

*

I hit the grass hard, my knees buckling under me. A shock of pain bloomed in my feet, but it didn't last. I stood slowly and walked toward the front door. The brass knob was warm in my hot hand. The door was made of thick wood, painted white, with nine small square windows in a grid. Three columns of three. The window closest to the door handle was not made of smooth, clear glass like the others. It was cloudy, scratched-up plastic from an old break-in. The door and porch had a thin layer of dust on them from the dry summer and nearby tomato harvest.

I turned the knob, pushed the heavy door open, and sighed in relief as the cool air hit my hot skin. Once I'd closed the door, I strode into the kitchen and turned on the sink, reveling in the cold water as it flowed over my hands and forearms.

I leaned over the sink and splashed handful after handful of water on my red cheeks and the back of my neck. Feeling better, I turned off the sink and pulled a clean dish towel out of the drawer and dried off my hands, arms, face, and neck. When finished, I hung the towel on the handle of the refrigerator.

I pulled a glass out of the cabinet, filled it to the top with cool water, and leaned against the counter while I drank it down in large gulps. The sensation of the cold water in my mouth and throat was a relief. I drained the glass and turned to refill it when I saw Joey standing near the refrigerator. I stopped, glass in hand midair over the sink.

"See, you didn't need my help, did you, dummy?" He flipped his head to the side to get his bangs out of his eyes.

I squinted at him, making my face as stern as I could. "Yeah, I got down. I don't need your help, Joey, ever. For anything."

Joey opened his mouth, about to talk, when both of us froze. We listened as the garage door creaked open and our mother's car pulled in. She closed the heavy wooden garage door with a thud. The house didn't have an automatic garage door opener. She had to do it by hand.

Mom walked into the living room through the door adjoining the garage. Her cheeks were flushed, and she looked tired, eyes drawn. Brushing the back of her hand across her forehead, she looked at us standing in the kitchen. I gently set the glass down on the counter.

"Hi, Mom," Joey piped. His eyes were full of unanswered questions as I knew he tried to gauge her mood.

She let out a long breath, walked into the kitchen, and dropped her purse on the counter next to the dish rack. We scooted out of her way and into the living room as she looked at the mess of water on the counter and kitchen floor that I had made while getting cleaned up. She turned on her heel and locked her eyes on us.

"Who made this mess?" she hissed.

"Me," I answered.

"Well, clean it up," she said sternly and stepped away from the sink.

I pulled the dish towel from the refrigerator handle and wiped up the water that was on the counter, and then I stooped down and dabbed at the water on the warped wooden floor.

"Don't use my kitchen towel on the floor," she shrieked. I flinched. "Jesus, Vivian, you're eight years old. You should know better by now." Her voice dripped with disgust and resentment.

Joey watched from the safety of the living room. I could hear him popping his knuckles, a habit when he was anxious.

I got a wad of paper towels and wiped the water off the floor, tossed the paper towels in the trash, and headed to the garage to put the dirty dish towel in the hamper.

"Vivian. I want you to take a shower tonight. You're filthy and you stink."

"Yes, Mom," I replied meekly, closing the door behind me. I sat down hard on the warm concrete step in the stifling garage, the dish towel hanging limply from my hand. I listened to the engine of my mom's car ping and click as it cooled.

Inside, I could hear her high-heeled shoes click on the wood floor as she headed for her bedroom in the back of the house. We wouldn't see her again for the rest of the night. Joey and I would have to fend for ourselves for dinner.

Sweat formed on my face and neck again as I let out a shuddering sigh.

*

I snapped back to running on the beach, still shuddering, and took a deep breath. I caught the aroma of my childhood garage: car exhaust, dust, and hot cardboard all mixed in with the scent of the ocean and tide. Aware again of my surroundings, I noted we had reached Morro Rock and were running on the narrow road that ended in a parking area on the west side.

Jared slowed when we reached the lot, and I followed suit. We were both breathing heavily and walked around in circles as we recovered. My ears, cheeks, thighs, and hands were bright red and stung from the cold and exertion. Despite the chill in the air, sweat beaded up on my face and under my shirt. Jared was also ruddy and had managed to sweat through his shirt around the collar and down the back.

Our circling slowed as we caught our breath. I leaned against a large rock that edged the parking area and looked out at the ocean. Jared stopped and stood beside me, giving me a timid smile, his chipped front tooth gleaming briefly.

"Where'd you go this time?" he asked.

"Bernadette's house."

Silence fell between us as I watched the ocean and Jared watched me. Gulls circled menacingly close to some fishermen as they returned to their truck.

Ready to head back, I started to push off the rock. Jared startled.

"Viv," he said quietly. I blinked and turned toward him, caught off guard by the nervous look in his hazel eyes. They were exceptionally green with flecks of gold in the early morning sunshine.

"Yeah?"

"Remember when we used to be roommates? How much fun we had?"

"Yes! I miss living here. I actually get homesick for this place sometimes even though I'm not from here," I answered, chuckling, trying to fend off his nervous energy.

Jared took a deep breath, straining his sweaty shirt. His face turned serious as he exhaled.

"Come back, Viv. You can move right back into your old room. We'll have fun, just like we used to." He paused a beat, gauging me. "Come back. But this time, I would like us to be together, not just roommates."

My brain raced. I held a neutral expression, forcing myself not to interrupt him, but rather to hear him out and let him say what he needed to say.

"I want a life with you, Viv. I knew I always liked you, but it wasn't until you moved out a couple years ago to transfer to UCD that I realized just how much. We've been through a lot together. Shoot, all the way back to basic training at Fort Jackson. Will you give it a try? Give us a try?"

His voice dropped off. His quads and hands were clenched, and I could see him forcefully relax them.

I shifted. The cold of the rock seeped deep into my body through my thin running shorts. I watched the seagulls circle for a moment as I chose my words carefully.

"I love you. I can't, Jared. I'm in school still. I'm about to finish my senior year. I've got a job I love. I'm supposed to co-captain a field hockey team for the Bay Area league this coming summer." I wasn't able to quite look him in the eye as I listed off my commitments. I focused straight through his eyes on what was behind him.

"Exactly, Viv. Wrap up senior year, graduate, and move back down here. You can get another bartending gig in SLO. You can help coach the field hockey club at Cal Poly if you still want to be involved in hockey." He shifted his eyes just a hair and looked uncomfortable as I continued to gaze right through him.

I didn't reply.

The optimism on his face melted away into disappointment.

"Okay, Viv," he whispered.

I pushed off the rock and began hopping up and down, shaking out my muscles, warming up for the run back. Softening the neutral expression on my face, I gave him a mischievous grin, raising my left eyebrow slightly. He looked back at me, confused.

"Jared. In all of the years that you've known me, have you ever seen me date a guy?"

"No. In the Army, we were just too busy and rarely on the same rotation. And when we were roommates, you'd never tell me where you were going when you went out. You're a private person, and I've always respected that." He started stretching as he said this.

I stopped hopping and grinned at him again.

"Dude. I don't do straight guy dick. I'm a big old queer. The nightclub I work at is a lesbian nightclub. You're a hell of a catch, but you're seriously not my type." I reached out, slapped his ass hard, and sprinted off down the road toward the beach.

Jared hesitated and then chased after me. He easily caught up on his strong legs. We ran side by side down the berm and along the cove where we could see surfers in wetsuits paddling out to the waves.

We got into a comfortable pace. Jared seemed to be processing the news. I could sense that he had spent countless hours imagining a life with me, and I had just brought all of that crashing down.

"Really?"

"Yes, really. I'm really gay. Super fucking gay. I kept it to myself for so long because of being in the Army. Don't ask, don't tell is bullshit, and it forced me back into the closet. I saw so many of my friends lose their entire careers. Solid, dedicated soldiers, discharged because of who they loved." I broke off for a moment to regulate my breathing. "Ever since I moved up to Sacramento to go to UCD I've been much more open about it. I work at a lesbian nightclub, for Christ's sake."

"Does your mom know? I mean jeez, I don't see good ole Bernadette being very open-minded about stuff like that." His tone sounded incredulous.

"Yup, she was the first family member I came out to. She didn't seem all that surprised, actually."

"Wow, Bernadette has come a long way," he said.

I grunted. "Hardly."

We ran the rest of the way back to the house in silence, pacing each other, knowing so well how to gauge what we each needed just by our strides, breathing, and posture, and adjusting accordingly.

Back at the house, we took turns showering, and shared breakfast. Jared was not his usual chatty self. He was withdrawn, silent the entire time. After breakfast, he stood in the doorway to the guest room as I packed up my duffel. I made one last trip to the bathroom, slung my duffel on my shoulder, and walked down the front stairs to my truck. Nineteen stairs. Nineteen wooden stairs that I knew so well. Every loose nail and creaky board.

Jared leaned against the warm metal of my front fender as I tossed my bag into the bed of my truck. He spread his arms and I leaned into him, wrapping my arms around his waist. He held me for a while as I rested my cheek on his shoulder and listened to the sounds of Highway 1 mixed with the Pacific Ocean crashing onto the beach. He released me abruptly.

"You're sure?" he asked, holding me by the shoulders, at arm's length.

"Yup, I'm sure. I can be your friend, as always, but that's it. I love you, and I've always got your back, BB."

"All right," he said absently. In all the years I had known Jared, I had never seen him pout, but I understood.

I climbed into my truck, buckled my seatbelt, fired up the engine, and rolled down the window to let in some fresh air.

"You gonna make the trip north for my graduation party?"

He gave me an unenthusiastic nod and a wave as I pulled out of the driveway.

Chapter Three

Every time I returned from SLO, I brought cider to my mother. Just before getting onto Highway 101 in SLO I stopped at the Apple Farm gift shop and bought a jug of frozen apple cider. The clerk wrapped it neatly in brown butcher paper.

On the way out I lingered in the garden, taking in the explosion of flowers and the tinkling of water from the water wheel. Reluctant to leave the peaceful garden, I placed the jug in the ice chest behind my seat and got back on the road.

The radio signal faded as I drove over the grade between SLO and Paso Robles so I put a CD into the disc player, *Recovering the Satellites* by Counting Crows, and downshifted for more power as my truck bogged down on the steepest part of the grade.

"Oh, Jared," I said as guilt washed over me for dashing his hopes. It was obvious how disappointed he was, but I knew how resilient he could be and was sure that our friendship would make it through.

At Paso Robles, I cut over on Highway 46 and then Highway 41. At some point the Counting Crows CD ended, and I swapped it out for U2's *The Joshua Tree*. I took off like a shot once I hit I-5 north at Kettleman City, blowing by orchards, dairies, cattle ranches, vast wide-open vistas, and foothills.

The closer I got to Sacramento, the more anxious I became. My stomach grew tight, as did my grip on the steering wheel. I had not done any of my school assignments over the weekend and had taken Saturday night off from work. Saturday nights were usually the highest earning nights of the week for me, so I knew I had missed out on at least two hundred dollars in tips.

I pressed my foot down harder on the accelerator. My little Ford Ranger ate up mile after mile. Finally, I reached Sacramento, took the Q Street exit, and made my way through Midtown. I snagged a parking spot at the corner of Twenty-fourth and Q, right outside of my apartment building.

With cooler in my hand, duffel bag on my shoulder, and stiff legs, I wobbled down the stairs to the door and unlocked it. Once in the dingy underground lobby, I walked up a flight of stairs to the first floor. The building was quiet, nobody in sight in the lobby or corridor.

The first-floor corridor was a long bland hallway, with windows on the left side and apartment doors on the right. The walls were painted a dull white, and the floor had thin blue carpet. The odor of the hallway hung somewhere between urine and curry.

My studio, #106, was just as I had left it, neat and sparsely furnished. While I fully appreciated interior design, I did not have a knack for it, so I stuck to keeping things utilitarian. One futon, one small coffee table, one folding chair, one card table in the connecting kitchen, a low table against the wall with a small television and DVD player on it. My books, CDs, and DVDs in neat rows on the floor along one wall. In the corner was a small three-drawer dresser that held my clothes. On top was a small freshwater fish tank. The calm burbling of the tank's filtration pump was a constant.

On the walls were neatly framed photos, including one of my basic training platoon, one of Jared in Class A's earning his stripes, one obligatory picture of me in BDU's laying prone in the mud while lining up a shot at the range, M-16 at the ready. One of my friend Bear astride her motorcycle, which she had adoringly named Champagne.

The studio was essentially a square room with a small kitchen, and an even smaller bathroom branching off it. The western-facing wall had the only window, which ran the studio's entire width and looked out onto Twenty-fourth Street and the apartment pool. Directly underneath the studio was the underground parking garage, so I never had to worry about treading lightly for downstairs neighbors.

I dropped my duffel and the cooler on the futon and carried the frozen jug of cider into the kitchen. I squeezed the jug into the freezer next to two other jugs of cider from my last trips to SLO. Apparently, I hadn't visited my mom in a while.

Next, I unpacked the duffel, chucking dirty clothes in the hamper and lining up my running shoes next to my boots in the closet.

I was thrilled to find that all my fish were alive. It was a small tank with a heating unit, a light, and a filter constantly circulating the water. I put some flakes into the tank and watched the fish eagerly swim to the surface.

Dinner time. I prepared a simple meal. Chicken, broccoli, and brown rice cooked in vegetable broth. I ate it while leaning against the counter in the kitchen, looking out of the window on the far side of the studio.

My ears screamed with tinnitus, so I focused on the sounds of Midtown. Cars drove by, people walked along the sidewalk chatting, doors slammed, dogs barked, and the warning signal clanged every time a light-rail train came into the stop on Twenty-fourth Street.

Eventually, I slipped into some black boxer briefs, a sports bra, well-worn jeans that hung on my ass just right, and the usual tight black tank top. I added some black ranger boots and a wallet chain. I fixed my bun and spritzed it with hairspray so it would hold up during my shift.

On the way out, I grabbed my tip bucket, which was full of my work gear: wine key, shaker, strainer, and bartending guide.

As I headed out, the brisk air hit me, and I hunched my shoulders as goose bumps raised up on my arms.

I made the short drive down to Twenty-first Street and *L* and parked across from the club. Scanning the block, I grinned. From the look of things, it would be a busy night. The sidewalks had plenty of people, the parking spots were mostly gone, and the restaurant next door was banging.

Just outside the entrance to the club I heard the bass line of dance music vibrating inside. Drawing in a deep breath, I said, "Show time."

Nobody enjoys a moody, distracted, or depressed bartender. I always put on a show at work, playing the part of the steady-handed and hard-to-get sporty butch barkeep.

Grasping the brass handle, I pulled open the door and slapped on my customary smirk. I nodded to the security officer, who was seated at a lectern in the entryway. She looked like the Marlboro Man with a mullet, and was one hard-ass, old-school, stone butch.

"Hey, Buck."

"Hey, Viv," she replied.

I put a little swagger in my step as I walked behind the bar to my station and exchanged a half-assed nod with the bartender at the other end of the long, highly varnished bar. My regulars greeted me from their stools.

Time for prep work. I pushed through double doors to the back bar. The large dance floor was mostly empty. Tick, the DJ, looked down at me from his booth and gave me an exasperated shrug as I scooped ice into a five-gallon bucket. Over the sound of my ice scoop, I heard Tick transition from "Crazy in Love" to "Hey Ya!", which drew more people to the dance floor. Even some of my regulars left their stools and walked through to the back bar.

I filled up garnish trays with lemons, limes, olives, and sickeningly red maraschino cherries. My manager materialized with a cash drawer, which we counted out together before I signed off on it. She was a sporty, fit, feisty woman, though her eyes were puffy and her voice was raspy. Despite it being almost ten at night, she was nursing a hangover and had me make her a Bloody Mary with a Red Bull back.

I'd worked with her long enough to know she was resilient and would be up on top of the bar dancing in no time. Sundays were Coyote Ugly night, which was usually a pretty big draw for our customers, and she was the star of that show.

There was a line forming at the door. Buck methodically checked IDs, took cover, made change, and stamped hands. Women, with a sprinkling of gay men, began filing in, filling up the front bar, and spilling over into the back and dance floor.

I spotted my bar back bypass the line and squeeze through the door. She walked behind the bar and promptly slapped my ass.

"Good to see you, Jen," I said as the sting on my ass cheek faded.

Jen tucked an American Spirit cigarette behind her ear and began stacking clean pint glasses at my station and inside the cooler.

"How'd last night go? I don't think I've ever missed a shift on a Saturday night."

Jen grabbed two bar towels. She tucked one in her belt and the other in my back pocket.

"You missed a doozy, dude. This place was at capacity all night. The windows were all fogged up. There was literally condensation dripping off of the ceiling in the back because of all the people dancing their asses off back there."

"Who covered my station?"

"Amy," Jen said, rolling her hazel eyes.

"Did she tip you out?"

"What the fuck do you think?"

I shook my head and scanned the room, grinning as women began lining up at my station and filling the barstools at my half of the bar.

"You ready for this?" I asked Jen.

She nodded confidently.

"Coyote Ugly, baby!"

Her hazel eyes sparkled, and she hopped up and down excitedly, her wallet chain jingling.

"And awayyyy weee go!"

I stepped to the bar, addressing the first woman in line. Tick had just turned up the volume of the speakers in the front room, so she had to shout her drink order over the music.

Time passed quickly. Pouring beers and shots, mixing cocktails, ringing up orders, filling the till and my tip jar. And of course, entertaining my customers. A couple of times I lay down on the bar and women took body shots off me. I always wound up with a five or ten-dollar bill in my sports bra when I hopped back down.

At midnight, Tick blared the air raid siren. Jen and I had everyone clear their drinks and purses off the bar as our manager Sheila stepped up on top of it. She was wearing a black bra, low-cut black slacks with her G-string peeking out the back, and heels. All the women in the front room hooted and hollered, standing back to take in the view.

I handed her a bottle of Everclear with a spout on it. She strutted the entire length of the bar, pouring Everclear into the shallow trough that captured over pours and spills. Her heels clicked on the varnish. At the far end, she handed the bottle to Jen and nodded at me. I took a book of matches, struck one and lit the entire matchbook up. Excitement flooded me, and my cheeks grew hot as I held the flaming matchbook over my head, a massive mischievous grin on my face. Everyone quieted down. All eyes were on me. Primal infatuation with fire had grasped everyone's attention.

When I dropped the matchbook into the bar trough, a line of fire rose up along the entire length of the bar. The women exploded in a raucous cheer, and Sheila began strutting again, her hips gyrating.

"Pour Some Sugar on Me" blared from the speakers. I was fairly sure Sheila's previous career had been as an exotic dancer, but she wouldn't confirm or deny that fact. Either way, her moves were hot, and the crowd responded.

The flames quickly died down, so I grabbed the soda gun and flushed the trough out with water. As the song ended, Sheila climbed deftly down off the bar, and Tick somehow transitioned to "The Humpty Dance," which nearly cleared the front room as packs of women headed to the back dance floor. A few couples who had been cuddled up in the booths stayed behind to continue their conversations. Jen jumped into action, spraying cleanser on the bar and wiping it down.

The night wound down after that, and by closing time the bar was almost empty. Buck locked up and walked around pulling down the shades on the windows facing Twenty-first Street. Jen collected abandoned glasses, beer bottles, crumpled bar napkins, and coffee cups from every corner of the place.

I had a neat line of shots on the counter near my tip jar. Several people had offered to buy me a drink, and I had taken them up on it, promising them I'd drink them after closing. One by one, I dumped the shots down the sink at my station, holding my breath the entire time. The stink of alcohol had triggered fear in me since childhood. But bartending brought in decent enough money that the tradeoff was okay for the time being. Tips were my lifeblood. I just didn't drink the stuff and had no patience for drunks.

I took a seat at the bar. My legs and feet howled after running in the morning, driving for hours, and then hustling all night. Taking the pressure off brought on hot throbbing and a cramp in my foot.

I counted my tip jar, pulling out the damp and crumpled bills one at a time. Some were damp with beer, others with boob sweat, because a surprising number of women used their bras as purses. I just never knew what fluids I was dealing with.

My tips came to a hundred and forty dollars. Not bad for a Sunday night at a lesbian nightclub in Sacramento. I stuffed twenty-five bucks into Jen's pocket as she walked by with her hands full of pint glasses. She gave me a wink in return and made her way to the other two bartenders to see if they would tip her out too. Next, I counted out my drawer and handed it off to Sheila.

The bartender from the back bar walked swiftly by, headed for the bathroom. I soon heard her vomiting in the echoey stall. Like clockwork, after every shift, she would make herself puke before she counted out her drawer. She said it kept her from getting hangovers and cleared her head so she could count out her drawer and drive home.

I tucked my tip money in my boot and Buck walked me to my truck. She was silent, head on a swivel, her calloused hands clenched into fists. Buck worked as a tow truck driver during the day and could knock out just about any jackass who caused trouble in the bar.

"G'night, Buck," I said as I got into my truck.

Buck grunted and broke her stoic straight face to give me a quick grin.

"G'night, kid. Oh, hey, your bro came by the bar during day shift. He was looking for you."

"Pfft. He probably just wanted me to front him some cash or a drink."

"He was trashed. I made him leave because he flipped out after he saw some guys kissing."

"What an asshole. He knows damn well it's a gay bar. If he doesn't like it, he can go to any of the straight bars downtown. Sorry 'bout that, Buck."

Buck clucked her tongue and headed back to the bar, her rugged stride carrying her across the street in four quick paces.

Midtown was mostly quiet. I made it home in under five minutes, and by some miracle, I got a parking spot on Twenty-fourth Street right near my building.

People in the neighborhood knew I was a bartender, which means cash. And at 3:30 in the morning, not many good Samaritans were out.

I took a deep breath, hopped out of the truck, and took fast, long, confident strides to the lobby door. Shoulders back, chin up, hands balled into fists. Ready to fight.

I made it to my studio unscathed. I pulled the cash from my boot and put it in a small safe that was tucked away under the bathroom sink, hidden behind a big box of panty liners and a small bin with bottles of lotion and sunscreen in it.

Finally, I pulled off my boots and stripped down to boxers and a fresh tank top. Once I'd folded out the futon, I grabbed a blanket, shut off the lights, and immediately fell asleep in the blue glow of the fish tank light, listening to the burbling of the tank filter and the whir of a passing light-rail train.

Chapter Four

My last quarter at UC Davis passed in a blur of rigid routine. I was taking sixteen units so that I could graduate on time. It took some serious time management skills. Weekdays I was up early, on little sleep after shifts bartending, commuting to Davis on my motorcycle. Parking permits were ridiculously expensive on campus, and there was no guarantee there would even be a parking spot. Motorcycle parking was much easier.

I gravitated back and forth between lecture halls, the library stacks, and benches on the quad. After my last class of the day I would change into running gear, which I kept in a locker I had commandeered at the Rec Hall.

If it was raining hard enough, I would do endless laps around the indoor running track, sprinting the straightaways and jogging the short ends, sometimes running the stairs in the upper deck seating. On days when the weather was decent, I ran around the Arboretum, which was just over four miles.

The Arboretum trail was usually a tranquil place, switching back and forth between dirt and paved trails, going under footbridges, and the canopy of a small redwood grove, past native plants, and open grassy areas where students lounged in the sun with their textbooks. Springtime on campus was gorgeous.

Yet, just before finals, I became aware of an unwelcome visitor creeping up in the back of my mind, its calloused hands ready to put me in a stranglehold. I had defeated it in the past, but PTSD with anxiety is a persistent motherfucker.

One afternoon, I took my usual seat in the enormous theater-style lecture hall on the second floor of the art building. Aisle seat in the third row, close to the door, directly in front of the professor's lectern.

Dr. Juda walked in, and there was a lot of hushed rustling as people took their seats. He was sharply dressed, as always. A crisp dress shirt, silk tie, pleated slacks, glasses, and a subtle pink triangle pin on his shirt collar. He began without delay. The lights dimmed, and the first slide popped up on a huge screen at the front of the lecture hall. A painting I knew well. Rubens' *Samson and Delilah*. Massive. Larger than life. Bodies crowded together, muscle and fabric in candlelight. The portrayal of Samson being betrayed by his love, under a statue of Venus and Cupid. Love was Samson's downfall.

As Dr. Juda began his lecture, I couldn't absorb anything he was saying. I sat, pen suspended over a blank page of binder paper, while the students in front of me were hastily jotting down notes.

My mind reacted like a startled flock of birds, thoughts racing in every direction, too fast to grasp. Breathing harder, I tightened my jaw. I gripped my pen with such intensity that the plastic began to make a small crackling sound. I closed my eyes and tried to do the breathing exercises my old counselor had taught me, but I was already too far into it and couldn't force myself to focus enough to do them.

Fight or flight. Fight or flight. Fight or flight. But never freeze.

I knew, rationally, that I was not in any danger. In fact, I was quite safe in that lecture hall, even in 2004 post-Columbine Davis. I squeezed my eyes closed harder, trying again to get control. I was hot. My palms sweaty. I couldn't breathe right, and then nausea began to taunt me.

I could hear Dr. Juda in the background and made a concerted effort not to make a scene. My eyes snapped open but couldn't settle on any one thing in the room.

I quietly picked up my notebook and backpack. Every ounce of my being wanted to bolt out of the lecture hall, but I managed to make a smooth, quiet exit, catching a disapproving glare from Dr. Juda's TA on my way out.

My footsteps echoed in the empty lobby as I galloped down the stairs and out of the double doors. I turned right and headed for the Arboretum, which was behind the art building. My breathing shallow and quick, and high in my throat. I couldn't get enough air. Fucking air hunger. I imagined that was how small, scared rodents breathed when cornered by a predator.

I cut through the trees and came out at the top of a hill above the duck pond. I dropped my backpack, notebook, and pen on a bench. Sitting down heavily, I was finally able to gain enough control to do the breathing exercises.

In through my nose for a count of five, hold it for a count of two, breathe out through my mouth for a count of five. Over and over and over until eventually my breathing steadied, my heart rate slowed, and the nausea subsided a bit.

And there I sat, and sat, and sat. Watching joggers pass by on the path below, students walking in packs, and parents bringing their toddlers to feed the ducks at

Spafford Pond. The scene rolled out before me while I sat there, vacant and exhausted, until I eventually laid down on the bench, tucking my backpack under my head as a pillow.

The sky was a watery blue as the sun continued retreating to the west and cumulus clouds scuttled by. The temperature held at a perfect seventy-six degrees. I drew in a deep breath and my core finally relaxed.

Dusk would arrive soon, and I disliked riding my motorcycle after dark. I needed to go, but lingered a bit longer, allowing my thoughts to wander and drift in the fog of emotional fatigue.

I thought about poor Jared pining after me, about my alcoholic brother, about the longest of my days in the Army, about my last crushing bout with anxiety right after my discharge, about fucking my ex in an alley at San Francisco Pride, about fucking that same ex in a public bathroom at gay prom, and finally about learning how to ride my bicycle as a kid on the street in front of my grandparents' house.

Finally pulling myself out of the haze, I realized the nausea was gone and I was hungry and dehydrated. Dusk had arrived. I sat up, packed up my bag, and walked at a fast clip to the distant parking lot.

Riding back to Sacramento, I berated myself for giving in to the panic, for missing an important lecture just before finals. That wound me up again. I attacked myself over and over, screaming into my helmet as I bombed at breakneck speed across the Causeway in the dark.

How can you be so weak? If you could fight for survival in the field, why can't you sit through a damn lecture, out of harm's way?

"You've gotten soft, you sorry sack," I growled.

A past therapist's repeated advice came to me then. *Wrap yourself up, Vivian. Give yourself the compassion you would give to someone else. Nurture the sad, lonely child inside you who was never nurtured.*

The floodgates crashed open. I cried, hard, all the way up Q Street, the visor of my helmet fogged up.

I pulled into the underground garage of my apartment building and parked in the spot assigned to my studio. The small garage was full of cars, but there wasn't anybody around. I stayed in the saddle and took off my helmet, the pads soaked with tears.

My sobs echoed around the garage. I cried because I was angry with myself. I cried because I was ashamed that I was crying. And I cried for myself for having been so invisible as a kid. I cried for the giant gaping hole that had been growing in my chest over the last year. A vacuum of need. Needing attention, needing love, needing to be nurtured, and having no idea how to go about getting those needs met.

The security gate slowly rattled open behind me. Hurriedly, I wiped my face on my sleeves, hopped off the bike, and busied myself unclipping my backpack from the back seat. I grabbed my gear and headed for the door that led to the lobby.

Hands full, I awkwardly unlocked the door as the woman who had just parked approached. She was dressed in an immaculate dark suit that fit well. A sheriff's department ID badge hung from her neck on a US Navy lanyard. She was tall. Really tall. Solidly built, with broad shoulders.

I held the door open for her, my eyes cast down, hoping she would pass by quickly. But she didn't. She stopped and took the weight of the door from me and stood in front of me in the threshold.

She waited. I finally looked up at her, knowing my face was red from crying, my eyes glassy. I looked her right in the eye and realized that I recognized her. She lived on my floor, just down the hall from me.

I tried to configure my face to look like someone who was having a normal day, and even gave her a small grin, but I knew my eyes and blotchy red face betrayed me.

The woman continued to stand in front of me, studying my face. So, I studied her right back. Her hair was pulled back into a flawless bun. Her skin had a slight olive tone to it under her tan. I figured she was about thirty. I realized I was attracted to her, and heat bloomed as my neck and cheeks flushed even more.

What the fuck are you doing, Viv?

I moved to walk through the door.

"Thanks," I said, since she was still holding it open.

"I've been there," the woman said.

"You've been where?" I asked, internally questioning my own motives as I turned back to her.

"Where you're at in your head. I've been there. How long ago were you discharged?"

I wondered how the hell she knew I had been in the service and then realized some of us can recognize each other. A certain posture, a certain stride, a certain look in our eyes.

"Four years ago," I said.

"Are they helping you at the VA?" she asked.

I looked at the ID badge hanging from her neck. The photo showed the woman a few years younger, not smiling. Her name was printed in bold letters beneath the picture.

ANGELA SORENSON

"What do you think, Deputy Angela Sorenson? Do you think the VA gives a shit about me and my mental health?" I was immediately ashamed for my tone, biting my lip. "Sorry," I said, looking back up at her.

"No need to apologize. Like I said, I've been there. I'm not trying to make you feel awkward or embarrassed, I'm trying to say that I get it."

I looked at Angela's suit again. She saw me looking and seemed a bit shy about it.

"I—I had court today. I'm normally in uniform."

I shook my head, conveying that there was no need for an explanation.

"I'm sorry. I've overstepped," Angela said, her tone losing some confidence. I shook my head again.

We both flinched as the automatic security gate in the garage began to open. The hypervigilance that plagued us both was apparent. It had been ingrained in us. Always listening, always scanning, always sizing up every person.

It was exhausting.

Angela cleared her throat.

"What are you doing tonight?" she asked.

"It's Friday, so I work tonight. I'm Viv, by the way."

Clutching my helmet under my elbow I extended a hand. Angela shook it. Her grip was firm, her large hand wrapped around mine.

"Ang," she said, and paused. "Okay. Well, you should stop by sometime, Viv. I'm in apartment one-oh-one. First door at the top of the stairs. I mean it. I know I'm a stranger to you, but I've been there. If you want to talk, or whatever, come over."

A car door slammed, followed by a trunk closing. Footsteps echoed around the garage.

I stepped out of the doorway and into the lobby. We both said hello to our elderly neighbor as he shuffled by in a burgundy velour tracksuit, headed for the elevator. I waited until the elevator doors closed behind him.

"That elevator is a fucking death trap," I said.

"I always take the stairs," Ang said with a chuckle.

"Look, I've had a really fucked-up day, and I need to go get my head right and get ready for work," I said.

"Yeah, of course. No worries. My offer still stands. I work weird hours, but if my light is on, you're welcome to come by," she said.

My eyes started to well up. I sniffed the tears back and strode across the lobby, taking the stairs two at a time.

I put my helmet and backpack away and dropped down onto the futon. I gave myself five minutes to lie there with my emotional hangover.

When my five minutes were up, I jammed it all down, drank three big glasses of water, and got my ass ready for work. I couldn't be late.

Chapter Five

"Show time," I said as I pulled open the door to the club. I nodded to Buck and got to work. The dance floor was packed, and every barstool, chair, and booth bench had a queer ass on it. The line at my station had been at least five people deep since we had opened. Tick was absolutely killing it in the DJ booth. Being busy was how I liked it. It left no room to dwell on things and helped me pull myself out of the hole I had fallen into earlier in the day.

I finished ringing up a sale on the register, my back to the bar. In the huge mirror along the wall over my register I saw the next person in line step up. My core immediately tightened. An explosion of adrenaline burst throughout my body.

It was Ang. I braced myself, put on my bartender smirk, and turned around. Ang's eyes grew wide as she recognized me, but she quickly got herself in check and threw me a confident, cocky smile.

"Hey, what can I get for you?" I asked. The same question I asked over and over again every night.

"Uh. Hey. I knew you were a bartender, but I didn't realize it was here," Ang said as she gestured to the ceiling.

I saw the women in line behind Ang start to get restless.

"What can I get for you?" I asked again, smiling.

"Right. Um. A Guinness, a Corona, and two bottles of water."

I got to work on the tap pouring the Guinness and pulled a Corona and two waters from the cooler. I popped the top off the Corona, jammed a lime wedge in it, and lined the drinks up on the bar in front of Ang.

"No charge. I got it," I said.

"You sure?" Ang asked, hesitant.

"Yup. I got it," I said again.

Ang got a guilty look on her face as she deftly picked up all four drinks between her fingers. She didn't spill a single drop of the Guinness. She started to turn away and then stammered. "I'm on a first date. It's not going well. My friends set it up right after you and I talked in the lobby earlier," she said, as if she felt obligated to explain herself to me.

I shrugged. "Try and enjoy yourself," I said and moved my focus to the woman squeezing around Ang and already shouting a drink order at me over the music.

As the night carried on, I caught glimpses of Ang and her date through the crowd. They sat at a table most of the night, visibly straining to hear each other over the music. Both looked uncomfortable, and I wondered why they carried on with the date even though they clearly were not hitting it off.

Bartenders, we see a lot. New flames, break-ups, good dates, horrible dates, assaults, drunks, overconfident people, and introverts. People pairing off to snort coke in the bathroom. All out fistfights. Tips, wallets, purses, and cell phones getting swiped off the bar. Sex workers subtly picking up dates.

I had even seen people fucking on one slow, lazy Sunday afternoon the previous summer.

*

All of Sacramento's dykes were at a Monarchs game. The bar would fill up as soon as the game ended, but right then the place was nearly deserted. I had gone outside to get some air in the narrow breezeway between the bar and the building next to it. It was basically a narrow brick hallway with no roof. The breezeway was closed off on both ends, an alley to nowhere. A lot of our customers used it as a smoking area.

I stepped into the breezeway and found a really hardcore butch sitting on a barstool, her back up against the brick wall. She had on jeans, motorcycle boots, and a button-up shirt. Her wallet chain hung halfway down the leg of the barstool. She had her face buried in the tits of a high femme who was straddling her, the heels of her stilettos hooked in the rungs of the barstool. The butch had her arms firmly around the femme's waist, supporting her. The femme was slowly riding up and down on the butch's enormous mocha-colored cyberskin cock, which I could see standing tall from the fly of her jeans.

I stood in the doorway and watched for a few seconds, holding eye contact with the femme, who was smiling at me dreamily. I cleared my throat and the butch finally looked up at me, her expression content, relaxed. Neither one of them stopped what they were doing. They just kept right on going and looking at me.

"I'll give you a few, and then I'm sending Buck out here."

The butch gave me a nod. I walked back into the bar and stood guard at the door. The last thing I needed was another customer, or the club owner, walking in on them. But what the hell, might as well let them have some fun for a few.

*

There had been countless times Jen and I had clambered out the side door to empty the heavy bins of empty beer bottles into the dumpster, with Buck in tow to make sure we didn't get mugged, only to find some guy on his knees giving head. The guys always looked embarrassed and covered their faces while scampering off once Buck started barking at them to move the fuck along.

I was amused at how many guys decided that a dank, piss-and-puke-spattered alley was a good place to get—or give—head. And I usually recognized them as customers from the bar. Why didn't they use the bathroom stalls or go under the DJ booth like everyone else?

Watching romances and dramas play out in the bar as I went about my work was sometimes challenging for me. I knew the players and could often predict the potential fallout before it happened, but since it was not my place to get involved, I had to remain a bystander to it all. That night I got to watch Ang navigate a bad date.

While closing up, I had her on my mind and enjoyed the sparks crackling throughout my body. I made a deal with myself. If Ang's light was on when I got home, I would knock on her door. Judging by how her date went, I doubted Ang would have brought the woman back to her place.

I parked in front of the building around 3:30 a.m. and looked up at the first-floor windows, which were about one story above street level. I knew Ang lived in the first apartment, just above the lobby and stairs.

Her windows were dark.

I was immediately deflated. *You idiot. What did you expect? She probably didn't give you a second thought tonight.*

I went to my studio in silence.

Chapter Six

I finished up finals despite the stranglehold that anxiety had on me. I often woke up exhausted, tangled in my sheet, with a sore jaw and the insides of my cheeks chewed up. On mornings like that, I'd stand in the bathroom rinsing out my mouth and spitting bloody water into the sink.

Appraising myself in the mirror, I knew damn well the stress of finals was not why I found myself in that situation. I'd lived a whole other life in the military before making a hard landing back into civilian life. I had siloed all thoughts about that time in my life and had no intention of ever examining them again, but in the meantime, I'd continue spitting blood into my sink and fighting the urge to bolt out of lecture halls, movie theaters, libraries, and just about everywhere I went.

I'd even had a severe anxiety attack while on a run, which sucked because running was how I kept myself sane; it gave me time to process things. But on one recent run down Twenty-fourth Street, a wave crashed over me. I ran faster and faster, my mind spinning, fighting the urge to turn around and go home. I became frantic.

I observed everyone around me going about their daily lives in relative peace. Cars lined up at the stop signs. A landscaper using a leaf blower on the sidewalk. I registered these things but couldn't focus on them. My heart was racing much too fast, my breathing short and shallow. Nausea clenched my throat.

It got to the point that I was sprinting down the sidewalk, not stopping at crosswalks, not caring if a car plowed over me. Random thoughts flitted in and out of my mind, nothing sticking. A small, rational piece of me was still there, trying to take the reins. Sweat dripped from my body as my pores opened up in the heat of Sacramento in June.

A block ahead, I spotted a dog walker. She had a bunch of dogs on separate leashes, all walking side by side and taking up the entire sidewalk. My eyes focused on the turquoise fanny pack the dog walker was wearing. I ran full tilt toward her, tunnel vision on her fanny pack as it swayed from side to side with her slow ambling stride.

I quickly closed the gap between us and knew I should slow down or stop or try to squeeze past the dogs, but my panicked mind just couldn't make the adjustment.

She clearly heard the fast approach of my sneakers on the pavement because she looked over her shoulder and quickly sidestepped to her right, yanking four of the dogs along with her. She had created just enough space for me as I blew past her.

"What the fucking fuck!" she shouted at me.

I didn't respond. Saying sorry wouldn't change the situation. I was an asshole, and I was out of control. I continued sprinting down Twenty-fourth Street, block after block, not looking for traffic, not stopping at intersections.

Finally, as I closed in on *D* Street my lungs and legs were burning so much that I had no choice but to slow to a walk. Embarrassed, I cut over to Twenty-third Street and jogged back to my apartment.

My body was absolutely depleted. I collapsed on the futon when I got home and slept the entire day away, waking only to go to work that night.

Chapter Seven

Graduation day had arrived. It was over one hundred degrees by 10:00 a.m., as all the graduates stood outside the Rec Hall waiting for the procession inside.

I didn't have much to say to my classmates but was personable whenever someone approached and offered me their congratulations. I hadn't made any close friends during my time at UC Davis, so I couldn't relate to all the people hugging and jumping up and down excitedly.

Sweat ran down my back.

Inside the Rec Hall my mother may or may not have been waiting to see me walk across the stage. She had also put together a graduation party in my honor. Friends and family had traveled from all over the state to celebrate my accomplishment.

All except Jared. Jared had cancelled without an explanation, leaving me crestfallen. Jared had been my rock for years, so his absence hit me deeply. I knew I needed to make time to call him.

My family was very small, and my generation in particular was almost nonexistent. So, everyone turned out for occasions like graduations, weddings, and funerals, which often doubled as family reunions.

As I marched into the Rec Hall, I kicked away the emotionally flat wet blanket that I had been dragging around, and a tentative surge of pride and excitement took its place. The sound of the crowd died down as the procession music began to play, on repeat, as hundreds of us filed in and took our seats, creating a sea of black polyester.

I numbly took in all the speeches and pomp.

When it was my turn to walk across the stage another surge of pride hit me, and tears welled up in my eyes. I bit back the tears and strode across confidently, my shoulders back and my chin up.

It was over before I knew it.

Taking my seat again, I realized I had to sit there for at least another hour as the rest of the graduates went through the motions.

I untied the blue ribbon wound around the rolled-up piece of paper I been presented with. Inside was not my degree, but rather instructions on how to get it at a later date. Terrific.

*

High School Graduation. Toomey Field, 1994. There was nobody in the bleachers for me. My mother, Bernadette, could not be around crowds of people or be in situations where she couldn't easily extract herself. I understood that she had agoraphobia but was still disappointed. And there was no excuse for why Joey wasn't there, aside from the fact he was probably sleeping off a bender on someone's couch.

Idly scanning the crowd, I was surprised to spot Bernadette standing in the grass at the edge of a set of bleachers. She had positioned herself so that she could see the stage and graduates but was away from the throngs of people. I was grateful for the effort she had made to be there, as I knew it was no small feat.

The boy in the seat in front of me pulled a brown paper bag out from under his robe. He elbowed his buddy in the ribs, and they both giggled as he opened the bag and dumped it out.

A pile of frantic white mice hit the ground and scattered in every direction. The girl sitting next to me clicked her tongue in disapproval. Kneeling, she managed to catch two of the mice and tuck them gently into the pocket of her flowing hippy skirt.

When I looked back up, my mother was gone.

*

A hand on my shoulder brought me back to the Rec Hall. It was time for the procession out into the relentless heat of Davis in June.

The party at my mom's house was a blur of family members hugging me and asking me, "So, what's next?" I didn't like being the focus of all the attention and didn't have a plan for what was next, so I deflected by asking people questions about their jobs, lives, and kids. For the most part it worked.

Ever the bartender and scared little sister, I was keeping an eye on my brother, who had showed up for the party. I kept count of how many beers he drank. I had never seen anyone drink beer after beer after beer that fast. I stopped counting when he finished the eleventh bottle. He was really good about always having one in hand to make people think he was nursing the same one, but that wasn't the case at all.

I was irritated that my mother was even serving alcohol. Nobody else drank. It was the typical enabling bullshit, and it settled in my gut like a hot coal.

The party wound down by early afternoon. I hugged everyone as they left, further embarrassed by the final round of congratulatory remarks.

Joey, not showing any sign of being drunk, got into his truck and drove away, down the street we had grown up on. I stayed behind and helped Bernadette clean up, gathering plates, napkins, and cups from all over the house and back porch. I began washing everything by hand. Bernadette had never repaired the dishwasher when it had broken eighteen years earlier.

She collected all of Joey's empty beer bottles and lined them up for me to rinse. I clenched my jaw as the hot coal in my gut rose up as rage in my throat. She hovered, watching as I washed the dishes and utensils. Each time she didn't approve of how I had washed something, she would sigh, take it out of the dish drainer, and put it back in the sink, just like when I was a kid. I bit back resentment. Years of it were piled up, waiting to cascade out of me.

Not looking at her, but focusing instead on the dishes, I spoke. Though the words were forced, I worked to keep my tone even. I said them because I knew they were expected. What I wanted to do, though, was tell her off.

"Thank you, Mom. The party was really great. I know it was a lot of work. I appreciate it."

Bernadette nodded and chatted happily about how nice it was to see all the family, all the while putting an occasional dish back into the sink for me to wash again.

I kept washing dishes until they were all clean, dried, and put away. I rinsed out all of Joey's beer bottles and lined them up on the old, avocado-colored Formica counter. The bottles stood there, wet and gleaming, between us. I snorted at the sight of them and went into the bathroom to change my clothes.

Aside from graduation day, it was also Sacramento Gay Pride, and I had to be at the bar, which would be absolutely slammed, much earlier than usual.

The bathroom had not changed at all since I was a kid. Faux marble countertop. Broken knob on the sink. Worn-out, tan linoleum on the floor.

I dressed in a white beater, long black Dickies shorts, and black boots that were polished with parade gloss. I looked down at the tattoos on my upper arms, chest, and shoulders with a grin.

On the way out of my mother's house, I filled my water bottle and we exchanged a stiff hug. I tried to ignore her sighs and disapproving glances at my clothes and tattoos. Opening her front door, I was blasted with heat.

"I really wish you'd stop getting tattoos," Bernadette called out to my back as I walked away.

I gave no reply aside from a sharp wave over my shoulder.

Chapter Eight

Midtown was hopping and parking was scarce, but I snagged a spot around the corner from the club. I stood out front of the bar. The massive floor to ceiling windows along Twenty-first Street were wide open. Raucous noise spilled out. Voices all combined to the point of white noise, punctuated with a few cackles from one of the gay boys sitting in a window seat. Beyoncé's "Crazy in Love" was pumping out of the speakers.

I climbed the steps and said "show time" to myself as I crossed the threshold.

I nodded to Buck, who was solidly stationed at the lectern, checking IDs and charging cover. There were extra security officers posted up in the back by the dance floor and one headed down the steps to stand out front. The tightwad bar owner only paid for extra security if he was expecting it to be a total rager, and being that it was Pride, it would be.

I took over my station from the day shift bartender, who looked exhausted. I jumped right in mixing drinks and pouring beers and shots nonstop, while doing my best to count out change and maintain my best flirty grin. And I sweat, a lot. It was hot. There's nothing quite like Sacramento in June, except maybe Sacramento in August.

Jen kept me stocked up with ice, pint glasses, tumblers, and garnishes. By 10:00 p.m. the place was completely packed, probably well past capacity.

Hopefully, the Fire Marshal didn't pop in. Tick blew the air raid siren, which prompted Buck and the other security officers to turn down the house lights and close up the front windows and door. City ordinance on sound levels was pretty strict, plus it kept the drunk people sitting near the windows from falling out onto the sidewalk.

I poured some Cosmos for a group of sorority girls decked out in glitter and rainbows. The one handling the cash slid a five-dollar bill across the bar to me for a tip. I gave her a nod and pulled the towel out of my back pocket to wipe a spill off the bar. Out of the corner of my eye I spotted a hand reaching around my next customer and snagging my tip from the bar. My brain changed gears in an instant and hot rage flooded my veins. I shot my hand out and grabbed the thief's wrist in a vise grip, digging my fingertips into the groove in his wrist where the radial and ulnar nerves come together. Over the music I heard him yelp. The woman standing at my station, between me and the thief, saw my face and immediately stepped out of the way. I yanked the dirtbag toward me until his belly was jammed up against the bar and continued to dig my fingertips into the pressure point on his wrist. With my other hand, I reached around, grabbed the shaggy hair on the back of his head, and slammed his face down on to the bar. That stunned him, so I took the opportunity to hook my elbow around the back of his neck and reach my hand around until I was able to dig my fingertips into the mastoid pressure point...just behind his earlobe.

All the women who had been standing in line at my station, and sitting at the bar, took a step back. They watched me with shock on their faces.

"Buck!" I shouted over the music. I continued to hold the guy down on the bar. Me on one side, him on the other. I anchored myself down by hooking my boots under the ice bin.

"Buck!" I yelled again.

Rage was pulsing through me so hotly, I wanted to rip the guy apart. I was so angry; I fought the primal urge to bite him. He smelled like beer and a week's worth of BO. I knew my anger was way out of proportion to his crime, which was how I kept myself mostly reined in. But...

I pressed down on both pressure points even harder. He squealed and kicked his feet helplessly. I pulled down more on the back of his neck and ground his forehead onto the bar top and leaned down until my lips were brushing his ear.

"Listen to me, you nasty little fuck," I growled through clenched teeth and spoke in a clipped, angry tone. "Do not ever come into this bar again. If I see you in here, I will break your clavicle. Do you understand?"

He nodded slightly and started panting. The smell of piss filled the air.

"Do you understand me?" I growled again.

"Yes. Yes. I understand." His voice was muffled by the wood of the bar and the music.

I looked up and saw Buck and two other security officers pushing through the crowd.

"Lucky you, I have to let go of you now. Are you going to behave?"

He tried to nod and squealed, "Yes."

Buck walked right up behind him and tilted her head at me slightly.

"I'm eighty-six-ing this piece of shit. I caught him stealing." That was all Buck needed to hear. People caught stealing from the bar or staff were dealt with firmly. I let go of him and my feet landed back on the floor. Buck grabbed him with one hand on the back of his collar. Her other arm hooked cleanly under his armpit in a half nelson. The crowd of women took a few more steps back, to give Buck and the other officers some room. My customers kept looking at me questioningly. My flirty, easygoing butch façade had come off and it left them confused. I had scared them.

"Hold it. I want his picture for my eighty-six book," I said. I dug around in the cabinet under my register until I found the old Polaroid camera. After our little dustup, the guy's hair was a mess, he had a huge red bump on his forehead, a fat upper lip, and blood trickling from his eyebrow. The two extra guards flanked Buck to get into the picture. I pointed the camera at them, and Buck's stoic face broke out into a rare lopsided grin. I looked at the guy one more time.

"Say cheese, douchebag."

Buck dragged Douchebag to the side door and shoved him out into the alley. I slid the Polaroid picture into the album that I kept with pictures of similarly scraped up and shocked-looking people who I had kicked to the curb.

My rage and adrenaline receded, leaving behind a massive thirst and full-body shakes. I downed two small cans of pineapple juice, which I normally used to mix Greyhounds and Melon Balls. Then I chased the juice with a bottle of water and was ready to get back to work.

Turning around, I saw all my bar stools full again and a line of women waiting to order drinks. I let out a sigh of relief and took their return as either indifference to my explosive behavior or an olive branch of forgiveness. There were two other bartenders working, and my customers could have easily gone to the other stations for drinks instead.

Jen swooped in with a bar towel and some disinfectant, wiping a few drops of blood off the bar and grabbing the crumpled five-dollar bill, which she put in my tip bucket.

When Jen was done, I cracked a cocky grin at my audience, clapped my hands together once, and started taking drink orders. I enjoyed the lingering thrill from roughing that guy up, but knew it was wrong.

By the end of the night, I had mixed enough drinks and served enough body shots to earn over three hundred dollars in tips. I tipped out Jen generously and was thrilled that despite so many transactions, my till balanced out perfectly.

Everyone went through their closing routines: counting money, doing liquor inventory, cleaning up, and hauling trash out to the dumpster. Jen groaned loudly every time she found something gross. Used condoms, puke in the corner, and even a slimy latex glove jammed into a potted plant. Pride night proved to be as eventful and lucrative as usual.

Chapter Nine

Lying on my futon, listening to the fish tank filter burble and the traffic passing by outside, I ran through thoughts about graduation, the party, and my shift at the bar. With a wince I remembered bloodying up the guy who had tried to steal my tip.

"Ahhh, shit," I groaned to the ceiling.

I rolled to my side and looked out of the window at the bright-green leaves on the trees.

I had no plan.

It had not even occurred to me that during senior year I should have been going to all the job fairs on campus and networking in the student employment center. Other students already had six-figure job offers before they had even finished finals.

But me, I had PTSD, a short temper, a degree in Geology, and no idea what to do with any of it. College had been so much about simply surviving each day that the bigger picture hadn't been on my mind, and I didn't have any kind of parents or mentor to provide guidance or show any interest.

It occurred to me that it was Sunday, and I had just graduated. For once, I didn't have to go to class or study, and I didn't have to work that night. While I was bummed that I wasn't on the schedule for Coyote Ugly night, I figured I'd better make the best of it.

I rolled over, grabbed my cell phone, and dialed my brother. It rang several times and then rolled to voice mail recording.

"Yo, this is Joey. Leave me a message. Or don't," followed by the obligatory beep.

"Joey. It's your sister. I'm going for a ride on the delta. If you wanna come, call me back in the next half hour."

I folded up the futon and paced my small studio for a while as I drank some tea, pausing to feed my fish before I finally sat down on the folding chair at the card table pushed against the wall in the kitchen.

I picked up the phone and dialed Jared. He answered on the second ring, his voice fresh and alert.

"Hello?"

"Hey, Jared," I said, and cleared my throat.

"Viv! Hey! What's up?" Jared's voice took on an edge of excitement.

"Hey. We all missed you at the graduation party yesterday. Mom kept asking about you."

"Yeah. I'm so, so sorry that I couldn't be there. You know I would have been if I could."

I really wanted to ask him the reason why he missed it but didn't. The new uneasiness in our friendship was very unwelcome. In the past, I would have had no issue giving him shit for missing something important and demanding an explanation.

"Yeah, I know." I paused and cleared my throat again. It was hoarse and raw from work. "Bernadette told me I need to marry you. She hasn't stopped with that since that time you called me at her house, all the way from Iraq. She thought you making that call was the ultimate gesture."

"Ohhh, Bernadette," he said with a deep, hearty laugh.

I heard the familiar sound of the hinges on his metal security door and the creak of the weathered wooden steps in front of his house.

"You sitting out front?"

"Yup. The weather is perfect today. It's so clear. I can see all the way past the oil rigs. The ocean is flat and glassy."

I closed my eyes as he painted the picture for me.

I shifted a bit and my beat-up old folding chair squeaked. I heard his foot scrape the wooden step. I drew in a shaky breath.

"I did it again, Jared."

He knew what I meant. He took a deep breath. I knew his T-shirt had to be straining across his broad back. I fidgeted with a pencil. He waited patiently. We had been through this conversation before.

"Some punk ass tried to steal a tip from me off the bar. I bashed his face into the bar top and dug into some pressure points. His ugly mug is probably a total mess today." I took a moment to breathe and think. "I can't keep living like this. Pinned down by anxiety, a short fuse for anyone who imposes themselves on me, and no plan."

The silence strung out between us. Jared seemed to choose his words carefully, waiting for the moment when he knew I was ready to hear him.

"You saw some shit, Viv. And you did some shit. You can't expect to just walk back into civilian life like nothing ever happened." He stopped, listening for me. I didn't interject. "And you don't need a plan for what's next. Not right now. What's wrong with what you're doing? Like you told me in January, you have a place to live, a vehicle, a job. So what if you weren't headhunted by some environmental firm or mining company? There's no need to rush. You're twenty-eight, and you've got a lot to process still. School was a good distraction, and now you can start dealing with the bigger stuff." He grew silent.

"Yeah," I said, feeling distracted. "I think I'm going to take a ride today."

"That sounds like a good idea," he said gently.

"Bye, Jared. Thanks."

"Bye, Viv. Take care."

As I was hanging up, I heard a woman's voice through the phone.

"Jared! Come back inside! Your show is coming back on."

"'Kay. Be right in," followed by the familiar beep as he hit the end button and hung up.

The corners of my eyes stung as I looked at the phone in my hand.

What the hell just happened? Did Jared skip out on my graduation for some chick? He wouldn't dare put some girl as a priority ahead of my graduation. We go too far back. We've been through too much together. He literally wouldn't even be alive if it wasn't for me.

I growled and stood up, gathered my riding gear, and left without hearing back from Joey.

Chapter Ten

I took the Jefferson Boulevard exit off Highway 50 and headed south through the outskirts of West Sacramento. The farmland opened up all around me once I got past the fledgling housing developments. There were row crops and orchards as far as I could see. I passed huge ranches on the back side of Clarksburg. Horses, goats, sheep, and even an agitated emu in the pastures.

Jefferson Boulevard eventually dead-ended at Courtland Road. I turned west and followed it for a bit, slowing down to cross Miners Slough on a narrow bridge. Then I turned onto Highway 84, which was a narrow, twisty two-lane road of rough pavement atop the levee. On my right was Miners Slough. On my left was a steep drop down to the expansive farm fields on the other side of the levee.

I didn't come across many cars. Every once in a while, another motorcycle would pass by, heading north. I'd give the rider a little wave and usually got a wave in return. I saw fishermen, their trucks parked precariously down on the steep banks of the levee, their lawn chairs set up in rows. Some even had pop-up tents for shade.

I focused on navigating the twists of the road. Shifting up, shifting down, listening to the engine, and enjoying how responsive and agile my bike was. I had mastered riding and appreciated how well the frame and seat fit me.

Eventually I came to the convergence of Miners Slough and Steamboat Slough. I pulled off the road down a narrow driveway to the docking area of the Ryer Island Ferry. The ferry was docked on the far side of the water, so I parked my bike, shut it down, and climbed off.

My ears rang in the sudden silence as I pulled off my helmet and gloves and got a water bottle from the tank bag. My legs were really tight from the ride, so I walked back and forth across the driveway, trying to loosen them while I took big pulls on the water bottle. I watched an otter floating lazily near the shore.

There was the sound of a motorcycle approaching, its pipes throaty and popping as the rider downshifted. I guessed it would be a Harley, and as it pulled up to the dock, I saw I was correct. The rider parked next to my bike and killed his engine. I walked over to greet him as he got stiffly off his bike and took off his helmet.

"Hey. Good day for it," I said, pleased to see another rider.

"Definitely! Where are you headed?" he asked as he scratched his sandy-colored beard.

"Oh, just doing a big loop. Sac, Rio Vista, Dixon, Winters, then some county roads around Davis and then back to Sac. You?"

"I'm almost home. Dixon. I bombed up 50 early this morning to the foothills, then made my way back through Latrobe and down the Jackson Highway. Wanted to get a ride in before it gets too hot."

He was older than me, maybe his late forties. He clearly had worked hard his whole life. His hands were calloused, and his neck and face were permanently red from being outdoors. He was short and solidly built. I could instantly tell he was a good guy and put my hand out to him.

"Vivian."

He shook my hand with a strong, solid grip.

"Jeff," he said. His bright blue eyes sparkled just a bit, and he pointed to my bike.

"That's a lot of bike. How many cc's?" he asked as he sized me up.

"It's an '03 Honda ST1300, so it's just shy of thirteen hundred cc's. The seat pan is low enough that it fits me perfectly. Don't you worry, Jeff. I can handle this bike just fine."

He grinned at me, a paternal look in his eyes.

I gave his bike a quick scan and couldn't hold back a grin. His bike was a Harley Sportster. It had a custom glittery purple paint job with pink pinstriping. I looked at him, trying to conceal my amusement.

He cleared his throat. "It's my wife's. She never rides it, so I have to take it for a spin every now and then to keep the fluids moving."

"Whatever you say, man," I said with a chuckle.

We both turned as the ferry started to move across the slough toward us. I stowed my water bottle, and we both put our helmets back on.

We took the ferry across the slough and rode out together. I enjoyed the views of Mount Diablo in the distance as I followed Jeff all the way to Dixon, where he gave me a wave as he turned into a new housing development.

I kept going through the small town and rode to Winters using the back roads. The road I was on, Railroad Avenue, cut right through downtown Winters, past Rotary Park, Steady Eddie's, and the Putah Creek Cafe.

Although downtown was only a couple of blocks, it was full of people window shopping, sitting on patios at restaurants, and cars vying for parking spots. It was lunchtime, and even though I was hungry, I opted to keep going. I really didn't feel like dealing with so many people.

I continued on, back out into the open farmland, enjoying the solitude of empty roads. Railroad Avenue soon turned into County Road 89.

Relieved to be out of town again, I flew along Road 89, my bike easily reaching one hundred miles per hour without even a hint of strain or wobble.

Soon enough, though, I realized that I had to pee. I slowed, looking for a place to stop. I was surrounded by open farmland. No trees or shrubs along the road. The few structures I saw were all farmhouses and outbuildings, so I kept going.

As I approached Road 27, I saw what looked like an old warehouse. It was all closed up, the metal siding rusty, the dirt lot empty and overgrown with Russian Thistle. It was perfect for a bio break.

I backed off the throttle and downshifted. The bike rapidly slowed under me. I pulled into the dirt lot and parked along the side of the structure. I killed the engine and hopped off quickly, yanking off my helmet and gloves.

My bladder was screaming for relief. I grabbed a tissue from my tank bag and jogged around to the east side of the building so I wouldn't be seen from the road. Dropping trou, I squatted against the side of the building. The heat of the warm metal siding radiated through the back of my shirt. Once I was finished, I stood, buckling my belt as the relief washed over my body.

The building was surrounded by row crops, and a breeze blew across the fields. The distant Sierra Mountains wavered in the hot air.

It occurred to me an abandoned warehouse like that would be a great spot for geocaching and I walked slowly along the side of the building, looking for potential geocache hiding spots.

I rounded the far corner of the building and stopped in my tracks. I was startled to see a car parked about twenty feet away. It was a rusted-out old Honda Accord, its windows rolled down. The burgundy paint was oxidized, and strips of the headliner hung down, fluttering in the hot midday breeze.

Some faint shuffling sounds came from inside the warehouse, and I realized I was standing directly in front of a rusty pedestrian door. I took a few steps back. My hands tingled and I balled them into fists.

It's just a farm worker getting some tools, dumbass.

But the hypervigilance that had kicked in would not go away. Something was off, and it made me bristle.

I reached down for my M16 sling and came up empty. I looked down at my boots on the dusty cracked ground. They were my scuffed-up riding boots, not military issue jump boots. My pants were denim, not BDU's.

I slipped away to another hot, dusty day five years prior. A day when RPG's and bullets filled the air rather than the sound of the breeze rustling crops. A day when blood was shed.

I took another step away from the building and forced myself to breathe. Breathe in the smell of freshly plowed soil, leather, gasoline, and the faint hint of a dung heap.

I slapped myself across the thighs, hard. Even through denim, the sound and sting of it helped bring me back. My thighs and palms burned. I did it again to make the point to myself.

The door to the warehouse opened, and a woman stepped out. She was wearing a tan backpack, whistling, and twirling a key ring on her fingertip as she walked toward a spigot near the door. Her long hair was brown and tightly permed. She was short but solid and moved like an athlete. Scanning her, I noticed that her hands and shirt were bloody. I coiled up inside, ready to fight.

The door closed heavily behind her, and she took a few more steps before looking up and spotting me. She stopped whistling as our eyes met.

I immediately shifted into a fighting stance. With no hesitation the woman charged at me. I got low and opened my arms because I didn't have time to try a side slip. As soon as the woman plowed into me, I wrapped my arms tightly around her.

We went down hard. I wrapped my legs around her waist. Dust and grit were immediately in the air.

I had a hard time keeping a grip on her torso because of the backpack. I worked my arms up until the crook of my elbow was wrapped around the back of her neck, holding her as close as I could. She bucked and tried to roll out of my grip. I locked my right foot into the crook of my left knee and squeezed the woman's guts. She grunted as I clamped my thighs down around her, restricting her ability to get a full breath. She was solid and strong, deep down in her core.

Adrenaline and rage surged through my body, and a clear lucidity took over. I was in my element, and apparently so was the woman I was hanging onto.

I tucked my head up under her chin to avoid getting headbutted. The woman responded to my hold by rearing up on her knees, taking me with her. She slammed me down onto the ground. The first blow knocked the wind out of me, and gravel dug sharply into my back. She did it again and again, pounding my back onto the rough ground as I clung to her.

I needed to disrupt her, so I reached up with my free hand and started raining a barrage of short, sharp hammer fists against her right temple. She switched tactics and pressed her body down heavily on top of me.

I kept punching her temple. I had grit in my mouth and spit it out into the woman's collar. She managed to reach with both hands under her chin and grip my forehead, pushing down fiercely.

My neck wasn't strong enough to withstand all the pressure that was being applied. I let my neck relax and the back of my head hit the dirt. This opened up a crucial gap between us. Just enough space for her to headbutt me. I saw a bright flash as her forehead crashed down on the bridge of my nose.

I stopped punching her in the temple and my grip behind her neck slacked just a hair in that instant. I tasted metal in my mouth and down the back of my throat. I coughed as I sucked in grit and blood.

The woman wasted no time trying to break my grip. She slid her forearm across my windpipe. I acknowledged that she had the upper hand when it came to grappling. I was going to have to find another way.

There was blood in my eyes, and I didn't know if it was mine or hers. It burned like a motherfucker as I tried to blink it away.

The woman continued to press her forearm relentlessly down on my windpipe, and I let out an involuntary croak. Blood ran down the back of my throat and collected there.

I spit a mouthful of grit and blood into her face as I released my hold on her neck. I got a grip on her backpack and flipped it up over her head until it was in between us. The woman was sputtering and cussing at me for spitting in her face.

I released my legs from around her waist and pulled my heels up into a butterfly guard, placing them on her hips. With my feet I pushed her up and away with all my might.

Immediately the pressure was off my windpipe, and I gasped for air, choking and gagging, as the woman landed on her hands and knees a few feet away. I wound up with the backpack in my hands, so I threw it behind me and scrambled up onto my feet as quickly as I could. Still choking, I spat blood into the dirt.

The woman was slower to rise. Her hair was in her face. She hesitated just enough that I realized I had an opening. I moved in and booted her hard in the gut. Once, twice, three times. The woman grunted and gagged and dry heaved.

I took a second to breathe, assess, and scan the area around us to make sure there wasn't someone else coming at me. It occurred to me that I could either finish her off or take my chances and back away. I kicked the woman solidly in the gut one more time to make my point.

Then I backed away until I stood next to the backpack. My hands shook with rage, but I pushed it back before self-defense crossed over into manslaughter. My head spun and ached. My ears were ringing loudly, and blood flowed freely from my nose, down my lips and chin.

The woman grunted and gagged and spat and finally stood up. Blood flowed from her temple, and she had a red bump rising in the middle of her forehead where she had headbutted me.

The woman's keys were in the dirt between us. I kicked the backpack back a few feet and stepped back some more, signaling to her to get her keys.

She hunched down and got them, shaking the dirt off them. Her eyes shifted quickly from me down to the backpack. Her jaw set and eyes narrowed.

"Nope," I said.

"Fuck you," the woman said, her voice strained. She was in pain. "Who the fuck are you anyway? What are you doing out here?" she demanded, motioning to the empty field, dirt lot, and rusted-out building. "I thought you were a goddamn cop!"

I stood my ground and didn't say a word as I panted, blood and sweat dripping off my chin. It was in my mouth, between my teeth, on my tongue.

The woman swiped at the blood drying in her hair and on her temple.

"Fuck it," she said and walked over to the old Honda. She climbed in, fired it up, and drove around the building, heading for Road 27.

I stood there, listening to the gravel crunch hollowly under the car's tires on the other side of the building, and then realized the sound had stopped.

My bike was parked on the other side of the building. I grabbed the backpack and sprinted the length of the building, dropping the pack just before I rounded the corner.

The Honda was stopped a few feet from my bike, and the woman was writing down my license plate number. Finished, she winked at me and drove out of the lot, heading east on Road 27.

"Fuck!" I shouted and kicked at the gravel. "Fuck! Fuck! Fuck!" I knew a simple reverse license plate search would reveal my name, and any resourceful person could get my personal information with that.

My nose had stopped bleeding, and I could feel the blood drying on my chin and upper lip. I pulled up the collar of my T-shirt and wiped at the blood, which mostly just smeared it around more.

I dug around in my tank bag and pulled out my cell phone and a small flashlight. I jammed them both into the front pocket of my jeans. Popping my bike into neutral, I pushed it around to the north side of the building, picking up the backpack along the way. I parked near the pedestrian door, put the bike in gear, and locked the steering column.

Flashlight in hand, I took a deep breath, listened, waited five seconds, and pulled open the door. The phrase "fatal funnel" bounced around in my head. Echoes of past urban warfare instructors pounding into us how dangerous a doorway could be.

I stepped quickly through the doorway and took an abrupt step to my right. I pressed my back against the wall. The door creaked shut on its rusty hinges and the warehouse fell into darkness.

I stood still with my eyes closed, letting them adjust to the dark. When I opened them, I could see there was some dim light seeping in from gaps in the metal siding and roof.

Scanning the huge dim warehouse, I found that it was mostly empty. A few stacks of crates, pallets, an engine on a mount, some old tractor tires.

Off to the right there was movement, low to the ground. I held the flashlight up beside my cheek and flicked it on.

"Anyone here?" I called out as the strong beam of light from the flashlight lit up the area to my right. Several feral cats skittered away. All except one. In the beam of my light was a cat, crouched down. Its fur was white, and its left ear had been clipped.

The cat did not run, but instead stayed crouched in place, sniffing at something on the ground next to it. I took one step toward the cat. It looked in my direction, and I saw blood all around its mouth and flecked on the white fur of its chest.

Sweat formed on my face and under my shirt. It was stiflingly hot in the warehouse. The air was so still.

I took several more slow steps toward the cat, curious, keeping my flashlight trained on it. It started to tense up as I approached and finally bolted away when I got within five feet.

It was then I saw what the cat had been gnawing on, and it stopped me in my tracks. A pair of hands. Human hands. Just lying there in a small puddle of blood on the warehouse floor. I bent over and looked closer. Shining the light on them, I noticed the hands had what looked like silver spray paint on the fingers and under the nails.

"What the fuck?" I said quietly to myself. My voice sounded small in such a large empty space.

I began sweeping the beam of my flashlight back and forth along the dusty floor. It didn't take long to find what I was looking for. About ten feet away from the hands was a man. He was laying on his back, his arms spread out, each one ending in a raw, fleshy stump.

I stepped up to him slowly, trying not to disturb anything that may become evidence. I shone the light on his face. His eyes were closed. There was silver spray paint all around his mouth and nose, and the word PERVERT was scrawled across his forehead in black marker.

"Pervert? Are you a pervert?" I asked the body on the floor.

He looked young, maybe twenty. His hair was cropped short, with a good fade. His face was clean aside from the silver paint, and a very precise mustache. He looked fit. His T-shirt and jeans were clean and new. His leather sneakers were perfectly white. He clearly put time into his appearance.

I'd encountered enough mangled bodies that seeing this one did not elicit any sort of reaction out of me. I squatted down next to him and placed my fingertips on his carotid artery. I was intrigued to find that he was warm, his skin was slick with sweat, and he had a pulse. It was weak, but it was there.

I stood up, pulled out my cell phone, and flipped it open with my thumb. The little green screen lit up. I dialed 9-1-1 and hit send. It rang six times before I got an answer.

"Emergency services. Are you calling to report a fire, medical emergency, or crime in progress?"

"Yes, sir," I said.

"Which is it?" the dispatcher asked impatiently.

"Medical emergency, sir. Inside a warehouse out in the county at the intersection of Road Twenty-seven and Road Eighty-nine."

"What is the emergency?"

A keyboard clacked as the dispatcher hurriedly typed.

"There is a man here. His hands have been cut off. He is unconscious, but he has a pulse," I said flatly, reporting the facts.

"You have an unconscious man with a pulse whose hands have been removed. Is that correct?"

"Yes."

"Do you know what happened? Was it an industrial or farming accident?"

"No, sir. I don't think so. I saw a woman walk out of the building with blood on her hands and shirt. She assaulted me. I fought back, and she left in an old burgundy Honda Accord. She went east on Road Twenty-seven."

I heard more quick keyboard strokes through the phone.

"Okay, ma'am, I have people on the way. Please do not leave. What is your name?"

"Okay. Thanks." I flipped my phone shut, ending the call.

As I slid the phone in my pocket, the adrenaline from the fight started to trickle away. My nose began to throb. My back ached where I had been repeatedly been thrown down and ground into the gravel. My throat was tender, and it hurt to swallow.

I looked down at Pervert and knew there wasn't anything I could do for him. It was too late for tourniquets. He would either bleed out or not. I walked to the door, pushed it open with my elbow, and stepped out into the blinding sunlight.

I welcomed the sunlight after the stifling air of the warehouse. The door thumped shut behind me, and I sat down, hard, in the shade cast by the building. I took off the backpack, put it in the dirt between my feet, and leaned against the wall to wait.

After a few minutes, sirens approached. First to arrive were a fire engine and an ambulance. The paramedics and EMTs hustled up to me with all their gear. I pointed toward the door, and they filed into the warehouse.

Next came several sheriff's deputies, the engines of their cruisers pinging after the sprint out to the remote warehouse.

The rest of the day was a jumble of questions by investigators, fending off EMTs who tried to tend to my injuries, and a trip to the sheriff's department for more questioning. Questions about the backpack. Questions about the fight. Questions about the woman. Questions about why I had been there. Fingerprinting, nail scrapings, photos of my injuries. Eating a tasteless sandwich that someone placed in front of me. Downing bottle after bottle of water.

Finally, a numb motorcycle ride back to my studio at dusk.

Chapter Eleven

Back home, I soaked in a hot bath, my head leaned back, an ice pack across my eyes and nose. The hot water stung all the little cuts and gashes from the gravel.

I wondered how differently the day would have gone if my brother had been with me.

The water turned murky gray with a pink tinge, and when I drained the tub it left a gritty ring.

I stood up and showered, scrubbing at my arms and back, feeling blooms of pain each time I passed over a scrape or bruise. I saved my throat and face for last, carefully wiping at the dried blood on my upper lip and chin. I tentatively ran my fingers along the bridge of my nose and was relieved to find it was not broken, though it throbbed and hurt like a son of a bitch.

An adage from my time in the service spilled from my mouth.

"Too easy. Too easy."

My voice was hoarse, and it hurt to speak. I knew I still had gravel in my back but was too tired to deal with it. I dressed in some boxers and a beater, shoved some tissues up my nose so I wouldn't bleed on my pillow, fed my fish, and curled up on the futon. Sleep hit me over the head.

*

"Darn it, Joey! I'm going to be late to soccer practice," I shouted as I stood in the front yard, hands on my hips, looking up into the crabapple tree.

My soccer jersey was itchy and hot. Burgundy polyester. The house key hung around my neck on a long string, tucked under my jersey, the metal resting warmly against my belly.

My bicycle was up in the crabapple tree. It was a short tree, but tall enough that I couldn't easily get my bike down from its perch in the crotch about five feet up between the two trunks.

Joey laughed from where he was reclining in the shade on the concrete front steps of the house. I was on my own.

I climbed up the tree to the branches above my bike and managed to get the frame unwedged from where it was resting. The bike was heavy and awkward, but I was just a scrappy little nine-year-old kid. I gave it a yank and a push, and my green men's ten-speed crashed down to the ground below.

Joey looked on, amused, as I jumped down and scanned my bike to make sure nothing was broken and then I checked the little red digital watch on my wrist. The watch I'd gotten from saving up fruit snack box tops and sending away for it.

I still had to ride across town to soccer practice; I was going to be late. Anger welled up inside me. My neck and face flushed. My jaw clenched and my stomach tensed. I hated to be late.

I charged across the lawn at Joey. He looked momentarily surprised but managed to stand up from the concrete step and tackle me in the grass. He pinned me easily, using his size and weight to his advantage.

I was not playing. I raged and brought my knee up sharply, hitting him square in the balls. He yelped and rolled off me. I was still boiling angry, so I got up on my knees and punched him in the arm as hard as I could. My knuckles immediately hurt.

Joey's face was twisted, and I knew I was in trouble. He let go of his balls and sat up with a grunt. Without even blinking, he wound up and punched me right in the nose. Blood began to flow, and my eyes welled up immediately. He grinned down at me.

I got up, stumbled to my bike, and got it upright. I threw my leg over the huge frame and rode away from the house. My eyes stung and watered as I pedaled down the street. I had to get away from him.

Just as I reached the end of the block, Gail came around the corner on her bike. She took one look at me and pulled her bike to a stop in front of mine, forcing me to stop. I could barely reach the ground as I stood on my tiptoes to keep from tipping over, the crossbar of the bike pressed uncomfortably into my crotch. It was much too big for me. But it's what my mother had gotten for me at the used bike shop in town, so I had to make do. I'd grow into it eventually.

Gail was wearing scrubs, probably just getting off her shift at the hospital. She looked at me gravely.

"Hey. You okay?" She eyed my bloody nose, chin, and jersey.

"Hi, Gail. Yeah, I'm okay. I fell off my bike. I gotta go though. I'm late for practice."

"Vivi, you know I'm a nurse. Let me get you cleaned up. I have everything we need at my house." She paused. "You don't have to go home right now. I promise."

I looked away from Gail and shifted my weight from one foot to the other. Someone's air-conditioner kicked on with a loud whir.

"You know you can't go to practice like that. Heck, your nose might even be broken. Let me clean you up and check it out, okay? I won't make you go home. I promise."

I nodded and followed Gail to her small duplex. We parked our bikes under the carport, and I shuffled shyly behind her through her tidy, efficient house to a spotless, modern bathroom. She had me sit on the counter.

Gail used wet gauze to gently wipe away the blood that had dried on my upper lip and chin. The bleeding had stopped, and bruises were already spreading underneath my eyes. Gail gently prodded my nose and declared that it was not broken.

I paid close attention to everything she did and watched her face, so close to mine, as she worked. Concern and concentration creased her brow.

My knee was also badly skinned up and had bits of grass and gravel ground into it. Gail sprayed something on my knee, and it immediately stung and burned. I sucked in my breath sharply. The spray had a strong medicinal smell to it.

"This is not going to feel good," Gail warned as she held my skinny leg under her arm, firmly against her hip. She took what looked like a scrub brush and began scrubbing at the wound on my knee. I immediately swallowed back a howl and bit the inside of my cheek, trying to stay silent.

"It's okay to cry, Vivi. You don't have to be so stoic all of the time. Crying is not a sign of weakness, ya know."

I didn't know what stoic meant but made a mental note to look it up in my mom's enormous dictionary when I got home.

I sniffed in response. Gail finished scrubbing and dabbed the wound with more wet gauze. She sprayed something else onto it that also stung, but only a little bit.

"All right, kiddo. Good as new," she said cheerfully as she gently released my leg. "You need to ice that." She pointed to my face. "Come on."

I followed Gail into her tiny living room. She had me sit on the couch and hold an ice pack across the bridge of my nose. She brought me a glass of ice water and put in a VHS of Swiss Family Robinson. *I had never seen it before and was immediately drawn into the story while she went about her evening chores and prepared her dinner. The cooking smells were very different than what I was used to at my house. Gail's cooking had a full, exotic smell to it.*

As the movie came to an end and the credits began to roll, I snapped back to reality and looked at my watch. It was 5:45 p.m. My throat clenched and my heart pounded as I hopped up, seeing stars. I shakily took my empty glass and warm ice pack into the kitchen.

Panicked, I said, "Gail, I've got to go. I'm late. Mom's home already."

She stopped stirring a steaming pot and gently placed the wooden spoon on the counter.

"Okay. Okay. Hey, please try to ice your nose some more tonight and keep that knee clean."

She could see I was coming unwound.

"Um, hey, Vivi, it's going to be okay," she said, placing her hand on my shoulder.

My shoulders shook as I sobbed silently. Huge tears streamed down my swollen face, and my nose began to throb.

Gail watched me, concern creasing her brow once again.

"Vivian, it's okay. It's not so late."

"Nnnooo, i-it's n-not okayyy," I said through my tears, hiccupping from crying so hard. "The rule is, w-we have to be home w-when she g-gets h-home from work."

I tried to stop crying and catch my breath, swiping at the tears with the bloody front of my jersey, and winced as I discovered how swollen and sore my face was. The carefree time watching a movie on Gail's couch had dissolved, and I knew I had to face my mother.

"I've got to go home, Gail. Thank you," I said as I jogged out to the carport. I hopped on my bike and waved at Gail as she watched me through her kitchen window, frowning.

I pedaled hard, racing back up the block to my house. The door was locked. I wiped the rest of my tears and pulled the house key out from under my jersey. The white string it hung on was dirty and frayed. I unlocked the deadbolt, took a shuddering breath, and walked into the house.

*

My head swam as I sat up, disoriented. Light filtered through my window. There was an urgent knock on my door, so I stood up gingerly. Stars exploded in front of my eyes and vertigo hit me. I stood still for a moment to clear my head before striding to the door. The soft carpet under my bare feet and the cool air on my bare skin worked to center me.

Looking out of the peephole into the hallway, I saw Ang. She was in uniform but had a cover shirt on over it. I unlocked the deadbolt, opened the door, and stood back.

"Hey. Come in," I croaked. I tried clearing my throat a few times which made it feel like I had swallowed glass mixed with sand.

Ang looked at my face with a frown and walked in. She peered around my sparsely furnished studio and sat on the edge of the futon, eyeing the tangled sheet.

I sat on the other end of the futon and tried breathing through my nose but couldn't. Still in my boxer shorts and tank top, my head throbbing, I looked down and saw that my arms and legs were covered in deep purple bruises. I knew my face and throat were probably a horror show too.

Embarrassed, I reached up and pulled the wadded-up tissues out of my nose and examined the dried blood on them and then shifted my eyes back to Ang. The fish tank bubbled faintly, and the light-rail alarm clanged outside.

"What time is it?" I asked, clearing my throat again.

"Just after three in the afternoon," Ang said, her eyes still locked on mine, concern all over her face, wrinkling her forehead.

"Wow, I don't think I've ever slept that long before. I must be getting old," I said, trying to make a joke.

I gazed out of the window. Ang shifted slightly and cleared her throat.

"Vivian, sorry to just show up, but I don't have your number, and I wanted to check on you."

"Are you checking on me in an official or personal capacity?" I asked, pointing at the duty belt bulging under her cover shirt.

"Personal," she said, sounding a touch insulted.

"How did you even know I had a tussle yesterday?"

"Uh, Viv, you had more than a tussle." She took a breath and went on. "We got a BOLO from the Diablo County Sheriff's office out there to keep an eye out for the suspect vehicle. We got the basic details of what happened so that we would know who we were dealing with if we tried to do a traffic stop. I was nosy and called my buddy at the Diablo SD to get more information, and he gave me a bit more. Including stats and a description of you and your motorcycle. No name. You and your bike are unique, though, you know."

I nodded slightly.

"Why did you decline medical? You really need to get looked at."

I shrugged and gestured at my body. "Nothing's broken, and I have a minor concussion at best. I've been through far worse than this."

"Did they offer you a crisis counselor or a victim advocate?"

"Yeah." I heaved a sigh, suddenly impatient at the mention of counselors.

"Are you going to call and make an appointment with the counselor?"

"No. I'll be okay in a few days. Only time can dull this. I've been to crisis counselors before. I'll take a pass this time," I said flatly.

"I'm worried about you," Ang said.

She reached across the futon and put her hand on my shoulder. With that touch, I instantly deflated.

We sat like that for a while as I cried silently, my body shaking, big tears rolling down my swollen face and dripping off my jaw onto my bruised thighs.

Eventually the tears stopped. I took a few deep breaths, and carefully wiped my face on my tank top.

"I may look like shit, but I have no doubt that she does too. I worked her over pretty good in the end. I'm fairly sure she will have some internal bleeding from all of the times I booted her in the gut. Or a broken rib at the very least. And she'll definitely need stitches on her temple where I opened her up."

I flexed my hand. It was sore.

"That'll teach me to take a pee break on private property," I said with a halfhearted chuckle.

Ang's frown finally cracked, and she gave a small laugh. "You're lucky one of the deputies didn't cite you for it! Trespassing and public urination," she said sarcastically. "Well, if you won't get medical attention and won't go to a crisis counselor, can I at least feed you?"

I hesitated and then realized that I was incredibly hungry.

"Yes, you can feed me."

Ang beamed.

"Okay! Great! I'll go get changed and pick something up for us. How about you meet me at my apartment around sixteen thirty?"

"Yup, okay."

"Good. And, uh, I'm going to need to dig that gravel out of you, so maybe some wine too?"

I nodded.

*

Our first order of business was to remove all the gravel from my back.

Her bathroom was similarly appointed to mine, though hers was bigger because her place was a full-size apartment with a bedroom.

I peeled off my tank top, wincing as my sore muscles flexed and cuts reopened with the movement. I leaned against her bathroom counter. Ang went to work with tweezers. Silence fell between us as I gritted my teeth and she concentrated on the task at hand. Occasionally I'd hear a click as she dropped a piece of gravel onto the countertop.

It was a slow, laborious process. Eventually Ang straightened up and declared me gravel free. She wiped my back down with hydrogen peroxide, which stung like a motherfucker, and then glopped antibiotic ointment on all the gashes before covering them up with gauze and medical tape from her first aid kit.

I was starving and tried to maintain some semblance of manners as I wolfed down the mashed potatoes and tri-tip that she had gotten from Jack's Urban Eats.

Afterward, we spent a few hours talking and listening to CDs. She sipped on some Merlot while I worked on a glass of water. Our conversation flowed smoothly, and a spark began to kindle between us.

Topics bounced around from embarrassing work stories to stupid things we did in high school. Unfortunately, I had a slight distraction as I kept an eye on the time.

When eight o'clock rolled around, I got up delicately from where I'd been sitting in the middle of her living room floor.

"Thank you so much for dinner and for digging that gravel out of me. I have to go get ready for work."

Ang stood up too.

"There is no way you can work tonight. You need to recover. You can barely walk down the hallway! And, no offense, but have you looked in the mirror? You look as beat up as I am sure you feel."

"I've got to. I'm the only bartender tonight. It'll be slow tonight since it's Monday, but tips are tips. And besides, it's better for me to be distracted right now."

"If you stick around, I'm confident that I can keep you distracted," Ang said with a smirk.

My heart raced as her words and smirk registered. I bit the inside of my cheek to hold back my own grin.

"Ooh, so tempting," I said. "But I really need to work. And besides, you haven't shown me your labs yet, so nobody's pants are coming off anyway."

"What?"

"I don't hook up with anyone until I've seen their STI test results."

"Seriously?"

"Seriously," I said and turned for the door. "Thank you so much, Angela, for everything today. This was exactly the recovery I needed."

"Call me Ang," she barked as I walked out the door.

"Whatever you say, Deputy Sorenson," I said as I closed the door before she could see the flush rising in my face and the stupid grin I was wearing.

Chapter Twelve

The next day, I got a text from Ang saying she had gone to the lab for STI testing. I slipped a printed copy of my test results under her apartment door.

As the weeks passed, I worked, healed, and spent time with Ang. I avoided watching the news and dodged calls from the local news outlets. Apparently, my name was out there, and they wanted to talk to me about my dust-up out at the warehouse.

My bruises went from purple to blue to brown to yellow. I fielded a few calls from Sergeant Brickhouse, who was investigating the case. He had a variety of follow-up questions.

Once my nose had healed enough, I spent a lot of time motorcycle riding, running, and lounging at the tiny apartment pool.

Most of the people who lived in my building worked the day shift, so Ang and I often had the pool to ourselves. She was working nights, and that left us with plenty of time during the day to spend telling each other about our lives, showing off old photo albums, and comparing scars and the stories behind them.

I was falling really hard for Ang, and I let it happen. I trusted her, and it helped that she was attentive, caring and patient. I willingly fell in headfirst. And despite the chemistry between us flaring up to impossible proportions, I didn't allow any intimacy beyond lots of cuddling and making out.

While in the glow of new relationship energy, or NRE, I still had to watch my back, and Buck kept a close eye on me at work.

Eventually, the call I had been anticipating came. It was Sergeant Brickhouse. He wanted to come by.

I buzzed him in and heard his heavy gait coming down the hallway. He rapped on my door with his big, Hulk-sized knuckles.

"Hi, Vivian," he said as I opened the door.

"Hi, Sergeant. Come on in."

He stood awkwardly in my entryway. His large frame and shoulder bag took up a lot of space in my small studio, and he was aware of it. He had on khaki slacks, a tan belt, a crisp white dress shirt, and nice navy-blue blazer. His badge was clipped near his belt buckle, and I could see a faint bulge under his arm from his shoulder holster. He had an enormous class ring on his right ring finger with the Marine Corps emblem stamped just to the side of the big burgundy-colored stone.

His head and face were closely shaved. His neck thick and strong, leading to enormous traps that popped under his blazer. He was a big dude.

I moved my helmet off the folding chair in the kitchen and set the chair across from the futon.

He looked relieved and daintily took a seat on the small chair. It creaked under his weight, but it held. I sat on the edge of the futon.

"It's been a while. What can I do for you?"

"I've got some news for you. We're getting ready to make an arrest. I'm going to need you to look at a photo lineup. We've already got a match on the prints from some items in the backpack, but I'd like you to look anyway."

"You know eyewitnesses are usually unreliable, right?"

He ignored my smart-ass comment, pulled a sheet of paper out of his bag, and handed it to me. He gave me instructions, and I methodically looked at each picture on the sheet. They were all women with dark, permed hair, and similar facial features and builds to the woman I had run into at the warehouse.

After looking at each one carefully I pointed to the second picture in the bottom row.

"Her," I said, hearing an unexpected edge in my voice.

"You're positive?"

"Yes. That's her," I said, looking into the eyes of the woman who had had her forearm firmly across my windpipe, her face just inches from mine. She had grinned at me coldly while she tried to kill me.

Her eyes in the picture were angry. She seethed. The set of her jaw reflected the massive chip on her shoulder. Her disgust at being arrested and photographed was apparent. It was an old mugshot, but it was definitely her. No doubt about it.

"We've dealt with her many times. She's a slippery one, has a whole network of associates who will let her hide out with them, so she has given us a run for our money before. But it's only a matter of time before we roust her out."

"What's her deal? I ask, because she said the reason she attacked me was cuz she thought I was a cop. Clearly, she doesn't like you guys."

"Her deal is that she's a product of a system that failed her as a kid, and now she's following in her parents' footsteps. On top of that, she's a big fish in a small pond.

We've only ever busted her for petty shit, but we know she's up to a lot more. Sex trafficking, for starters. Just haven't gotten enough on her for the DA to actually agree to press charges. If I had to put money on it, I'd bet she whacked Mister Johnny Long's hands off because he messed with one of her working girls. But he isn't talking, and I already know she won't say a word to us when we finally do haul her in."

I nodded. Sergeant Brickhouse had me circle her picture, initial, and date it. He collected his stuff and stood up to leave but paused in the entryway.

"We're going to get her, Vivian," he said.

"I'm not worried. I can take care of myself," I said. "But I haven't watched the news. What happened to the guy I found in the warehouse? Johnny, you said his name was?"

Sergeant Brickhouse nodded.

"Mister Long survived. But he won't tell us anything. He is scared out of his wits. Once he stabilized, we arrested him. He had a warrant out for stalking. It was a misdemeanor charge, but enough to at least get him into custody so we can keep an eye on him."

"You put a guy in jail who has no hands and rumors he's a perv? Damn, Sergeant. He'll be eaten alive."

Sergeant Brickhouse grunted and moved on.

"That backpack you got off her was a jackpot. Her fingerprints and his blood were all over the machete she used."

A chill went up my spine.

"A machete? That bitch is brutal."

"That's for damn sure," he said as he headed for the door.

Ang was walking up to the door as I opened it. There was an awkward moment as Sergeant Brickhouse said goodbye, and Angela waited out in the hallway for him to leave. She gave him a nod when she saw the badge clipped to his belt.

We waited until Sergeant Brickhouse had disappeared down the stairs to the lobby, and then Ang stepped up to me and gave me a quick but close hug.

"Hey, babe, how are you?" she asked as she stood nervously in the corridor. I wondered why she seemed so anxious.

"I'm great. You?"

"I'm good. Good. So, I've decided to start training for a century ride in the fall."

"A century? Wow, that's impressive and quite a commitment," I said, raising my eyebrows.

"Um, do you work tonight?" she asked.

"No."

The nervousness dissolved and Ang smiled devilishly, pulling an envelope out of her back pocket.

"My STI labs. All clear, as promised." It appeared her patience with my abstinence had ended.

Fair enough. Let's see if she can handle what I have to offer.

"Excellent," I said and took the envelope from her. With my other hand, I grabbed the front of her button-up shirt, pulled her into the studio, and pushed her against the wall.

"Stay," I said, and Ang stayed.

Her breath quickened. Her mouth was slightly open, and her eyes were pinned on me as I closed and double locked the door.

Standing in front of Ang, I pulled the lab report out of the envelope and reviewed each page. All her tests were indeed clear. Nodding, I folded the paper back up and put it in the envelope, which I placed on the floor by the door. I did everything just a foot away from Ang, and I took my time. The tension was building between us, crackling like a livewire.

Straight faced, I stood squarely in front of Ang. I could smell her musky cologne mixed with a floral shampoo, a combination that was unique to her and that I had come to know. I looked up at her.

"How tall are you, Ang?" I asked, an authoritative edge to my voice. I knew damn well how tall she was.

"Six feet, three inches, sir," Ang replied, her throat tight. That made for an eight-inch height difference between us. I nodded again.

Ang got an obstinate look on her face. "Do you think you can handle that?"

"I have no doubt I can handle you," I replied, my tone steady and stern.

I grabbed the front of Ang's shirt roughly and pulled her away from the wall, flush against my body, paying close attention to her breathing and body language, and I determined that my impression of her had been correct. She was definitely a submissive. But I suspected she was also a bit of a mega bottom.

She bit her bottom lip and held her breath.

I looked up into her eyes and commanded, "Breathe."

Ang's eyes fluttered for a second as she regained her focus. She drew in a deep breath and let it out slowly.

"Are you here, with me, right now?" I asked. She nodded. I let go of the front of her shirt.

"Is that a yes?" I demanded.

"Yes," Ang replied, her hands clasping and unclasping.

"Yes? Yes, what?" I hissed.

"Yes, sir."

"Good."

I nodded and stepped back, looking her up and down, taking in every detail, assessing. Ang stood, hands fluttering against her thighs. The tension built in her eyes and in the creases around her mouth.

Ang was waging war against that coiled spring inside her. She wanted to reach out and touch me, but as a submissive bottom, she knew better. So, she waited for instructions, her eyes wide. Mouth still slightly open.

"You're armed." It was a statement, not a question.

"Yes, ankle holster, right leg," she replied haltingly.

"That's what I thought. Take it off and give it to me."

I stood back patiently with my hand out as Ang squatted down, pulled up the leg of her jeans, and removed the holster. A small semi-automatic pistol was nestled snuggly in it. Ang stood up and placed the holster in my hand. We were still in the narrow front hall of my studio, and Ang's broad shoulders and tall frame made for close quarters.

"Put your back against the wall," I said.

Ang pressed her back against the wall.

I pulled the pistol from the holster and examined it. A Ruger LCP, black on black. I deftly hit the magazine release and caught the magazine as it dropped out. I racked the slide back, ejecting the round that was in the chamber. After locking the slide, I placed the holster, pistol, magazine, and spare .380 bullet carefully by the door, on top of Ang's STI results.

"Take your boots off and place them, neatly, next to your holster."

Ang quickly removed her boots and put them next to the holster. She looked back at me. I shook my head.

"They aren't evenly placed, and your laces are hanging out. Do it again. Neatly."

Ang looked at me with confusion on her face.

"Put. Your. Boots. Back On. Do it again," I said firmly.

She quickly snapped into motion and did as she was told. She went through the whole thing again, but the second time, she ensured that her boots were lined up perfectly and the laces were tucked in. I nodded my approval.

We went through the entire exercise, over and over, with every single item of clothing that Ang had on until she was standing, naked, with her back against the cold, white wall. Ang knew I was testing her, just as she was gauging what kind of a top I was. So far, my style seemed to be exactly how Ang liked it. Stern but calm, disciplined, direct, confident.

I knew I would find Ang's hard limits and not push her past them. The way she looked at me showed that Ang trusted me and already knew I would take care of her. She knew that because of the foundation we had already built and because of the exercise I had just put her through. It was clear to me that she could, and would, submit completely to me, which was a responsibility I took very seriously.

I looked Ang over again, taking her all in. I spent extra time to gauge her expression and facial features. Looking for hesitation, doubt, fear. There was none. I ran my eyes over her strong, broad shoulders and small breasts. Her mons and labia were completely hairless, and her overall muscle tone impressive. Traps, deltoids, abs, obliques, quads, calves, all toned and firm. I nodded my appreciation.

Ang did not have any tattoos. Her skin only marked by the occasional scar.

I drew in a deep breath and slowly released it. I ran my fingertips along Ang's arm, shoulder, trap, and then I slid my fingers up the back of her neck and into her hair at the back of her head. I curled my hand into a fist, pulling Ang's hair, hard. I checked that I had a proper grip. It was even, and I was satisfied with it. I tugged Ang's head back. She immediately groaned.

I got up on my toes and whispered into Ang's ear.

"What is your safe word?"

Ang took a sharp breath.

"Red light," she said as she breathed out.

Ang's body had already started to respond. She had goose bumps, and her nipples were hard. Her breathing had become shallow. I could see her pulse pounding away in her carotid.

My grip still firm in the hair on the back of Ang's head, I stepped toward the futon.

"Come with me," I said.

Ang did as she was told.

Chapter Thirteen

I hunkered down behind a low rock wall. Gravel dug into my knee as I pulled a fresh M16 magazine out of the pouch on my LCE. The chatter of rapid gunfire came from my left and errant bullets whizzed by, too close for comfort, pinging off the rock wall. As I shouldered my weapon a high-pitched sound bloomed in my ear, and I awoke with a start as my cell phone rang shrilly. Releasing the shadow of an M16, I reached out and grabbed the shrieking cell phone off my coffee table. The phone's small green screen showed that a blocked number was calling. Ang stirred next to me as I answered.

"This is Vivian."

There was no reply.

"This is Vivian," I repeated evenly.

"I've got you," the caller said. It was a woman's voice, in a steady yet mischievous tone.

I immediately recognized the voice. I gripped the phone tighter and steadied myself.

"You've got nothing." I paused, pacing myself. "Have your broken ribs healed yet? Are you still pissing blood?"

"Fuck you, dyke," she said, sounding disgusted.

I chortled in amusement.

"Thanks. I will."

"I've got you," the woman said again.

I sighed, already tiring of the exchange.

"Pffft. All right, then. Have yourself a great day," I said, laughing as I pressed the end button and disconnected the call.

"Hooo-leee shit!" Ang exclaimed.

I rolled toward her and propped myself up on my elbow, grinning smugly at her. Her eyes were bright with excitement.

"What?" I raised an eyebrow at her.

"Are you fucking serious? Was that the woman from the warehouse?"

"Yeah."

Ang looked at me, speechless, mouth hanging open slightly.

"Yes, yes. I know. I'll call Sergeant Brickhouse later and let him know."

I looked at the window and saw the orange glow of sunrise in Sacramento.

"Have you peed since we finished last night?" I asked Ang, directly.

"Umm, no," Ang said, looking slightly embarrassed.

"You didn't follow my instructions. Go pee. Now. No UTIs on my watch."

"Yes, sir," Ang said with a grin.

The boundaries and roles that reigned the night before had fallen away when we had finished playing. But Ang liked calling me sir, so she continued to use it even when it wasn't required of her.

As she got up from the futon and headed for the bathroom I smiled proudly. There were still red, hand-shaped welts on her ass and up the back of her thighs, as well as purple spiderwebs from broken blood vessels within the welts.

I nodded to myself, satisfied with my work.

*

I caught Sergeant Brickhouse on his desk phone and told him about the call.

"Vivian, I highly advise against antagonizing her like that if she makes contact again." His voice was heavy.

"Well, that's no fun," I replied.

"I'm serious," he scolded and sighed deeply. "Now listen up. We went in full force to execute her arrest warrant, but she wasn't at any of her usual spots. We tossed her shithole of an apartment and found information about you. She clearly did her homework. Your phone number, address, where you work, registration info on your bike and truck." He sighed again. "We didn't get her. You're really going to need to watch your back. Can you go on a trip out of town for a little bit? She's on the run or holed up somewhere."

"Mm-hm. I can take off. What's her name, anyway?"

"Crystal Wylie. Several of the deputies are familiar with her. She's no stranger to the County Jail. Also, we've impounded her beater of a car, so I have no idea how she's getting around."

"Hm," I grunted, thinking through my options. "Yeah, I know somewhere I can go to get away for a bit. I can't go right this second though. I need to sort my shifts out with my boss and see if my landlord will feed my fish for me. But it'll be today."

"Okay. Keep me posted, and I'll let you know if the situation changes."

"Thanks for the heads up, Sergeant."

"You're welcome. Watch your ass, kiddo."

Kiddo. Really?

"I will."

Hanging up, I looked out of the window at the tops of the trees.

As I considered leaving town, I thought about work, and Ang, and how I would handle things if Miss Crystal Wylie tracked me down. I opened my phone and dialed Jared, who answered on the third ring.

"Hello," he said, annoyed.

"Hey Jared! How's it going?"

"Good. Things have been good." He cleared his throat. "How about you?"

"Things have been a little bumpy. I've got so much to tell you. I was hoping I could come down there and visit for a while. We can get caught up, go for some runs, the usual."

There was an uncomfortably long pause. Normally, Jared would have jumped at the chance for me to visit. I frowned.

"I don't think that's a good idea," he said haltingly.

A woman's voice hissed angrily in the background.

"I'm sorry, Viv. But no, please don't come down. It's not a good time. And you probably shouldn't call me for a while."

Disappointment washed over me. A level of disappointment I hadn't felt since I was a kid. He had already missed my graduation, and now, for the first time, had turned me away. I was floored. Jared was my best friend. The guy who had always had my back and had literally saved my life on more than one occasion. My stomach began to hurt. I was at a loss for words.

"Oh. Um. Okay."

"You take care, Vivi."

"I'm trying. Is everything okay, Jared?"

He lowered his voice. "Not even remotely. But I'm figuring out a way to handle it."

"You know you can call me any time. Whatever you need. I'm here for you."

"Thanks," he said. It sounded like his throat was tight and he was choking back tears. He hung up.

I stared at the little cell phone in my hand. "What the fuck?" I said, incredulous. Confusion and disappointment fought for top ranking. I knew I couldn't solve the problem in that moment. I had to get out of town. But concern for my friendship with Jared weighed heavy across my shoulders.

I knew Ang was working a twelve-hour shift on patrol and likely couldn't talk. I sent her a text.

> *Sgt. Brickhouse told me to leave town. Will keep you posted.*

My landlord agreed to feed my fish, and I apologetically asked my boss for more time off. Sheila had been very understanding since the mess at the warehouse. She agreed to cover my shifts for a while and would hold my job for me, which was very generous in that line of work.

I made a few more calls to arrange a place to stay in Guerneville and to pick up some shifts at a queer bar there that I used to frequent. Even though the summer season was winding down, they still said they'd be glad to see me and give me some work.

I packed my duffel with warmer clothes and running gear and pulled fifteen hundred dollars in cash from the safe under my sink before texting Ang again.

> *Update: For your eyes only. Heading to my usual spot in G-ville. Want to come up on your day off?*

Ang worked twelve-hour shifts on a rotation. Three days on, four days off. Then four days on, three days off. Round and round.

Yes. Sounds great! Let's talk details after my shift.

I grinned and added my gear to the duffel bag. Harness, lube, condoms, gloves, a selection of cocks, and a stiff boar's hair brush. All set.

The drive was surprisingly smooth. I didn't hit the usual traffic on Highway 37 or Highway 101. By the time I got to Guerneville it was late. I made a quick stop at the Safeway to get supplies and headed across the river to the cottage where I always stayed. The innkeeper was waiting and welcomed me warmly. We chatted for a few minutes, getting caught up since my last visit. Thankfully, my favorite cottage was available, and I paid cash up front.

Due to frequent flooding of the river, all the cottages were up on stilts, with parking underneath. The entire property was ringed with massive redwoods that rustled in the breeze as I hefted everything up the stairs to my cottage. Nineteen wooden stairs.

The cottage looked and smelled exactly the same as it always did. My core relaxed as I put away the groceries in the kitchen, my duffel in the bedroom, and my dopp kit in the bathroom.

I had time to kill before Ang got off work, so I decided to take a soak in the hot tub. I walked along the elevated walkway, past other cottages, relieved to discover that I had the hot tub to myself. I turned on the jets and lowered down slowly into the steaming water and took in the night sky, which was impossibly full of stars.

I thought of other times I had looked up at the night sky. As a little kid wearing a stiff ruffled dress and Buster Brown Mary Janes on a humid Fourth of July, lying on the grass listening to the gentle waves of the ocean, waiting for the fireworks to start while Joey and the other kids ran around hyped up on sugar trying to catch fireflies.

As a middle schooler, I used to sneak out of the house at night. I had figured out how to get up onto the roof of the school and would lie up there, the roof warm on my back as it radiated the heat from the day. Looking up at the stars with the sound of Highway 113 in the background, I would disconnect from the chaos at home.

As a high schooler, I had gone to many parties in the farm fields outside town. Country music blaring from someone's truck speakers. Those parties usually involved a bonfire, the guys getting too drunk and the girls getting way too caught up in gossip and shit talking. Fistfights were common. I would sit in the bed of my pickup and watch the satellites go by. The raucous noise of the party so close to me, yet I was encapsulated in the back of my truck, somehow at the party but also very alone.

As a soldier, out in the field with my unit for a training exercise. On the perimeter for fire guard. It was late and dark and humid. A warm breeze blew through the scraggly pines. Cicadas trilled all around me. I was filthy and stank of days of salty sweat, caked in red dirt. Smudges of camo still on my face, neck, and ears from the day before. I was hungry. Despite dousing myself in DEET, mosquitoes hovered close by. Looking up through the trees and letting it all fall away. The moon was full, and the stars shone brightly. I spotted the twinkling lights as an airplane flew by high overhead, and realized a couple of hundred civilians were all heading somewhere for work or for pleasure, totally unaware of the soldiers on the ground sleeping the dreamless sleep of those whose bodies have been completely wrung out.

I also remembered the times when we weren't playing war games, on foreign soil and in grave danger. Advancing in the dark. Our senses on overload, trying to hear and see everything and anything. Even then I had found one short moment to pause and peer up at the stars.

As I sat in the hot tub in Guerneville, I considered how the night sky looked the same to me, no matter where in the world I was.

The hot tub timer clicked, and the jets turned off. I took that as my cue to go. Wrapped up in a towel, I scurried along the elevated walkways, my swim trunks dripping a trail behind me, my skin steaming in the cool night air.

As I passed each cottage, I heard snippets of conversations, laughter, TVs, music, and one fussy baby. Cold, wet, and alone, I passed by little bubbles of family and love and connection.

Back in my cottage I shed my wet swim trunks and sports bra in the bathroom and hung them up to dry in the shower. The nights were much colder there, so I got into some sweats and made peppermint tea.

I sat on the couch with a mug of tea, reading one of my favorite books: *The Wind-up Bird Chronicle* by Haruki Murakami. I had beat it up so much that I had to use a strip of clear packing tape to keep the front cover on.

In some ways, I identified with the main character, Toru. He lived a solitary life and completed every task thoughtfully and completely. Like Toru, I was adrift, unclear of what the future held.

I was deeply engrossed in Toru Okada's world when my cell phone pinged, startling me.

Finally off shift and home. Okay to call you now?

I looked at the time. It was just past 1:00 a.m. I sent her a quick reply.

Yes, please.

I set down the book and sat up a bit. Cold, I grabbed the throw blanket and put it across my lap and legs. I took a sip of my tea, which had also grown cold. My phone rang loudly, breaking the silence.

"Hey, how are you? How was work?" I asked.

Ang chuckled in response. "I'll answer those questions. But first, a sergeant told you this afternoon to get out of Dodge, and you've already made it happen. You don't fuck around. I'm impressed."

"You shouldn't be so surprised. You know I make shit happen. And besides, there is a sociopath out there who seems to think she needs to take me down."

"You did kind of ruin her post-maiming getaway. Plus, dude probably would have bled out if you hadn't shown up. So now she has one witness and one victim, both alive to tell the tale. Not ideal when you're trying to get away with a slow, torturous murder."

"You've got a point," I said wryly.

"Anyway, I'm good. Work was a hot mess. Got involved in pursuit of a stolen vehicle, and then went on a call where I had to remove and impound all of the firearms from the house of a DV." She paused and took a deep breath, exhaling slowly. "That's enough about work."

Taking the hint, I changed the subject. "So, they have a massive zip line course out here, which in itself is awesome. But these zip lines are up in the canopies of the redwoods, like two hundred feet off the ground. If you're game, I'll get us on their schedule," I said, my voice taking on the excitement I felt.

"That sounds amazing. I'm in! I'll be there in a couple of days. I'm really looking forward to spending some time with you."

"Me too. Have a good night. Get some sleep."

"G'night."

I got up and checked all the windows and doors to make sure they were closed and locked. There were nine points of entry on the cottage, including the front door.

I turned off all the lights and collapsed on to the queen-sized bed. It was so much bigger and softer than my futon. I sank into it, enjoying how my body immediately relaxed. Sleep began to pull me under when the cottage phone rang. I sat up, on edge. I let it ring two more times and then answered.

Making my voice stern and commanding I grunted out, "Yes?"

A man cleared his throat nervously.

"Yes?"

"Uh, hey, Vivian," the man stammered.

I did not recognize his voice. I heard him shift. My mind raced.

"Uh. Hey, dude. I think you've got the wrong number."

"Oh. You sure?" he said with surprise in his voice.

"Yeah. Nobody here by that name. What was it? Valerie?"

"Nope. Vivian. I'm trying to find my friend Vivian."

"Sorry, man, I'm not much help. Have a good one."

I hung up and sat still in the bed, my mind working through all the scenarios I could think of.

I reached under the pillow to the cool space underneath and brushed my fingertips across the familiar hard plastic of my stun gun.

Somebody knew where I was. I wasn't at all surprised but still had a twinge of irritation. I turned the ringers off on my cell phone and the cottage phone, deciding that sleeping was the best option, and lay back down, my hand resting on the palm-sized stun gun.

Sleep overtook me quickly, pulling me down into the darkness, and my subconscious gleefully began its nightly ritual of strangling me.

Chapter Fourteen

I awoke as the gray, pre-dawn glow tinged around the edges of the curtains. I was tangled up in the sheets. My jaw was sore, and the inside of my cheeks had long thin welts from clenching my teeth. My palms had little cuts on them from my hands being balled up into fists all night. That hadn't happened in a long time.

I showered, ate breakfast, packed up my small day pack, and drove to the state park. I sat in my truck and immersed myself in Toru Okada's world until a ranger raised the US and California flags and opened up the main gate and the visitor's center.

The chill air hit me as I stepped out of the truck. I had on a beanie and a fleece jacket over my running gear. A few other visitors walked with me to the big trail map. I gave it a once-over to confirm that the ridge trail was open and the route had not changed and then took off at a trot in the direction of the trailhead behind the visitors' center.

The ground was covered in ferns, leaves, and fallen redwood needles. Overhead, the sky was closed off by the tall canopy of the redwoods. Sound traveled strangely there. It was muffled but also carried very well.

When I reached the trailhead, I picked up my step to double time. The trail was a narrow dirt path which immediately inclined as it climbed up the base of the hill. After about a half mile, the trail had a flat area similar to the landing in between two flights of stairs. I paused to look back on the trail behind me down below. There were a few hikers going at a slow clip near the trail head. Drawing in a deep breath, I smelled a faint hint of wood smoke mixed with the earthy aroma of decaying plant matter and damp earth. Turning to face the next section of trail, I realized shit was about to get real.

In front of me was a steep incline. The hill looked like it had stairs cut into it, but the steps were actually a massive, ongoing tangle of tree roots that were so well worn by hikers and runners they looked polished. Up beyond the tree root stairs, the trail went through a series of endless switchbacks as it wound its way sharply up through the forest.

"All right, Chastain. Take that fucking hill."

I ran, climbing the steep tree root steps up the hillside at a quick, steady pace. Halfway up the relentless incline my lungs and quads begin to burn. My pores opened up despite the chill. My breathing was labored, so I focused on evening it out. I listened to my feet pushing off the trail, step after step. The scratchy sound of grit ground between my shoes and the tree roots.

Just as it seemed my lungs would burst, I reached the top of that incline, and without losing momentum, picked up the next section of the narrow trail, which wasn't as steep. I kept on at a jog to allow my body to recover, even though it screamed to stop and take a break. But I knew if I stopped moving right then my legs would seize up in the cold.

Nausea overtook me. I spat a few times into the underbrush as my mouth flooded with saliva.

I called a fast-paced marching cadence quietly to myself.

"Take the hill," followed by slapping my hand twice on my thigh.

Take the hill, slap slap,
Take the hill, slap slap,
Take the hill...

*

The deep voices of my squad repeated after me as I called it out. I led them on a hellish red-dirt trail, broken by sharp volcanic rock. Our boots were caked in red mud. My nose was running from the strain, so I stopped calling the cadence and blew a snot rocket.

"Sorry, Pollock," I said to the soldier behind me.

"Ain't nothing, Sarge," he said between labored breaths.

The soldiers farther back grunted, sniffed, spat, and coughed as they ascended the trail at a rapid step. All kitted out with full rucks, LCE's, our M16s slung at our sides, and Kevlar PASGT helmets.

I kept a steady pace, slipping in the slick mud now and then. My helmet was incredibly heavy. I knew it weighed about three and a half pounds. The nylon webbing inside dug into the top of my scalp, causing hot spots, which were really aggravating. The leather sweatband stuck to my damp forehead.

"Fuckkkk," I said quietly to myself.

"Yup," Pollock said matter-of-factly.

I heard more slipping and cussing and grunting as my squad struggled. I wanted to stop right there and rest, and I knew they did too. But stamina, endurance, and timing were the order of the day, so I kept on. We were on a timed ruck, and our time would be compared against the other squads in our company. We were determined to keep our top ranking.

I flipped through my memory for another cadence. One I knew would raise their spirits a bit. As my left boot hit the ground, I began calling it out in a strong, steady voice. In unison, they called it back to me.

Seen an old lady walkin' down the street.

Seen an old lady walkin' down the street.

She had a ruck on her back and jump boots on her feet.

She had a ruck on her back and jump boots on her feet.

I said, "Old lady where ya goin' to?"

I said, "Old lady where ya goin' to?"

She said, "US Army Airborne Schoooollll."

She said, "US Army Airborne Schooollll."

I said, "Hey, old lady, ain't ya been told?"

I said, "Hey, old lady, ain't ya been told?"

Airborne school's for the young and the bold.

Airborne school's for the young and the bold.

She said, "Hey, young punk, who ya talkin' to?"

She said, "Hey, young punk, who ya talkin' to?"

I'm an instructor at the Airborne school.

I'm an instructor at the Airborne school.

Cause I'm hardcore.

Hardcore.

Lean and mean.

Lean and mean.

Fit to fight.

Fit to fight.

Rock.

Rock.

Steady.

Steady.

Rollin'.

Rollin'.
Ready.
Ready.
Rock.
Rock.
Steady.
Steady.
Fit to fight.
Fit to fight.
Lookin' good.
Lookin' good.
Hollywood.
Hollywood.
Our voices echoed through the trees, and my squad pushed on.

*

At last, I passed the tree line and reached the ridge. My heart was beating so hard I could feel it in my throat. The trail flattened and straightened as it followed the ridgeline. I jogged it and finally stopped once my breathing and heart rate had slowed a bit.

I unclipped my small day pack and slid it off. The cool air hit the sweat on the back of my fleece and gave me a chill. I dug out my water bottle, a banana, and protein bar and sat down slowly on a boulder beside the trail, careful that my quads didn't go out on me as I lowered myself. Cold radiated into my haunches from the rock.

Slowly, I ate the banana and protein bar, and sipped on the water as I took in the view. The horizon to the east and south revealed Napa and Sonoma and all the surrounding vineyards nestled in rolling hills. The air on the ridgeline was a touch warmer and smelled of the ocean. Not far to the west was Highway 1, Jenner, and the wide-open Pacific Ocean. I knew the ocean was there. I just couldn't see it.

There were horseshoe prints on the trail where the hiking path intersected with the horse trail. Hoofbeats approached, and soon a row of horses filed by as they headed east. The horses kept to a comfortable, slow walk. They, too, had just climbed that mountain and were recovering. The riders were all silent as they took in the vistas.

I gave the lead rider a nod, and he nodded back. His posture and clothing showed he clearly spent a lot of time on horseback. He looked to be in his early fifties. His face was red and weatherworn.

The people on the horses behind him were definitely tourists. They all seemed a bit tense and weary yet excited, dressed in colorful sweatshirts and jackets, sunglasses pushed up on their heads. The horses knew the way and moved on along the trail.

After the group had passed, I stood up and began stretching slowly and methodically. Once I was finished, I took a quick look around to be sure I was alone and squatted behind the boulder and peed.

Back on the trail I snapped the chest and hip straps of my pack and continued jogging the ridge trail. The entire ridge trail loop was just over five miles. When I was trail running, the descent usually took me less than half the time as the ascent and was always an adrenaline-pumping experience.

As the trail steepened, I had to think quickly since every step could end in a terrible tumble if I didn't land properly. My brain worked in overdrive to process it and make all the calculations on where to step and when, not to mention my thighs and feet were quite numb at that point, and my knees threatened to explode with the impact of each downward step.

But I loved the sheer madness of it.

Chapter Fifteen

Back at the cottage, I ate, showered and, somewhat recovered, made some phone calls, and then walked across the river on the footbridge. Tip bucket and work gear in hand, I crossed the main drag to the gayest bar in the small town.

Wealthy queer folks from the Bay Area owned vacation homes there, which is why a gay bar could survive. Their little gay haven away from the hustle and bustle of the city. Walking through the front door of the bar, I skipped my usual pre-work mantra.

It was dim inside, and as my eyes adjusted, I smiled, seeing that nothing had changed since my last visit. Rough wood-paneled walls, billiards in the back, a few small tables, and a rectangular bar smack in the middle of the place, with bar stools all the way around it. It smelled like beer with a slight hint of stale pot and cigarette smoke.

Duran Duran's "Rio" was on the jukebox.

"Ho-lee she-yat. Look who's here. If it isn't Viviana herself, in the flesh and blood," the bartender said, giving me a wide grin. "They told me you were coming, darlin', but damn, it's been a while. You don't call; you don't write. What's a fella to think?"

Several of the men sitting at the bar chuckled, all regulars who I recognized. They were mostly older white men, cruising for otters, cubs, and twinks. I had spent enough time there to know each of their tastes in drinks and men.

"Hey, Jack-o. You're looking sexy, as always," I said, grinning at him.

"Don't you know it," he replied with some flair, spinning around slowly so I could get the full picture.

He was in his fifties, wearing Wranglers, and a tight white T-shirt. He had faded Navy tattoos on his tan, muscular forearms, a handlebar mustache, and an orange bandana hanging out of his left back pocket. Exactly the type of bartender anybody'd expect to see in a place like that.

I raised my eyebrows at Jack and pointed at the orange bandana.

"Looking for some fun, are ya?"

"Daddy gets what Daddy wants. Anything, anytime, baby," he said with a wink as he opened up the flip top section of the bar and I stepped through.

I put down my tip bucket, set up my gear, and got to work as "No Diggity" started playing on the jukebox.

The night passed quickly as I got into the groove of that bar.

*

Back at the cottage, I drew in a deep breath, cell phone balanced between my ear and shoulder. My feet and legs were screaming from the beatings they took between the trail run and ten hours of bartending. I let out a groan, glad to be off my feet.

Ang chuckled, her voice low. I could tell she was tired after her twelve-hour shift. We'd been chatting about our respective days and there was a comfortable pause in the conversation.

"I'd say I'm worried about you, which I am, but I know you can take care of yourself."

Defensiveness boiled up, pushing aside the comfort and calm I had been lying in. "Yup. I can. You need to trust that I can take care of myself."

"I do. I do," she said and paused. "And now I think you need to put your hand inside those boxer briefs and take care of yourself for me."

"Only if you do the same," I said, amused.

"You're on. I've already gotten a head start. Your voice at night, tired, mellow. So hot."

I lay back in the bed and propped the phone between the pillow and my ear and slid my hand into my boxer briefs. Ang's breathing picked up, which immediately turned me on.

*

The next two days followed the exact same routine. Up early, reading in my truck until the gates opened at the state park. Trail run on the same trail. Back to the cottage to clean up and eat. Then walk across the footbridge to the bar. Work my shift. Walk back to the cottage. I did it exactly the same way, for the benefit of whoever was tracking me, if anyone was tracking me. I could feel it in my gut that I had a tail, just hadn't pinned them yet.

On my fifth day at the cottage, I woke up anxious but energized. Ang was going to meet me at the zip line place in the afternoon. I didn't have a shift at the bar to worry about that night. I was looking forward to showing her some of my favorite places and spending time with her.

As I got ready, I threw my usual stuff in my day pack: water, banana, protein bar, tissue, pen, geocache tracker, folding knife. The knife was something I had picked up while in the Army. It had a belt clip, the handle was OD green, and I kept it sharp. All week I had been wearing my stun gun clipped to the waistband of my running shorts, my shirt pulled down over it, and that day was no exception.

I parked in the lot at the state park. There was only one other car, on the far side of the lot. A nondescript white sedan. Probably a rental. Children bounced around in the back seat, and a man in the driver's seat read a newspaper.

I dug around in my day pack, pulled out the geocache tracker, and fired it up to see if I could get a signal through the dense canopy. Success. I had a signal, and there were caches nearby.

I had finished *The Wind-up Bird Chronicle* and moved on to *Valencia* by Michelle Tea. I was on my third reading of it, and the cover had started to break away from the binding. I read *Valencia* until the park opened.

I slung the lanyard of the GPS around my neck, tucked my pen behind my ear, and hopped out of the truck. I jogged into the park, following the coordinates to the closest cache. Behind the visitor center, I found a tiny magnetic cache stuck to a light pole. It was well-camouflaged. I opened up the canister and pulled out a tiny scroll that contained the log. I added my name to the strip of paper, rolled it up tightly, and slid it back into the canister. I stuck it to the light pole, tossed the GPS tracker and pen into my day pack, and jogged to the trailhead for the ridge trail.

I made decent time as I ran up the steep tree root steps and on up to the ridge. My legs were still sore and fatigued from the previous runs but getting moving helped loosen me up. By the time I reached the top I was totally gassed. I probably should have taken a rest day to let myself recover.

I sat on the usual boulder to hydrate and refuel. The air on the ridge was a few degrees warmer than the previous days, and it smelled more like pine than ocean. The breeze had shifted. I shed the beanie and light fleece and shoved them into my day pack. I stood up and began going through my stretching routine, getting my body ready for the rest of the run. No one nearby, I squatted behind the boulder and peed.

Just as I was about to stand up, I heard the sound of a boot crunching on gravel on the trail. It was very close; behind me and to my left. I did not outwardly acknowledge that I'd heard the footstep. Instead, I looked at the sky, admiring how clear and blue it was, and then stood, pulling up my shorts as I went. I placed my hand gently on my hip, along my waistband, and turned around.

Sure enough, there was Crystal.

Her hair was pulled back into a tight braid, and she was dressed for a hike. I spotted a small scar on her temple where I had opened her up before. She was holding my day pack. *Shit.*

"Howdy," I said chirpily as I walked around the boulder and back onto the trail.

She dumped the contents of my pack on the ground and pushed the items around with the toe of her sturdy hiking boot. *Rude.*

"Great day for a hike," I said.

She scowled at me and nudged my GPS with her foot. "What the fuck is that?"

"It's a GPS, made especially for geocaching. A Geomate Junior," I said cheerily, trying to throw her off with my enthusiasm.

She nodded.

"Sooo, I'd really like to start running again before I cool down too much. Muscle cramps, ya know. They're a bitch."

I placed both my hands on my hips and smiled at her. My left hand was still an inch from the stun gun, clipped to my shorts. I was enjoying messing with her and decided to keep pushing.

"I'll be sure to tell Sergeant Brickhouse that you say 'Hi.'"

I took a step toward all my gear that was in a loose pile on the ground.

"Uh-uh," she said, shaking her head at me.

"How'd you like the hike up here?" I asked. Watching her, gauging her.

"Cold. I got an early start. Really early."

"So, do you vacation here a lot or—?"

"Stop trying to be funny," she said, cutting me off.

"I'm fucking hilarious once you get to know me."

She grunted.

I looked her directly in the eyes and cast all friendly demeanor to the wayside.

"All right. What the fuck do you want, Crystal?"

"Just needed to have a little chat and wanted some privacy." She winked at me. A grin twisted her lips, dimples forming on both cheeks. A hint of disconnect fell across her eyes. The look on her face gave me a moment of pause.

This chick is crazy.

I feigned impatience.

"Well, here we are, not a soul around. Say what you came to say. You're wasting my time. I've got shit to do today."

I was doing what I could to control the tone and mood of our interaction. I found she was easily manipulated in that way. As I escalated, she escalated. As I brought it back down, she came back down. I was trained to do it. I knew exactly how to manipulate and control an interaction. Right on cue she mirrored my impatience.

"Hey! You're wasting *my* time. You think I enjoyed hiking up here in the dark?" She paused, looking briefly to the horizon. "The sunrise was nice though."

I shifted my weight and looked at her. She shifted her weight as well.

"So, they're gonna catch me. They will. I can't leave NorCal 'cuz I've got...obligations. And when they do get me, this whole fucking thing is going to go to trial. And guess what? You're gonna have to get up in front of a judge and a jury and tell them what you saw."

I put on my best impertinent face. "Jesus fucking Christ, Crystal. I don't need a goddamn civics lesson. I know how the judicial system works."

I caught the sounds of footsteps and voices coming up the trail. Two hikers came into view as they crested the ridge.

"Good morning." I kept my tone cheerful as they approached.

"Good morning," they answered in unison and laughed. They looked like they were probably married, in their thirties, and fit, wearing matching wide-brimmed sun hats, khaki shorts, and hiking boots, and using walking poles. They didn't stop to chat or rest but rather kept on moving along the trail at a steady pace.

Once the couple had rounded the bend and were out of earshot, Crystal dropped her voice, her tone harsh.

"Listen, asshole. You have two options. You either respond with *I do not recall* to every question they ask you about all of this, or you meet an untimely and slow demise."

I looked at her and considered her proposal. I also considered killing her. It sure as hell wouldn't be my first time wiping out a waste of oxygen like her.

I also considered the context. This wasn't some raping, pillaging enemy soldier in a warzone who I could make disappear. There was law and order and a justice system here, and she was right. They would catch her. I decided I couldn't justify her death.

Then I considered our previous meeting, and I knew she would try to fight me. I also knew she was a far superior grappler. If she got me on the ground, it may not end well for me.

"Really, Crystal? You're going with good old-fashioned witness intimidation? Weak. You followed me all the way to Guerneville and to the top of a damn mountain for this? You've been watching too much bad TV. Why didn't you just catch me at my apartment or work?"

"The cops know who I am around Sac. I was keeping tabs from a distance. When I saw you packing up your truck, I figured perhaps a short vacation is what we both needed. Besides, there's nobody to hear you scream up here."

I laughed loudly. A hearty belly laugh meant to distract her while I took another step toward her, closing the gap to about five feet.

Her face reddened. I'd embarrassed her, which I found amusing. The grin on my face must have been the last straw for her because she charged at me, just as I knew she would.

I was ready for her. I had already pinned another one of her weaknesses: She was very predictable. I planted my right foot solidly on the dirt trail and delivered a brutal push kick directly to her sternum. All her weight plowing into me almost knocked me down, but I had been ready for it and was able to stay upright.

As my left foot slammed into her, with all her own momentum adding to the pressure, her lungs emptied, and something in her chest cracked. She immediately began gasping for air, while still trying to lunge at me.

This is one tough bitch.

I shuffled back a step to avoid her fists. As soon as there was an opening, I stepped up close to her and grabbed the front of her shirt. I delivered a head butt to the bridge of her nose. The sensation on my end was akin to being punched in the forehead. Stars bloomed in my vision. She grunted but didn't cry out at all. I took a quick step back. Her nose bled heavily, and her eyes teared up from the sting of it. I stepped in again and punched her in the nose, crushing it. A solid right cross. I put my hip into it. That did it. She whimpered and stopped advancing on me. I kicked my backpack and the pile of my stuff behind me.

My forehead hurt, but not nearly as much as I was sure her nose did. She leaned her hip against the boulder, her hand pressed into her sternum, her breath shallow. There was a steady *tap, tap, tap, tap* as her nose bled onto the dirt at her feet. She wasn't even trying to keep an eye on me.

I was mildly disappointed that I didn't have an excuse to use my stun gun on her.

I just wanted to get the hell out of there. Shoving everything back into my pack, I took quick glances at her and behind me to make sure no one was approaching. Crystal stayed put.

I made a mental inventory as I put everything back in my pack and had the sick realization that one thing was missing. My knife. I scanned the trail between us, and the ground alongside the path. Nothing. I shook my head.

Damn it.

I slid into my pack and clipped the straps at my chest and hips. Crystal heard the clicks, which seemed to bring her back. She looked at me fiercely and wiped at her nose, smearing blood all across her cheek.

"Okay, so, it's been fun running into you and all, but I need to head out now," I said. "I'm on a schedule today."

"I won't stop." Her voice was angry and garbled as she tried to talk through the blood trickling down the back of her throat. She groaned and rubbed at her sternum. My foot had left a nice dusty shoe print in the middle of her shirt. She spat a wad of red mucus into the dirt. We both looked at it.

"But why is that? Why won't you stop? What's the point? Every time you pop out from wherever it is you are holed up, just to fuck with me, you're putting your own self at risk of getting tagged by the cops." I kicked at the dirt with the toe of my running shoe. "Seems like a stupid fucking risk, if you ask me."

She cleared her throat and hawked another bloody loogie into the dirt. "Loose ends. I don't like 'em."

"Loose ends? I am *not* the loose end you need to worry about. Your loose end is sitting in jail right now, with no hands, mind you...he's probably wishing he had died after all. He's your loose end, not me."

Clearly in pain, she was practically folding in on herself as she leaned against the boulder. Rubbing at her sternum, she just glared at me.

"So, that's it? That's all you've got for me? Pfft. See ya around, Crystal," I said with a grin and jogged away along the ridge trail.

As I ran, I assessed the situation. I'd somehow easily bested her that time, which was unsettling since I knew how strong of a fighter she'd been the last time. She had even fallen into my ridiculously simplistic trap of keeping the same routine every day.

Have I overestimated her? A small-town bully who happens to be a sociopath. Maybe she isn't as cunning as I gave her credit for.

But she may or may not have my knife. It was all too easy, which made me suspicious.

I glanced over my shoulder and found I was still alone on the trail. I reached down under the hem of my shirt and unclipped the stun gun from my waist. I flipped the safety off with my thumb.

Soon I was past the tree line and back under the canopy. Adrenaline seemed to be pushing me along. My breathing was elevated but steady. The smell of rotting vegetation and wood smoke tinged the air.

I eventually overtook the couple who had passed us on the trail earlier. They were still walking at a steady measured pace.

Coming up quickly behind them, I called out, "On your left!"

They both sidestepped to their right, allowing me to carry on without slowing down.

"Thanks!" I yelled over my shoulder to them.

"You're welcome," they said in unison, which made them giggle.

As I left them behind, I smiled to myself. They were weird, but out there getting it done. Couldn't fault them for that.

The trail twisted and narrowed as it became steeper yet. A flicker of movement off to my right stole my attention and that momentary distraction caused me to slide in some loose gravel as the path made a sharp switchback turn. My left sneaker slid out from under me like I was on ice. I went down hard. Gravel and dirt bit into my bare forearms and legs. There was a hot slicing sensation as a jagged tree root gave me an impressive gash on my right shin.

I sat up as the dust settled and evaluated the damage. I couldn't triage any of it up there. It would all have to wait.

I grabbed my stun gun out of the ferns, glad I hadn't shocked myself during the fall, and gave it a once-over. The safety was still off, and the charge light was glowing happily. It was ready for service. I pressed the fire button and saw an arc of electricity jump between the prongs as it made a loud crackling sound.

A grin spread across my face. I got up quickly, shook off some of the dust, and got moving before the hikers caught up to me to see what a mess I was.

I took more care, watching for gravel and tree roots. Blood ran down my shin and soaked into my sock. The trail was technical and had switchback after switchback as it wormed its way down the mountain.

I finished my run and jogged slow laps around the parking lot to cool down. A few people walking to their cars gave me questioning glances. I was a mess, bloodied up and dirty. I circled my truck a few times looking for any vandalism or signs of tampering. All looked clear, so I hopped in and headed back to the cottage.

I drove past meadows full of late season wildflowers and tall lush grasses on the edge of town. Less Than Jake's album *Anthem* was in the CD player as I drove across the river. I sang along loudly, windows down, the adrenaline draining away.

My easy victory over Crystal brought me no joy. I still couldn't let my guard down.

Chapter Sixteen

It took some time to clean up the gash on my shin and the road rash on my arms and legs. I used tweezers from my dopp kit to pull out gravel and splinters, creating a bloody little rock collection on the cream-colored bathroom counter. Finally, I scrubbed off in the shower. Peering in the mirror, I knew there wasn't much I could do for the purple lump growing on my forehead.

I hydrated and ate. Somewhat recovered, I headed out, wanting to get to my date with Ang on time.

The drive to Occidental was smooth, the roads narrow and winding. The parking lot of the zip lining place was deep in the redwoods, the lot surrounded by tall trees, and bordered on one side by a creek.

The only signs it was more than just a random parking lot in the middle of the woods were a pop-up tent and an outhouse. There were a few other cars, but there wasn't anyone around.

I stood by the shallow creek and watched it flow slowly past, the water so clear I could see straight down to the gravel bottom. Little pools had formed, and minnows flitted about. Periodically I would hear the echo of people shrieking and hooting.

I looked down at my watch: 13:45.

A car pulled into the lot behind me, the tires crunching on loose gravel. The engine shut down and pinged as it started to cool. I turned and was relieved to see Ang's Subaru parked next to my truck.

Ang stood by her car and watched my approach with a huge grin on her face. She gave a quick glance to the goose egg on my forehead but didn't mention it. She had on a tight white T-shirt, navy-blue tactical pants, and her service boots. Her hair was pulled back in a tight bun identical to mine.

The butterflies in my stomach intensified as I got close to her. I reached up and grasped the back of her neck, brought her face down to mine and kissed her. She immediately responded to my firm, commanding touch and kiss, stepping up to me so that our bodies were just touching. I caught her bottom lip between my teeth and bit down exactly as hard as I knew she liked. She groaned and wrapped her arms around me, pressing her hips into mine.

I released her neck and lip and stepped back. Her eyelids fluttered but she quickly recovered.

"Hi," I said.

"Hey," she said back. Her eyes flicked again to the lump on my forehead.

"Good drive?"

"Decent. Hit traffic on the thirty-seven and one-oh-one, but here I am," she said, looking back down into my eyes, grinning.

"Here you are. Fuck. Thank you! I'm so glad you were able to come. Thanks for making the trip up here."

She nodded and I took her hand in mine as we walked across the lot. We took turns using the outhouse and then stood by the creek.

At 14:00 on the dot a beat-up pickup truck pulled up to the pop-up tent from a gravel service road. Six people sat in the back on benches.

As soon as the truck stopped, they jumped out of the back and began excitedly talking to each other. They all had thick Australian accents. One of them, a petite blonde woman, was clearly traumatized by the zip line.

She walked over to the creek and sat down heavily on the bank. She was pale and shaking and carrying on, her voice bordering on hysterical. "You're all out of your minds. Who does something like that? How could you take me up there? Insane!"

Her friends walked over to her but didn't do anything to comfort her. They continued to carry on and jump about excitedly. I knew immediately that I was going to love it.

A small party bus and two rental cars pulled into the lot and parked. The group of Australians piled into the party bus, the pale one moving the slowest. She got in last.

Ang and I exchanged amused glances and walked over to the pop-up tent, followed by the people who had just gotten out of their cars.

The person who had driven the pickup truck had set up a laptop and a small table under the pop-up tent and boisterously called us over to him. He reviewed the waivers, took our money, and had us sign our lives away. He raised his eyebrow at the state of my face, and I gave him a grin.

"I'm fine. Let's do this."

"Alrighty. Load up," he said, and we all climbed onto the benches in the back of his truck.

We bumped along a one-lane dirt and gravel service road. It wound around this way and that and then climbed a few hills. I lost my orientation since we were under a dense canopy. West? East? No idea.

I held Ang's hand tightly for the drive, our thighs leaning against each other. The warmth and the realness of her leg against mine comforted me, and I wanted to drown in that sensation.

Having spent so much of my life without physical contact, I was often overwhelmed by Ang's body touching mine. She was so solid, so warm, so present, and it provided me so much comfort. Something as simple as her thigh pressed against mine while taking a bumpy ride in the back of a pickup truck was monumental.

At the end of the road, the truck pulled into a lot. There were two small storage buildings and another that looked like a gift shop. It was strange to discover a gift shop at the end of a private road in the middle of the woods. There was a vaguely Jurassic Park vibe.

We climbed out and were directed to one of the sheds. Three employees waited for us. They were young and caffeinated and got us suited up in harnesses, helmets, and well worn, thick leather work gloves.

The goose egg on my forehead and road rash on my arms got concerned looks from the woman tightening my harness. I gave her a smile and asked how her day was going. She chirped a generic, "Great," and moved on.

We practiced clipping, unclipping, and braking. They had a short zip line that was about eight feet off the ground for us to practice on. We got the safety talk and then started the climb up the ladder to the first platform.

I made the ascent just behind Ang and enjoyed the view I got of her lean muscular ass framed by the tight harness.

The wood platforms were square and built around the massive trunks of the redwoods. The highest zip line and platform were two hundred feet off the ground. The zip lines were longer than I expected, strung out between the trees. Far below was the forest floor, mostly red dirt, boulders, and underbrush.

We all took turns zipping from tree to tree. Hooting and hollering and enjoying the rush. Everyone in the group was into it, no fear, no hesitation. It took us almost two hours to make it through the entire course.

While I was waiting for my turn to rappel back down to the ground from the final platform, I made some small talk and learned that the father/daughter duo in the group were on holiday in the US from Kosovo. Both were very attractive. The father's English was excellent. He shared that he was a psychologist and his daughter was a student at university.

I'd been deployed to Kosovo in 1999, as part of Operation Joint Guardian. The atrocity of the brutal ethnic cleansing of men, women, and children left a scar on my soul forever. I bit my tongue to stop myself from commenting on my time in their homeland. Instead, I welcomed them to the US and to California and wished them well on their travels. The daughter rappelled down with gusto, followed by her father.

I was silent on the ride back to the parking lot. Ang threw me a few concerned looks, squeezed my knee, and held my hand gently. After we all hopped out of the truck everyone dispersed, the others all hyped up on adrenaline still. I took a deep breath and let it all go, turning to Ang with a big smile.

"Okay. I'm back," I said. She smiled at me, relief apparent on her face.

"Welcome back! So, that was fucking amazing! Nothing like chancing death two hundred feet above the ground to get your heart pumping."

I looked up at her and gave her the sleaziest grin I could muster, cocking my left eyebrow up. "You get my heart pumping, babyyyy."

We broke into laughter and walked back to our cars, holding hands.

Another anxious group of thrill-seeking tourists were already under the pop-up tent signing their lives away.

Both of our cars looked a bit off kilter. After further inspection, we found that Ang's right front tire had been slashed and my left front tire was flat. My missing US Army knife was stuck down to the hilt in my tire.

"What the fuck!" Ang was incredulous. Our cars were parked next to each other's so it hadn't been hard for someone to walk between them and slash both of our tires.

"I've been making new friends," I said flatly.

"Clearly," she said.

"That's my knife." The fact caused a momentary startled look to pop up on her face before she locked it up and was all business.

Scanning the tree line, I walked around our cars. I pulled the knife out of my tire, folded it up, and put it in my pocket, glad to have it back. And also glad it had been lodged in my tire and not my neck.

"Well, no damsels in distress here. Let's handle this shit and get on with our afternoon. I bet I can change a tire faster than you. Wanna race?" I asked, giving her a wink.

"You're on," she said and immediately bolted for the rear liftgate of her car.

"Damn, woman! You're cutthroat," I said and dove under the bed of my truck to free my spare tire. It was neck and neck, but in the end, I had her beat by just over a minute.

"Not bad," she said.

We sat on my tailgate, out of breath, our hands black with brake dust and grime. As we caught our breath, we sat and listened to the creek passing by and the shouts of the next batch of people zip lining.

"So, are you going to tell me what happened?" she asked, turning to me.

"Hmm?" I grunted absentmindedly, my attention snapping back to her.

"Are you going to tell me what happened?" she asked again, her tone neutral.

"Well, once upon a time, a mommy and a daddy loved each other very much…"

She punched me in the arm and laughed.

"But seriously, I've been watching that red bump on your forehead swell and turn purple since I got here. Your arms are full of road rash, and you've been bleeding through your pants."

"Where?"

"There—" She pointed to my shin.

"Oh. That," I said with a shrug. "I took a tumble during my trail run this morning. And I also ran into my pal Crystal."

Ang narrowed her eyes.

"When?" she asked and immediately went into hypervigilant mode, scanning the tree line. She got up, unlocked her glovebox, and pulled out her ankle holster. She strapped it on adeptly and joined me back on the tailgate.

"This morning on the trail. I knew someone had been tailing me, so I made it really easy for them. More predictable for me that way too. Crystal walked up on me. We had a chat. We tussled a bit. Then I left. And I fell on my way back down the mountain."

I stopped, took a deep breath, and looked into Ang's eyes for a moment. She held my gaze and hesitated, then asked, "Is Crystal in any kind of condition to get herself back down off that trail?"

I bristled and bit back my temper.

"I didn't kill her, if that's what you're asking," I said, looking down at my hands nestled in my lap. The knuckles on my right hand were red and swollen from punching Crystal.

"No, no, that's not what I was implying. Really. It's just..." Ang paused, choosing her words carefully. "It's just, look, I know you are very capable of taking care of yourself, and that you'll defend yourself, when needed."

"Do you not trust my judgment?" I peered up from my hands and saw that look on Ang's face. Like she wanted to backpedal and take it all back. I kept going, letting her off the hook.

"Look. I disabled her just enough so that I could safely make it back down off that ridgeline without having to watch my back too much. And before you say anything, no, I am not calling Sergeant Brickhouse. At least, not yet. She'll be fine. Clearly, she is fine, she managed to track me here and stab my truck!"

I took a breath, and my temper melted away. I chuckled.

Shaking her head at me, she pursed her lips. "Okay, stud, let's get you back to your cottage so we can put some ice on that forehead. I'll also dig the rest of the gravel out of your arm and look at that gash on your shin. Between our two branches of the military, we should be able to patch you up. Either way, I'm good with tweezers and super glue. And if you're lucky, I'll also let you fuck me."

She slapped my thigh, hopped off my tailgate, and headed to her car.

Chapter Seventeen

Properly patched up and properly fucked, I lay on my side in bed. The bedroom was impossibly dark from the blackout blinds. Exhausted from the trail run, tussle with Crystal, and excitement from zip lining, I fought to keep myself from getting pulled down into sleep.

Ang spooned me. As cliché as it sounds, in that moment our bodies fit together perfectly. With her long legs and arms and her broad frame, she held me in a way I never knew I needed, and once I had it, I never wanted to lose it.

The warm smooth skin of her bare stomach and breasts pressed against my back. I was soaking it all in and fought sleep just to be able to prolong it. It was the first time I'd been content in a long time. I still had that gaping, sucking chest wound that wanted, no, *needed* some sort of something I hadn't figured out yet. In that moment, even *it* was calm.

I drew in a deep breath and released it. By the sound of Ang's breathing, she was still awake. Her arm was draped over my side, and she was holding my hand where it rested, nestled between my small breasts. I squeezed her hand gently.

She delicately cleared her throat and kissed the back of my neck gently, before speaking quietly into the pitch-black room.

"I wonder if we might set aside some time to talk?"

"Sure," I said groggily. "Anything in particular?"

"Yeah. I'd like to talk about us and nonmonogamy. About opening up."

A lightning bolt of anxiety shot through me and my gut clenched up. My eyes opened wide in the darkness, staring into the red numbers on the nightstand clock.

"Okay," I said. I continued to focus on the clock and tried to keep my breathing even and my body relaxed even though inside I was exploding, imploding, and clenching up all at the same time.

"Thanks," she said and squeezed my hand. Her breathing soon slowed and evened out until she was in a deep sleep.

All my drowsiness had dissipated in the hot rush of insecurity coursing through me. I lay as still as I could while my mind raced and Ang slept.

In theory, I strongly believed in polyamory and ethical nonmonogamy. In practice, I'd not had a good experience. My only experience with nonmonogamy had not been consensual. My partner at the time was deep in the queer BDSM community in San Francisco. I'd attended some meetings and functions with them.

One night, they came back from a queer BDSM meeting in SF and announced that they had found a top and would be getting involved with that person.

I was blindsided. Literally speechless. I did not advocate for myself. We never discussed boundaries.

So, it began.

At one point, they came back from a date with their top. They undressed to shower, and I discovered they had "SGT" cut into the flesh of their left ass cheek. Their top was a sergeant in the US Army and required that her subs call her Sarge.

Carving "SGT" into my partner's skin seemed like she had overstepped, but in reality, we had never set a rule about marks. I still said nothing, but I seethed inside.

What finally pushed me over the edge was when Sarge ended it with my partner. My partner was crushed and came to me for comfort. I couldn't. I could not be that person for them. I couldn't help them grieve and process the breakup. I had reached my limit and ended the relationship.

Afterward, I read several books on polyamory and ethical nonmonogamy to try to better understand. That's when I realized that, when done ethically, nonmonogamy wasn't bad at all.

Ang asking to talk about nonmonogamy was totally reasonable. But I knew Ang well enough to know she wanted what she wanted. So, us talking about it and deciding against opening up wasn't really an option. She wanted to open up our relationship, and that's how it would be...or I could take a hike. And that was a shitty situation to be in.

I watched the minutes pass by on the clock and listened to the sounds of the deep night. The creek burbling far below, the occasional swish and groan of tree branches in the breeze, a dog at the campgrounds on the next property over alerting us to something.

And then I heard the inevitable sound of a creaking step on the wooden stairs below, followed by a slight footfall on the walkway just outside. Then, the sound of someone trying the windows gently, one at a time. Ang still had her arm draped over me, so I grasped her wrist and slowly squeezed it, applying more and more pressure until I knew she was awake. She didn't say anything.

"We're about to have a visitor," I whispered.

Silently, we untangled and got out of bed. Ang pulled her collapsible asp off her nightstand, and I picked up the stun gun off mine. I had recharged it, so it was ready for service. I switched off the safety with my thumb. Still naked, we both trod lightly out of the bedroom, through the small living area to the adjoining kitchen. She was almost as good at the creep as I was.

It was incredibly dark, but our eyes adjusted. We stood off to the side of the refrigerator so that we were not visible from the large corner window over the kitchen sink. We'd intentionally left that window unlocked, the blinds halfway up. Every other point of entry was locked up tight, and all the other blinds were closed.

I stood on my tiptoes and confirmed that Ang's handcuffs, cuff key, pistol, and zip ties were all on top of the refrigerator. Just in case. We'd set a simple trap, and now we waited in the darkness to see if it would be sprung.

A gentle tread outside stepped from the living room window to the front door. Someone tried the door handle and found it locked. The delicate steps then went from the front door to the kitchen window. I heard the kitchen window slide open about an inch, followed by a long pause. Then the window slid open slowly in its well-greased tracks.

Adrenaline gushed through my body with every thump of my heart. We listened as someone nimbly climbed through the window and over the sink and then slid the window closed. I could see the outline of Ang, all six feet three inches of her, tensed and ready. Not an ounce of fear in her in that moment, and I adored her for that. We were in our element.

The intruder's rubber-soled shoes tapped lightly down on the linoleum floor as the person lowered off the counter. A few hesitant steps that paused in front of the refrigerator. It was so silent in the cottage my ears were ringing. The compressor in the refrigerator kicked on, and I had to stifle a flinch.

After a long pause the person took a few more tentative steps and turned. They stopped right in front of Ang, with their back to her. I was close behind Ang and watched as she struck like a viper. Her right arm shot out and hooked the pit of her elbow around the person's throat. She pulled their body snugly up against hers, tightening her arm until she had a secure choke hold. Tight enough to restrain, but not tight enough to make the person pass out.

Ang's free hand flicked out and the sound of her asp baton expanding out to its full eighteen inches was music to my ears. There was rustling as the person struggled to escape from Ang's iron grip. I stepped around them and flipped on the overhead kitchen lights.

What I found was Crystal flailing, trying to reach back and punch up at Ang, while also stomping down on Ang's bare feet. Crystal, a solid person in her own right, looked like a weak little ragdoll compared to Ang. Amid all of it, Ang didn't even flinch.

"We've got ourselves a visitor," I said sarcastically to Ang, who nodded back at me, a neutral expression on her face that said it was just another day at the office.

Crystal looked around frantically when the lights came on and took in the scene.

"Why in the hell are you guys naked?" she demanded, her voice straining as she forced the question out.

"Well, Crystal, it just so happens we were fucking. You should give it a try some time. Maybe it will make you less of a murderous bitch. It's a great release. Just a thought."

Crystal seemed to figure out that she couldn't get out of Ang's grip, and stopped flailing and stomping.

I stepped up closer to them, careful to stay out of range of Crystal's short, powerful legs, and whistled between my front teeth.

"Damn. Well, look at you. You've got some nice black eyes to go with that ugly crooked-ass nose. Did I break it?" I asked, taunting her.

"Fuck you," she hissed, and spat in my face.

I took a step back.

"You know, it's going to be really hard for us to stay friends if you keep being so rude to me. Maybe we can be pen pals once things cool down and you're doing time at Chowchilla."

I looked up at Ang. She was alert, but relaxed. Confident in her role. She gave me a quick grin and nodded to the top of the refrigerator. I reached up and grabbed the handcuffs, cuff key, and zip ties. The weight and coolness of the handcuffs were familiar. I stood off to the side and waited. Ang broke her silence and spoke in a clear, direct, no bullshit tone.

"This is what's going to happen. You and me, we're going to turn around, and you're going to put your hands on the wall. Do you understand?"

Crystal let out an angry sigh and nodded against the crook of Ang's arm.

Ang stood up to her full height, lifting Crystal's feet off the floor, and turned around. She took a step forward so that they were facing the wall. Crystal kicked her feet wildly and scratched at Ang's arm around her throat. Ang set her back down but did not release her.

"Hands. Against. The wall," Ang said sharply.

Crystal was coughing and cussing, but she complied. She hissed, "Damn, Ang. Why you gotta do me like that?"

I froze in that moment, thinking back to the handful of words I had spoken since flipping the lights on, and I was certain I had not said Ang's name. I got a brief chill but pushed it away, telling myself Crystal must have learned her name while stalking me.

Ang released Crystal and took a step back. She stood with the asp ready to strike, the veins in her arm popped, and tiny droplets of sweat forming on her back. When she was satisfied that Crystal was going to comply, she pressed the tip of the asp against the side of the refrigerator and collapsed it back down.

She kicked Crystal's feet apart and began a methodical pat down. She pulled item after item out of Crystal's pockets, dropping them on the floor and sliding them back to me with her foot. Rental car keys, a motel key card, a tan bandana, a small packet of spearmint gum, a burner cell phone, zip ties, a tampon, and a sturdy new set of rose clippers. I raised my eyebrows as I picked up the rose clippers. Nothing good could come from her carrying those, especially since I knew she had a proclivity for cutting off people's extremities. I placed all the items in a gallon size ziplock bag and placed it on the kitchen table.

After Ang finished searching Crystal's pant legs and shoes and poking around in the loose bun on the back of Crystal's head, she stood back up. She placed her left hand between Crystal's shoulder blades and pressed her against the wall. Ang reached her right hand back to me. I placed the cuffs in her hand, the metal now warm from my body heat. She expertly cuffed Crystal. Clearly, she had put handcuffs on people many, many times in her career.

I passed her the key and she double locked the cuffs, which were snugly in place. Crystal stood there, her forehead against the wall, feet still spread apart, and groaned. I figured her sternum was still sore from where I had kicked her earlier. Ang took Crystal roughly by the shoulders and turned her around so that they faced each other. Crystal was much shorter than Ang and didn't bother trying to look up at her.

"Sit," Ang directed. Crystal sat on the floor, her back against the wall.

"Legs in front. Cross your ankles," she said. Crystal complied. Head down, jaw clenched, hands tightly secured behind her back.

Ang squatted down near Crystal's feet. I handed her the zip ties, and she went to work securing Crystal's feet.

"Jesus fucking Christ. Can you please put some goddamn clothes on? I do not need to see your twat."

"Do not move from this spot," Ang instructed. Then she grabbed her pistol off the top of the refrigerator and walked toward the bedroom. I stood across from Crystal, stun gun still in my hand. We stared at each other the entire time Ang was getting dressed.

I turned my head only when Ang returned. She was dressed in khaki tactical pants, boots, and a tight black waffled thermal shirt. I could see the slight bulge of her ankle holster. The shirt clung tightly to her shoulders, arms, and across her strong back. She walked over to me, and I heated up just from being close to her. I handed her the stun gun, and she took my place, leaning against the kitchen table. She and Crystal locked eyes, and I went into the bedroom.

I dressed quickly in jeans, a long-sleeved T-shirt, navy-blue UC Davis hooded sweatshirt, and my trusty running shoes. Detouring to the bathroom to pee, I smirked when I saw my cock sitting on the counter with droplets of water still clinging to it and my harness hanging over the shower rod to dry. I finished up, collected my gear, and took it into the bedroom, where I stowed it.

Returning to the main room, I found Ang and Crystal were still staring at each other. I sat down on the futon and looked over at Crystal. She didn't acknowledge me.

I slid out my cell phone and dialed Sergeant Brickhouse's number.

"Sheriff's department. This is Sergeant Brickhouse," he said. It was close to 4:00 a.m., so I was surprised he sounded so alert.

"Sergeant, this is Vivian Chastain."

Crystal clenched her jaw as she heard who I was calling.

"Vivian! Hello there. What can I do for you on this lovely morning," he said, sounding amused.

"I've got Crystal Wylie detained. Can you send someone out here to pick her up?"

"Did you just say you have Crystal Wylie detained?" he asked as his voice went up a few octaves.

"Yes, that's what I said."

"Where are you?"

"I'm in Guerneville."

"Okay, okay. Give me the details, and we'll come get her."

I stared at Crystal the entire time I spoke to him. I rattled off the address and other details, and he said he'd have Sonoma County sheriff's department sit with us until he arrived. I told him I had an off-duty deputy with me, but he insisted that he notify Sonoma County SD.

After the call, I told Ang they were on their way. She collected her asp from the top of the refrigerator and locked it up in the ammo can she used to transport her weapons.

We all stayed put. Crystal on the floor, her back against the wall, legs stretched out in front of her, crossed and zip tied at the ankles. Ang across from her, leaning against the counter.

Me sitting on the futon, cell phone in hand.

Knowing how silence could put a lot of pressure on some people, Ang and I allowed the cottage to drop into deep quiet. Eventually, Crystal started talking.

"He had it coming to him. That punk ass." She paused, still looking down at her lap. "I don't need to justify myself to you. But just so you know, he deserved what he got. Fucking huffer. Got no brain left. And a sick-ass pervert. A real predator."

Crystal shifted her gaze to Ang.

"What I can't figure out, Crystal, is how you tracked me all the way to the zip line place. I get you finding the cottage, cuz you claim you followed me here. But I left you in a pile on top of a mountain, so the knife in my tire at zip lining makes me curious."

Crystal shrugged and shifted her gaze from Ang to me. "I'm just that good."

"I doubt that very much."

She shrugged at me again and looked back down at her lap. Ang raised her eyebrows at me and then we resumed our silent contemplation.

Thirty minutes later, a vehicle pulled into the lot below, followed by boots clomping rapidly up the wooden stairs. A firm knock on the door. I rose and stood to the side of the door. Peeking out through the curtain, I saw it was a uniformed Sonoma County deputy. I unlocked the door and let him in.

There wasn't much to say. He had clearly been briefed already on who Crystal was and what the situation was. He took up a post by the front door, leaning his butt on the side table. He was standing to Crystal's left and stared at her busted nose with amusement, while he quietly chewed a piece of gum. I could smell the faint aroma of spearmint mixed with his deodorant. I pegged it as Speed Stick. He was in his late twenties. Muscular and tan with short black hair and hazel eyes. He had a tattoo on his forearm of the 25th Light Infantry patch.

"Vincent," he said with a nod.

"Chastain," I said, nodding back.

"Sorenson," Ang said, also nodding at him. And then we settled in.

Almost an hour passed in a bubble of silence. Alert, but also in our own thoughts.

Crystal finally looked away from Ang, turning her gaze on me. I noted that the bruising around her eyes had settled in, and her eyes were more swollen. She drew in a long breath and let it out. My thoughts had drifted to our tussle on the trail earlier.

Pale watery light seeped in through the blinds over the sink. I looked at Deputy Vincent and Ang. "Coffee? Tea?"

"I'd love some coffee," Crystal said to her lap.

"Go fuck yourself," I said back. "Anybody else?"

Deputy Vincent and Ang both requested coffees, so I prepared it for them and also put a kettle on to heat up some water for my tea. Soon, the small cottage was filled with the aroma of coffee and peppermint.

I put a piece of bread in the toaster and poured mugs of coffee. I handed Ang and Deputy Vincent their mugs and gave Crystal a wide berth.

I returned to the kitchen, grabbed a banana and the dry piece of toast, and tossed them both onto Crystal's lap. She looked at me angrily.

"Eat up. You're gonna need it. Something tells me you've got a longggg day ahead of you," I said.

She shot daggers at me with her eyes and shifted uncomfortably. Her hands had probably fallen asleep a while ago, cuffed behind her back like that.

"Oh, can't reach? Poor baby," I said as I sat back down on the futon and sipped my tea.

Crystal looked back up at me, her jaw clenched. There was not even a drop of defeat in her expression. I had to give her credit for that. There she was, handcuffed and zip tied with Sergeant Brickhouse on his way to pick her up, and she still looked rock solid and ready to fight.

"Don't forget what I told you up on the trail," she said to me. Her voice was froggy.

"Oh, you mean that I'm going to meet an untimely and slow demise?" I said, amused.

I squatted down next to her. Ang and Deputy Vincent tensed up and set their coffees down but stayed where they were.

"Yes, I recall what you said up there. And you. Don't you forget what I told you up on the trail. About what I can do to you."

She cocked her head to the side and looked at me through her purple, swollen eyelids. I could see she was flipping back through her memory of our conversation and coming up blank. She narrowed her eyes at me.

"What? You don't remember?" I asked, sarcastically feigning hurt feelings. "Here, let me refresh your memory."

We were close together, and I didn't have much room. I cocked my arm back and delivered a short, sharp rabbit punch to the bridge of her nose. She cussed and tucked her chin down, trying to protect her face.

Ang and Deputy Vincent both sprang forward and pulled me back. They pushed me down on the futon. Crystal sniffled as blood began to trickle in a thin line down her upper lip. Silence fell over us again, aside from the occasional sniff and grumbles from Crystal.

I watched tiny drops of blood cling to her chin and then drip down and get absorbed by the front of her shirt. Her nose was destroyed, taking on a certain swollen flatness it didn't have before.

I could see Ang out of the corner of my eye throwing me looks and knew I was in trouble.

Sergeant Brickhouse and another deputy showed up before my tea got cold. There was a short discussion about how we caught her and how her nose got broken the day before. No doubt they would have to document it and get her medical attention.

Sergeant Brickhouse swapped out Ang's cuffs for his own and did another pat down of Crystal. We handed over the bag of items Ang had pulled out of Crystal's pockets earlier. Crystal complied without a word, head down, jaw clenched, vein throbbing at her temple just below the scar I had given her.

As they were guiding her out the door, I thanked Sergeant Brickhouse and said to Crystal, "See you later, pal. Have fun in lockup. I'm sure you'll make all kinds of new friends."

She didn't acknowledge me.

Sergeant Brickhouse and Crystal filed out, followed by Deputy Vincent and Ang. Ang closed the door behind her and walked down with them.

The sun had barely risen, the sky hadn't yet taken on any color beyond the light-gray of early dawn. I got up and opened all the blinds and then went into the kitchen. I took my time making breakfast. Toast with egg white omelets, oranges, and banana slices. I plated it all and sat down at the table to wait for Ang.

She came back in and locked the door behind her.

"God damn. I'm exhausted," she said as she sat down at the table.

She smiled and thanked me for preparing breakfast. She ate every single bit of food on her plate and then sat back in her chair, turning her attention to me.

I had already finished and was draining the last bit of cold tea from my mug.

"What the fuck was that?" she asked me, as if picking up a conversation that we hadn't finished yet.

"What are we talking about?" I countered. Defensiveness immediately jumped up, but I held it in check to see what she had to say.

"You know you can't just beat on someone, especially if they are in handcuffs."

"No, *you* can't beat on someone in handcuffs because you're a cop. I am average Joe civilian, so I have a bit more...wiggle room."

"That was battery," she said flatly. "Shit, you already broke her nose yesterday. That was excessive. I'm surprised Deputy Vincent didn't cite you."

"Well, he didn't."

She looked at me. I could see she was straining and holding back. Filtering.

"Look. Viv, I don't know much of the details of what happened to you growing up or what sort of stuff happened while you were in the military because you never talk about it. But I know that whatever it was, it's fucked you up." She paused, gauging me.

I looked back at her, my expression neutral while my brain spun.

Her tone softened a bit. "There's clearly some shit you need to deal with still. And I want to help with that, whatever it looks like."

"Jesus, you're so sweet. I just love it when people tell me how fucked up I am. I know I'm fucked up. I know I have stuff I need to deal with. I know I should be in therapy. But, really, I don't want to do any of that right now. And you know what? Being on edge the way I am and having a hair trigger are probably what kept me from getting myself killed by that bitch they just walked out of here."

She put her hand on the table and reached for mine. Inside I was boiling, but a tiny part of me knew that lashing out at her was not the right answer. Even though what she had said was harsh, the base of it was that she cared about me and wanted to help.

After a moment, I put my hand in hers.

"Okay, Viv. Well, when you do get there, and you're ready to work on some stuff, just know that I'm here to help however I can." She hesitated. "I was an absolute ball of stress when I left the Navy. It took a long time before I was ready to face it and tackle it. It took a lot of work...a lot of work. I backslid a bunch of times, and I'm still not free from some of it. PTSD is one mean motherfucker. It gets its claws into you and you can't really ever get them all the way out. At least...I couldn't. But now I can go about my work and carry a gun, and I trust myself to make good decisions and not nut up when things get stressful on the job."

I nodded, looking down at our hands. Both were tan, the veins visible, our knuckles calloused and scarred from hard work. Her hand wrapped around mine. A calming sense of being protected and cared for spread over me, and I soaked it in.

All my defensive bullshit drained away, and I opened myself up to her and to being cared about. I allowed the little kid inside me to pop up her head. A little kid who had been kicked around and ignored. Who had been treated like an inconvenience and a burden. A little kid who didn't know how to be loved. Still didn't know how to be loved.

My face flushed and my eyes started to well up. That lonely little kid always fell apart at the slightest bit of love or nurturing.

I feared becoming an incredibly needy partner. So instead, I had always remained present, but aloof. I had always been perfectly capable of giving plenty of love and attention, just not at receiving it. But with Ang, I sensed that I could. I had finally started to trust her.

I drew in a ragged breath, blew it out, and pulled back those tears.

"Thank you," I said.

"You're welcome. So, since we've both acknowledged how fucked-up we are, let's talk about us."

My throat tightened and I started to pull my hand away. She held my hand just a bit tighter and her eyes narrowed a hair.

"Viv, don't shut down. We really need to talk about this and do it together."

I nodded. "Okay."

"So, we've been monogamous the whole time we've been seeing each other. Honestly, that's not how I'm wired, and I never normally get involved in monogamous relationships. It just happened that when we met, I wasn't seeing anyone else. But I usually do. And I am completely at fault for not talking to you about nonmonogamy from the very beginning. I own that."

The sad, lonely little kid inside me immediately withdrew and curled up into the fetal position. It took everything I had not to do the same.

"Look, Ang, my only experience with nonmonogamy was not consensual and not ethical. While my partner at the time called it poly, I don't think I would even call it that at this point. So, this isn't something I can easily just jump into." I paused, gathered myself. Weighed my words. "I wake up every day and choose you. I choose us. I thought you did the same, but what I hear you saying is that you don't. That you're distracted by other people and not focused on us."

"I do wake up every day and choose us. I also think about other people, every single day. But us having other people in our lives who we love would serve to build us both up and strengthen what we have together. It is completely possible to love more than one person and not have that take away from either relationship."

I stammered. "I...I—"

"Look. Imagine you have a really great conversation on the phone with your buddy who you always talk about, Jared. And then later that day you have another great phone conversation with your friend Bear. Does your conversation with Bear take anything away from how you feel about Jared or the friendship you two have?" She gave me a hopeful look.

I thought about that for a bit, shaking my leg rapidly under the table.

"Look, Viv, you know I care deeply for you. We are magnetic. And we are a fucking inferno in the bedroom. Will you please give this some thought?"

I nodded. What she was asking for wasn't unreasonable, and my reaction was about my own baggage, which I needed to sort out. She was right though. She should have told me upfront that she was poly.

"Yeah," I said and realized how sad my voice sounded.

The hopeful look on her face faded, and she looked concerned again.

I cleared my throat. "Yes, I will think about it. But however this shakes out, I'm going to need you to be patient with me. Can you do that?"

She smiled and nodded. "Yes, I can do that. And thank you. Thank you for being open to talking about this and open to giving it some thought."

Doom settled into my gut because I knew Ang well enough to know she wouldn't settle for anything less than what she wanted. There would be no compromise.

I stood up from the table. "I'm going to go for a trail run. Out on the coast this time. Want to come?"

"No, thanks. I need to get some miles in on my bike."

She stood and wrapped me up in her arms. We hugged for a long time. Breathing together. Exchanging the amazing energy we always had when we were together, yet I had a pinprick of disappointment right in the center of my being. I tried to push it away, but it held firm.

Chapter Eighteen

We slowly separated and went into the bedroom to get changed. Me into running gear, and her into her cycling kit. We parted ways in the parking lot. I drove out to the coast to run the bluffs and ridge trails. And she headed out on her road bike to ride the River Road.

Not allowing myself to think about anything at all the entire drive to the trailhead, I focused only on the road. I parked at Goat Rock Beach, snapped on my day pack, and hit the trail. I ran mechanically along the bluff trail, passing a lot of hikers along the way. At Shell Beach, I turned east and started on the Pomo Canyon loop.

I was breathing heavily, my legs were warmed up, and my gait was smoothing out. As the trail began to incline, I allowed myself to start processing. My mind wouldn't settle on any one thing for more than a few seconds. Flitting around between the conversation with Ang about nonmonogamy, my run-ins with Crystal, and eventually, myself.

*

Myself. My ten-year-old self at a slumber party to celebrate my friend Gina's eleventh birthday. I'd been the first to arrive since I lived two blocks from her and had ridden my bike over, my stuff neatly folded in a backpack. I helped Gina greet all the other girls as they were dropped off, one by one, by their parents.

Every time we opened the big oak front door, I watched as each kid was given a big hug by their mom or dad, given a quick pep talk about acceptable behavior, and then told to have a good time.

We played games and chatted all afternoon. Following dinner, we had a vanilla birthday cake with chocolate frosting. Afterward we pushed the coffee table out of the way and set up our sleeping bags on the floor in the living room. We all crawled into our sleeping bags and watched a VHS of Lady in White. *It was frightening.*

At bedtime, Gina's mom and stepdad both came and told her good night, told her how much they loved her, and hugged her warmly. After lights out, I lay on my back, snug in my sleeping bag, and stared up at the silhouette of the ceiling fan in the darkness.

Hot tears slid silently down my face, pooling in my ears. I was ten, and I couldn't remember the last time my mother had hugged me. It had never really occurred to me that the sterile environment at home wasn't normal, because it was my norm.

But that day, seeing parent after parent hug their kids goodbye, even the fact that their parents were present to drop them off, made me so angry and so jealous. Angry at my mom for not being there for me and not giving a shit about me. And hotly jealous at my friends for actually having what I realized I so desperately wanted. I decided I was better off not knowing that my norm sucked so badly.

*

The coastal trail was busy. I wiped at tears hanging from my jaw. That angry, jealous little kid still lived inside me. Still needed to be loved and nurtured. Was still jealous of those who had supportive friends and families. Still didn't know what a secure relationship was like (well, except for Jared. He'd been rock solid before he flaked out on my graduation and started pulling away), and that was why nonmonogamy was so gut-shakingly scary to me.

I reached the summit and followed the ridge trail as it looped around. Eventually, I stopped for a short break and to take in the view.

The Pacific Ocean unrolled before me, as far as I could see, the water choppy. There were massive tankers far out on the horizon.

The gash on my shin had started to throb, but the wound hadn't opened back up yet. A huge bead of sweat clung to the tip of my nose. I blew it off, stowed my gear, and began running again. I finished the loop along the ridge and headed back toward Shell Beach, careful to not break an ankle or plow over a hiker on the way down.

I thought about my drunk brother, wondering when I'd get the call that he was dead in a ditch somewhere. I thought about my empty well of a mother. I worried about Jared. *What the fuck is going on with Jared?*

I headed north, back along the bluff trail toward Goat Rock Beach. Pods of dolphins swam a short way out. There were seals on the rocks far below. I smelled a skunk on the breeze. Saw scat on the dusty trail.

I thought about Ang. *Oh Angela.*

My heart clenched the instant I allowed myself to think about opening up our relationship. Fear gripped my core, tightly. My body responded in kind with a wave of persistent nausea which stuck with me the rest of the run.

*

On my way back to the cottage, I stopped by the bar to talk to Jack. I thanked him for the work and let him know I was leaving town. He hugged me and told me to come back any time. He still had an orange handkerchief dangling out of his left back pocket. That man was such a charmer, he hardly needed to flag.

I stopped by the cottage office, settled my bill, and let the innkeeper know we would be leaving in the morning.

When I arrived at the cottage, Ang wasn't back yet. I made us some lunch. A simple meal. Sandwiches on whole wheat bread. Smoked ham. Swiss cheese. Dijon mustard. And on the side a salad with greens, thinly sliced cucumber, grated carrots, chopped hardboiled eggs, and walnuts with citrus vinaigrette.

I put it all in the fridge and took my book out front. I found a sunny spot at the table on the porch and read for a while, engrossing myself in *Valencia*.

I soon heard the telltale humming of road bike tires hauling ass on pavement. The bike turned into the parking lot and came to a stop just below me. I looked down and saw Ang unclipping from her pedals. She hoisted the bike up on her shoulder and carried it easily up the stairs in large bounds. The cleats on the bottom of her cycling shoes clacked on the wooden steps. She put her helmet and her bike inside the cottage and came back out to give me a huge sweaty hug and kiss. We both had salt crusted on our clothes from our exertions.

"Hey," she said sheepishly. Her face was tense. Clearly, she had been mulling things over while out on her ride.

"Hey," I said back and gave her a smile.

The tension drained a bit from her face when she saw my smile.

We went inside and quietly ate lunch at the table. Then we stripped down and got into the small shower together. We both scrubbed off the dirt, grime, and sweat and stood under the warm water, hugging, enjoying the slippery feel of the water between our bodies.

Being in her arms centered me again. My worries about nonmonogamy melted away as the energy between us repaired itself.

I ran my tongue around one of her nipples, and then drew it into my mouth. She leaned into me and groaned. I gently moved her so that the shower sprayed her back, no longer flowing down between us, and got down on my knees in the cramped space. I reached around and grasped the backs of her thighs, just below her butt, and pulled her an inch closer. I ran my tongue around her clit a few times, and then drew it into my mouth. She groaned again. Her quads clenched up and her hips shifted forward as her hands found the back of my head and eagerly pulled me in.

*

Checkout time was at 11:00 a.m. Ang and I loaded up our cars and did one last check of the cottage before locking up at eleven on the dot. Not ready to separate, we sat on a bench off to the side of the parking lot. Redwoods towered over us, and I heard people packing up at the campground on the other side of the fence. The smell of wood smoke and pine sap was in the air.

Ang sat on the bench facing me, one leg on either side of my body. She had an old glass pickle jar full of coffee, lightened with milk, which she had placed on the table. We sat and spoke quietly, extending our time together. Neither one of us wanted to leave. We were both physically depleted from marathon sex and lack of sleep. I was in a haze, high on oxytocin.

We eventually parted ways and started the drive back to Sacramento.

I had my window rolled down, enjoying the fresh air as I wound my way along the River Road, then 101, and Lakeville Highway. I listened to Led Zeppelin. Every now and then, I would spot Ang's Subaru in the traffic behind me, her bike in the roof rack. Jimmy Page's guitar and John Paul Jones's bass opened up "Ramble On," and I turned up the volume as loud as I could stand as Robert Plant's vocals began.

When I crested the hill on Interstate 80 between Vallejo and Fairfield, the temperature rose at least fifteen degrees. I rolled up my window and turned on the air-conditioner.

The rest of the drive was smooth. Walking into my studio, I was glad to be home, although it smelled weird. Vacant. That smell empty apartments get. My fish were alive and darting about the tank.

It was early afternoon on a weekday, but I could hear my upstairs neighbor moving around, and his bathtub running.

My oxytocin cloud was starting to fade, and reality was settling back in. I unpacked my ice chest and duffel, putting everything back in its place, and filling up my clothes hamper.

I grabbed my jar of quarters and some laundry soap from the closet in the bathroom, and took everything to the laundry room, which was the next door down from my studio in the corridor. I loaded up the washer, popped in six quarters, and hit start. The machine kicked into gear, and I headed back to my studio.

As I closed the door, I heard water. Not like a sink left on, but more like water overflowing onto a tile floor. I followed the sound into my bathroom and saw water pouring from the ceiling through the light fixture and around the vent.

"Motherfucker! Again?"

I marched angrily down the hall to the manager's apartment and knocked loudly. He didn't answer, but I could hear him shuffling around inside. I pounded on his door some more. When he finally answered, I took in the sight of him. He looked like he hadn't bathed in a while and had probably been awake high on meth for a few days.

"Hey! That idiot upstairs from me is overflowing his bathtub. Again! My bathroom is flooding!"

"Oh, right, right. Okay. I'll go talk to him."

"Uh huh. And then?"

"And then..."

"And then someone is going to come clean up the mess in my bathroom and pay for any damage to my personal belongings. I've had it, Pete. This is the third time he has done this. Last time, the water leaked into my closet and drenched clothes, shoes, and boxes I had stored in there. No more!"

"Okay, okay. Yup. I'll be there in a few."

I spun on my heel and strode angrily back to my studio, muttering under my breath.

"Motherfucker."

Welcome home, Vivi. Home sweet fuckin' home.

*

A few days passed as I got back into my routine. Work. Running. Taking rides on my motorcycle.

I didn't see Ang. She was no doubt working and training for her upcoming century ride. I'd occasionally see her car in the underground garage, but I hadn't stopped by her place to say hi.

I needed time to think. I knew I was still too reactive to have another conversation with her yet about opening up our relationship.

Once the ceiling of my bathroom dried, it began falling onto the floor in clumps. The manager promised to fix it.

Hmph. We'll see.

I got ready for work in the dark. I was afraid to turn on the bathroom light and fan, for fear that the recent dousing had fucked with the electrical wiring.

It was *Coyote Ugly* night, and I knew it would be off the hook.

I walked down the corridor toward the stairs and hesitated in front of Ang's apartment door. I knocked, on the off chance that she was home.

After a short delay, she answered. Her apartment was dark, the shades drawn against the fading dusk. She was in pajamas, and her hair was down, her eyes sleepy.

"Oh shit. I'm sorry, I didn't mean to wake you. I'll go," I said, suddenly embarrassed and flushed.

"Hey. No, no. It's okay. I'm on nights again this week, covering for one of the other FTO's. What's up?" She leaned against the doorframe, crossed her ankles, and rubbed her hands over her face briskly.

"I'm headed to work, but I'd like to spend some time together soon. Talk. You've been on my mind. I miss you. I miss us." As the words were spilling out of my mouth my mind was screaming *shut up!*

Ang gave me a sleepy grin.

"Yeah. I'd like that a lot." She reached her hand out to me. I took it, and we stood like that for a moment in her doorway. Her hand was so warm and present in mine.

"How's that gash on your shin doing?"

"It's good. Healing." I straightened up. Preparing to leave. "Okay. See you soon," I said and gave her a small wink.

As I turned to head for the stairs, I heard the sound of a delicate sneeze come from the depths of Ang's apartment, just as she shut her door.

I paused at the top of the stairs, jaw clenched.

Nope. Not now.

I headed for work, wondering how I was going to be able to maintain my showmanship behind the bar after hearing that dainty, feminine sneeze come from Ang's apartment. I did manage, though, throwing myself fully into the role, flirting, tossing out winks and compliments, mixing some damn good drinks, and relying heavily on Jen to keep me hydrated and stocked up with clean glasses and garnishes. I made a killing in tips and held it together until closing time. Funny how people can fake their way through pain just long enough to get the job done. High functioning, I think they call it.

I hustled to finish my closing duties, tipped out Jen, and got myself home. Before getting into bed, I stripped out of my work clothes and got into my usual boxers and tank top. As I was folding out the futon and making my bed, my cell phone pinged. It gave me pause, given how early in the morning it was. I flipped my phone open and saw that I had a text from Ang.

> *Hey. I just got in and saw that your truck is here. Can I come see you?*

I was exhausted. It was closing in on 4:00 a.m., and I still wasn't sure what I wanted to do about Ang. But we didn't have to solve anything that night. She was probably just off work and exhausted, too, so I replied:

Yes, come on over.

I leaned against the cold wall and waited. Anxiety was trying to make an appearance. I took several deep breaths and did what I could to push it away.

A few minutes later I heard Ang's heavy footsteps in the hall and a light knock on my door. When I answered the door, Ang gave me a grin and stepped inside. She wrapped me up in her arms.

"I missed you," she said in my ear. "Thank you for stopping by earlier."

I nodded into her shoulder, hugging her back, and breathing her in only to find that she didn't smell the same. Instead, she smelled like she had been in a restaurant, and she was wearing different deodorant.

I led her in and folded the futon back up into a couch. We sat down and turned to face each other.

"No uniform. You didn't work tonight?" I asked, nodding to her clothes.

She looked quite dapper in khaki slacks and a navy-blue men's button-up. She had on some brown oxfords that didn't have a single scuff on them.

"No. No work tonight," she said and paused, her forehead creasing with concern. It was a look I was becoming all too familiar with.

"I...I was out on a date. Her name is Kate." She paused, and a chill fell between us. "I think you'd really like her if you would be willing to meet."

My brain stuttered, and my heart skipped a few beats before it started pounding. Adrenaline surged as I had a really strong reaction to the news.

I was hurt, which triggered anger. And then, my abandonment issues popped up, which doubled the anger. I worked hard to keep my face and body language as nonthreatening as possible, but it was a struggle. My hands tingled.

"A date?"

"Yeah."

"We haven't agreed to open up our relationship yet," I said solidly.

"Well, we talked about it at the cottage. And then you disappeared on me. You've been dodging the conversation, Vivian."

"What we talked about was me considering us opening up. And that's exactly what I've been doing. I have had a lot to work through about it and needed time to think. Jesus, it's barely been a week since we talked. You couldn't wait? You couldn't respect my request for a little bit of time to process?"

Ang gave me a look I couldn't quite decipher. It fell somewhere between empathy and apathy. Somewhere between caring about upsetting me and being annoyed.

"Look, Vivian. I'm poly. This is who I am. This is what I need."

"Yeah. I get that. I may not be experienced at poly, but I know enough to know that it should be done ethically and consensually. I haven't agreed to this yet, and we haven't even talked about boundaries."

Ang flinched just a hair when I mentioned ethics and consent.

Fatigue hit me over the head, and I had an overwhelming urge to lie down and sleep. My eyelids were heavy as I struggled to remain coherent and thoughtful in that moment with Ang.

Stay fucking focused, you idiot. This is important.

"You're right. We haven't talked boundaries. That's fair," she said, her tone formal.

A long pause strung out between us. I looked at her and waffled back and forth between trying not to pass out and trying not to choke the life out of her.

"I still don't know if I can do this. And if we do open up, I'm going to need you to be patient with me, because I already know there will be some rough days."

Ang's face lost what little empathy it had left, and her eyes went cold.

Right then I realized that while she may have been my submissive during sex, I was her emotional submissive, and she was a careless and cold top.

"Well, I can't be in a monogamous relationship with you. I've tried. I need more. I need to be true to myself. And after what you've just said, I don't know if a nonmonogamous situation will meet both of our needs. This relationship isn't good for you, Vivian. I can see it."

I was immediately frightened that she was about to break up with me, and inside I began to panic. To try to find the right words to stop the breakup. Desperation landed in my lap, and I fucking despised it.

"Ang, I'll decide what I can and can't handle. Don't tell me what I can handle. Okay. Let's give it a try. Let's open us up. But again, I'm going to need you to be patient with me through this. And I have to be your primary partner. There's no other way."

Ang looked at me hesitantly and then a huge smile spread across her face, wrinkling the skin at the corners of her eyes and along the sides of the bridge of her nose.

"Are you sure about this?"

"Yes. I'm sure. I don't give up so easily. I would regret it if I walked away now and didn't try."

Ang leaned across the couch, pulled me to her, and gave me a hug. I melted into her arms, and the doomed feeling in the pit of my stomach subsided a little bit. I drew in a breath to help myself relax and caught the residual scents from her date that were still on her shirt, and my eyes snapped open.

I realized I was still extremely angry that she had been out on a date with Kate, so we were already starting with a massive trust deficit. I gently ended the hug and sat back across the couch from her. Ang scooted a bit closer and took my hand in hers. I bit back my anger and swallowed the bile in my throat.

"Okay, let's talk about boundaries," I said.

Ang readily and enthusiastically agreed to every rule I listed. She didn't set any additional rules, though we talked until well after the sun rose.

I finally had to end the conversation, because I was so tired I simply couldn't think clearly anymore. I slept the entire day, alone, and woke up in time to make it to my shift at the bar.

Chapter Nineteen

A few days passed. I slept. I worked. I ran. I read. I kept my wounds clean. Ang and I had marathon sex a couple of times, and we didn't talk about Kate.

One afternoon, I made my way down to New Helvetia for a cup of tea and snagged a seat on the patio. I was engrossed in my copy of Kōbō Abe's *The Woman in the Dunes* despite the cacophony of Nineteenth Street. A couple of rowdy guys walked down the sidewalk out front, headed for the tattoo shop. The sound of an air compressor kicked in followed by the whine of power tools at the auto shop next door. A group of women sitting at the next table took a break from studying and began talking animatedly. They pulled out packs of menthol cigarettes and cloves and lit up with small silver Zippos. The patio was narrow, with minimal air circulation, so their smoke hovered lazily in the air. Their conversation was enough to finally disrupt my concentration on the book, pulling me out from one of Niki Jumpei's tantrums.

I was startled as the cell phone in the front pocket of my jeans rang. The ring was harsh, grating. I sat up in the chair, slid out the phone, and was surprised to see that it was Jared.

"Jared?"

"Yeah. Hey, Viv," he said, sounding sheepish.

"Hey, man. What's up? You okay?"

"Things haven't been good, but yeah, I'm okay. I'm sorry I've been such a shitty friend lately."

"Aww, hey, we're good. No worries. I'm glad to hear from you. You kinda dropped off the face of the earth. Do you wanna talk about it?"

"Nah. I don't want to get into it right now. I want to hear about you and what's going on in your world. Are you...dating?"

"Are you sure you want to hear about that?" I didn't want to add insult to injury since I'd turned him down.

"Yep. Spill it."

Yet, I hesitated, trying to be mindful about hurting his feelings, but I also really needed to talk to somebody about Ang. Back in the day, I could tell him anything.

Spill it. Okay, you asked for it.

"Everything is kind of a mess. Yeah, I'm in a relationship. She's my neighbor. And, get this, she's a Navy vet." I chuckled, and it was good to hear Jared chuckle back.

"You are so full of shit, Vivi. You always swore you'd never date a damn seaman."

I laughed harder when he said the word seaman, feeling like a silly little kid for a moment.

"Well, I broke my old drunken oath on that one. Now I'm out of the service, that stuff doesn't seem to be as important. And what makes it worse is that I know I shouldn't be in a relationship with her. This one is gonna hurt like hell. But I just can't walk away. The chemistry is so intense, and I love her. It's pretty fucked up. And of course, my anxiety has been ramping up. I'm trying to do good self-care, but that doesn't ultimately change the stressors."

"Okay, I hear you. But what makes it so intense? Like, why stay? You just said you know you shouldn't be in it, and that it's gonna hurt like hell. Sounds to me like you need to get the hell out."

I took a moment to consider Jared's questions. Questions I had been avoiding asking myself for months.

"You want the ugly truth of it?" I asked him hesitantly.

"Yes, of course. You know you can be brutally honest with me."

"Because she wants me. It has to be on her own fucked-up terms, but she wants me."

A long pause strung out between us as we both considered what I had just said. I immediately recognized that I was a jerk because Jared had wanted me, too, not all that long ago.

"I know that sounds nuts, but I've lived a pretty solitary life since I moved here. School, run, motorcycle, work. Repeat. I haven't branched out and made many new friends even though I've been here a few years now. I'm friends with some of my coworkers, but I keep that stuff mostly contained to work. I've dated casually, but I haven't had a spark with anyone here till Ang. She's...she just drew me in. Ang gets it. She gets me, where I've been, what I'm about. I'm incredibly attracted to her. We can't keep our hands off each other. The sexual dynamic is off the charts. And right now, I need to be wanted and needed."

"Viv," Jared said softly. "There will be other connections. Connections with people who don't give you a sense of dread for the inevitable day it crashes and burns. Connections with people who will enter into a relationship with you on equal ground, who will compromise with you to establish something that works for you both. Not something that is only on their terms, and makes you feel like shit half the time."

"But the other half of the time, it feels so damn good. And for now, I'll take it."

We both let out a sigh as what I said sank in.

"Viv, I know we've talked about it before, but I really think it might be helpful for you to talk to a therapist. In the past, your answer has always been a hard no. But keeping everything on lockdown isn't going to resolve anything long term. It's just going to keep on building up pressure."

I drew in a breath and gave it some thought. I looked around at the people on the patio and hoped no one was eavesdropping.

"I've been adamant about not wanting to get into therapy. Not wanting to think about, talk about, even acknowledge some stuff. But it's bleeding over into my relationship and life." I held my breath for a moment. "It's probably time." I nodded to myself.

"Viv, you're awesome, and I hate that you've been suffering for so long. I wish there was something I could do to make it all better for you. This will be really good. I'm not going to lie though. Once you get into therapy, it's going to make things harder for a while."

"Yeah."

"Okay, Viv, I'm gonna get going. Find yourself a good therapist and get cracking."

"I will. Stay in touch. And, Jared, thanks for calling."

"You've got it. Later."

"Later."

I folded up my cell phone and held it for a moment as I pondered my options for getting a therapist.

Do I go to the VA?
No.
Can I afford to buy my own health insurance?
No.
Can I afford a private practice therapist?
Dunno.

I was startled out of my thoughts by my phone ringing again. I was becoming that obnoxious person at the cafe who is on her phone the whole time. I rolled my eyes and answered a call from a number that I didn't recognize.

"Hello?"

"Hi, Vivian, this is Sergeant Brickhouse."

"Hey there, Sarge. What's up?"

"How've you been?"

"Good. Staying out of trouble. Keeping my head down."

"Okay. Okay. Good. Good," he paused.

"Spit it out, Sarge."

"Just wanted to give you a heads-up that they have set a court date for Crystal Wylie. I heard today that the DA has offered her a plea deal but haven't heard yet if she will accept it."

"A motherfucking plea deal?" I said, far too loudly.

The women at the table next to me all turned sharply. One of the women took me in, looking at my men's clothing and boots. The skin at the corners of her eyes tightened ever so slightly as she realized I was a dyke. She gave me a hard, disapproving glare. I gave her a snarky wink, and she quickly looked away. I contained myself and drew in a breath to calm down but got mostly secondhand smoke.

Lowering my voice, I brought my attention back to the phone.

"Sarge, a plea deal? That's complete horseshit. You and I both know she intended for Johnny to bleed out and die. Not to mention, she kicked the tar out of me and then stalked me. Intent, intent, intent! And she already has a record. She is a known entity. This isn't some one-off thing. She is dangerous."

Sarge grunted in agreement.

"And, they have a shit ton of evidence against her. It's not like this is some case based only on hearsay. You told me before that the backpack I got off her was a jackpot for you guys. Her fingerprints in his blood. The freakin' machete!" I hissed.

There was a long pause.

"That's just it. There is some question about whether or not the backpack, or anything in it, would be admissible as evidence in court. And we've heard murmurs that if that evidence is allowed in court her Public Defender is going to try and say you framed her and falsified everything in the backpack. We managed to verify your whereabouts leading up to when you ran into her at the warehouse. The ferry operator remembered you. And we located that Jeff guy who you said you talked to and rode into Dixon with.

"But they could still punch holes through that and say it was you who butchered Mister Long. He's been tight-lipped, so he won't clarify anything. The only person talking who saw Crystal at the warehouse is you. And you magically turned up with a bag full of evidence against her. I'm guessing that's a risk the DA isn't willing to take."

I sat there, silently submerged in thought. I could hear the buzz of the women nearby chatting, the din of machinery and power tools next door, cars passing by on Nineteenth Street. The sounds blurred together to the point where it was a low hum.

"There's more," he said.

"Oh, lovely," I replied and clenched my jaw.

"As part of the plea deal, they are dropping all of the peripheral charges involving you. The stalking, dropped. Multiple counts of battery, dropped. The telephone harassment, dropped."

"I don't really give a damn about all of those charges, but they cannot let her off easy for what she did to that guy."

"They can, and they might."

Silence fell between us. I watched as one of the women next to me lit another cigarette off the butt of one she had just finished.

"Look, I'll have one of our victim advocates send you a notice in the mail with the dates and details of her court proceedings. If they go with the plea deal, you won't have to get up on the stand for questioning, but you can still attend any proceedings if you want."

"Victim advocate." I let the words roll off my tongue. They were clunky and took too long for my brain to absorb.

"Vivian, you take care."

"This is horseshit, Sarge."

He sighed heavily. "I know."

I hit the end button and my phone immediately pinged that I had a new text message. The screen lit up with Ang's name across it and a little icon that looked like an envelope. I clicked the icon to open her message.

Hey there.

And for the very first time, I didn't care. I had no desire in that moment to engage in a conversation with her. I flipped my phone shut and angrily jammed it into my pocket, leaning back in the chair.

The metal frame bit into my back, and I focused on the sharp sensation. I pressed harder back into the chair until the pain of the metal cutting into my spine and ribs forced me to hold my breath and clench my jaw. Closing my eyes, I allowed the anger and frustration to flow through me and build up with the pain.

Should I have finished Crystal off when I had the chance?

I snapped my eyes open and leaned forward in the chair. The pain immediately dissipated, but the anger did not.

I drank the rest of my peppermint tea, which had gone cold, grabbed my book off the table, and took long quick strides out of the patio and down Nineteenth Street to where my motorcycle was parked. I seethed as I straddled the bike and zipped up my jacket.

What the fuck are you so angry about, Chastain? It's not like Crystal cut your hands off and left you to die in a hot abandoned warehouse. And so what if Ang is dating someone else? What the hell do you care?

I didn't know. Zings of adrenaline were pumping down my arms to my fingertips. I recognized that my anger was disproportionate to the situation and tried to get it in check as I sat on my bike at the curb.

The impulse hit me to ride back out to the warehouse where Crystal had hacked that guy's hands off and tried to snuff me out. It was good riding weather, and a ride would clear my mind. My stomach was in knots with anger. Not really knowing why I was having that level of anger made me even angrier.

"This is fucking stupid," I said matter-of-factly to myself. I snatched my helmet off the gas tank and yanked it on. I recognized that I was coming apart at the seams, that my mental health was not in a good place.

Therapy. I need help.

I rode home and bounded up the stairs to my floor.

In my studio, I pulled the Valley Rainbow Pages down from the top of my refrigerator and stood at the counter flipping through it until I found the section for counseling and mental health practitioners. If they were in the Rainbow Pages, they could handle a queer like me. Right?

I grabbed the cordless phone from the wall charger and called the first name I found that was in Midtown. It went straight to voice mail. I did my best to leave her a coherent message to inquire if she was taking on new clients. As soon as I hung up, I was overcome with a sense of relief. Layer after layer of anger began to fall away, and my head started to clear. And yet...

*

Sitting on an uncomfortable wooden chair, I swung my feet and picked at a hangnail. My scuffed-up sneakers pinched my toes, and I had scabs on both of my bare knees.

Mom and Joey were in their weekly family therapy session, and I had my weekly session of staring at motivational posters and reading Highlights *magazine in the therapist's empty lobby. It was after 5:00 p.m., and nobody else was around. I pondered why I was never included in the family therapy sessions. I choked back tears, swallowing hard.*

I could hear the low murmurs of Mom and the therapist talking, and the higher intonations when Joey spoke. Mom and Joey finally came back into the lobby, Joey frowning, which was normal for him after therapy. Mom passed a check to the therapist and snapped her purse shut.

My mom was tall and glamorous in her work clothes. A long flowing sage-colored skirt, cream-colored blouse, and heels. It was the end of the day, and her hair was still flawless, as was her makeup. I had a moment of wonder and hoped that I would grow up to be pretty like her.

She strode toward the exit with Joey in tow.

"Vivian, let's go," she said sharply. I hopped off the chair and gave the therapist a small smile as I passed. The therapist responded with a frown.

Chapter Twenty

I got an intake appointment with a therapist just in the nick of time. I had been living in crisis mode for so long that I was unraveling. My therapist was a queer woman named Alexia, who seemed to have her shit together. She charged one hundred dollars an hour, didn't take insurance, and wanted me to come in once a week, which was exactly what I did.

The expense was a strain on my budget, but I managed.

I got her up to speed fairly quickly on what the home environment was like while I was growing up. We talked around the fringes of my time in the military because I wasn't ready to get into that.

While respectful of my boundaries, Alexia was no pushover. She drove me hard and called me out on my bullshit frequently. I often had a hard time keeping eye contact with her, partly because I was ashamed of all the shit I was unloading on her, and partly because I realized I was a tiny bit attracted to her. But I wrote that off as my being attracted to any woman who showed care and concern for me.

She was older than me and had a penchant for tie dye, but something about her drew me in. I spent most of our sessions looking out of her office window while I spoke. The building across the street was under construction, which gave me a lot to look at rather than meet her gaze.

And Jared was right. At first, things got a lot worse. Talking with Alexia opened the floodgates.

Suddenly I hated my brother and mom more than ever. In my mind, they became terrible, selfish, heartless people. Opening up about my childhood further awakened that sad, lonely little kid who lived inside me, which rattled me to the core. And I found that the sad, lonely little kid was angry too.

Ang was really supportive of me being in therapy. She knew I was a private person, so on therapy days she would ask how I was and would often stop by just to give me a hug. But she never pried or asked for details.

Life moved on. The gash on my shin finally healed, and my landlord repaired the ceiling in my bathroom. I attended Crystal's plea hearing, sitting in the back of the stuffy courtroom and staring at the back of her head. She had somehow managed to maintain her perm while in jail.

She didn't turn around or look out into the audience at all. She only spoke to plead *nolo contendere*, no contest, and accept her plea deal. She seemed apathetic about the entire thing.

Her sentencing hearing followed not long afterward. The DA asked me if I wanted to make a victim impact statement to the judge. I declined. I had to refrain from telling the DA to go fuck himself for giving her a plea deal.

I didn't bother attending the sentencing hearing. At that point, I didn't need closure from Crystal, and I didn't have anything to say. I was ready to put the entire thing away and be done with it.

Chapter Twenty-One

Ang and I lay cuddled together in her queen-sized bed. Light streamed in from the floor to ceiling window that overlooked Q Street. She had a feather bed on top of her mattress, which was one of the most comfortable things I had ever slept on. We were tangled up in her big white down comforter. She never used a top sheet, so the smooth duvet cover slid along my skin when I moved. Her bed was far more comfortable than my hard, lumpy futon, which is why we often ended up at her place to fuck.

She let out a long, contented sigh into the crook of my neck as she nuzzled me. The feather mattress had molded itself perfectly around my body, and I wanted to stay in that exact spot forever. High on oxytocin, warm and comfortable, and skin on skin with my hot girlfriend.

And right on cue, Ang ruined the moment. She had developed a knack for abruptly starting tense conversations right when things were at their best.

"I have a date tonight. With Kate."

I immediately tensed up and rolled onto my side, away from her embrace. Suddenly, her bed was too hot. I kicked off the duvet and lay there with only my boxer briefs on.

"You're having a reaction," she said pointedly.

I couldn't respond without saying something shitty, so I kept my mouth shut.

"Jesus, Viv, is this how it's going to be every time I tell you I have a date?"

I drew in a long breath, counting up to ten as I did so, and then I held it for two seconds, and let it out slowly, counting to ten again, just like Alexia had recommended that I do whenever my temper began to flare. I chose my words carefully.

"Ang, I know that one of our rules is you inform me when you have plans with someone else. But here's the thing. We were just enjoying a really great time together. Just us. And then you inserted Kate into our time. Can you please, please, try to be more tactful in the future when telling me you have a date? Cuz doing it right now was bad form."

She started to speak but held back.

"Ang, now that we are open, I need reassurance more than ever. I need our time together to be focused on us. Can you do that? Please?"

"I'll try. But there is never a good time to tell you these things, Viv. You react negatively every single time."

"True. I'm working on it. I promise. But can you just work on your timing a bit? Do you see why telling me right now was not great?"

"Yes to both," she said with a tinge of annoyance.

I rolled back toward her so that we were face to face, and I gave her a gentle kiss.

"Thank you," I said.

Her expression softened, and she kissed me back.

"You're welcome, Daddy."

I took in a deep breath, trying to get the tension in my shoulders to release. Anger simmered within me, but I took it like the bitter pill it was, because the alternative of not having Ang in my life felt like the worst possible thing.

God damn it, Viv.

*

Walking through the heavy front door at work, I pushed aside my anger at Ang. I couldn't go into work distracted.

Buck gave me a nod from her lectern in the entryway, and I gave her a grin in return.

Soon enough, the place was packed, the music was blaring, and I was slammed. Jen hustled, keeping me stocked up. I was in a groove, banging out drinks, enjoying banter over the music with my customers, and having a great time as the evening flew by. It occurred to me at one point while pouring a beer that I hadn't been so happy in a long time. I welcomed the relief it brought.

The next customer stepped up to my station, and my knees went weak. My hearing cut out. I could still feel the bass from the music, but I couldn't hear anything.

Ang was standing at my station, looking fairly jovial and drunk. Her cheeks were flushed, and her arm was around the shoulders of a petite woman. The difference in their heights and builds was almost comical. Ang's hand dangling off the woman's shoulder had several club stamps on it, which meant they had been making the rounds of the bars in the gayborhood.

I made eye contact with Ang and then made eye contact with the other woman and gave her a quick scan. She was short, with a very narrow, lean frame, probably in her early forties. Veins popped on her arms and neck, and the skin on her cheeks stretched tight across her cheekbones. She had a very dark, uneven tan. Her baby doll shirt was skintight, and she looked at me nervously. I pegged her as a cyclist, probably a racer by the looks of how little body fat she had. In the seconds it took me to assess her, my brain kicked back into gear, and the sounds of the club came back at me full volume.

I tilted my head to the side, blinked, and turned my gaze back to Ang. I fought to keep my face neutral. I could see people behind them in line already getting impatient and shifty.

"What can I get for you?" I asked in the same tone I used for every other customer.

"Hey. Hey. Viv. This is Kate. I really wanted you guys to meet, and since we were already in Midtown, I figured we'd come say hiiiiii!" Ang slurred.

Kate shifted uncomfortably and gave me a lopsided *what-can-ya-do?* style grin.

I rested my hands on the edge of the bar, leaned forward toward them, and drew in a long breath, counting to ten in my head. Kate leaned back a centimeter, and Ang swayed. My instinct was to fly off the handle, but I did what I could to rein myself in.

"Ang, you're cut off. I can't serve you anything but water. Kate, what can I get you?"

I busied myself by pulling a bottle of water from the cooler, opening it, and passing it across the bar to Ang. She wore the expression of an insolent toddler but didn't say anything.

"I'll take a water too. Please," Kate said, giving Ang the side eye and looking embarrassed.

I passed Kate a water, knocked on the bar with my knuckles, and told them to have a good night. Confused looks passed between them as they stepped away from the bar.

I drew a deep breath into my belly, releasing my tightly clenched core.

The next customer stepped up, oblivious, and began rapid firing a huge drink order at me. I got busy mixing drinks and pouring beers while watching Ang and Kate wade through the crowd until they were standing near a booth by the tall front windows. They were talking animatedly over the noise, and Ang kept throwing glances in my direction. She was so tall I could easily see her over the crowd.

I lined up the drinks on the bar and rang up the customer. She and her friends gathered up the drinks and teetered off, trying not to spill on themselves or the jostling crowd.

I let out the breath I had been holding as yet another customer stepped up and began shouting her order over the chaos. My mind was racing, but I had to force myself to concentrate. I wanted to rage, but it was not the time or place. Besides, I was doing my best to not allow myself to default to anger anymore.

Ang was drunk, which was a major turn-off, aside from the fact that she had made a serious asshole move by bringing her date to my bar. I clenched my eyes shut for a second and began what would become my new poly mantra:

Ang can date other people. This is okay.

It doesn't matter.

It doesn't matter.

It doesn't matter.

Snapping my eyes open, I forced a grin at the customer, repeated her drink order back to her, and got to work.

I deftly poured a line of Cosmos, one Adios Motherfucker, and a Red Bull with vodka. I couldn't stand any of those drinks, but since they were all the rage, I made a lot of them.

The woman at my station was getting impatient. She huffed, dropped some cash on the bar, grabbed her drinks double fisted, passed them off to her friends, and left.

Another customer stepped up to my station and tried to get my attention by waving her hand at me. I turned my attention to the customer.

"What can I get for you?"

The customer rattled off a drink order, and I got going. Jen squeezed behind me with a tray of clean glasses, still hot from the glass washer, and she began stacking them behind me on the back bar.

Adrenaline and fatigue were colliding inside me, and I turned to talk to Jen, holding a shaker filled with ice and a Long Island Iced Tea. In the tight space behind the bar my hips were nearly pressed up against Jen's butt. She looked up and stopped stacking glasses. We made eye contact in the mirror behind the bar as I spoke into her ear.

"Hey, have you been practicing mixing drinks?"

"Yes," she said, confused.

"I need you to cover me for a bit. I need a break."

Jen looked at me, shocked. She'd never taken on full bartending duties before, and certainly not on a night when the place was packed.

"Should I get Sheila to cover you? She's the boss."

"Nah, it'll take forever to find her in this crowd. Just cover me. Please."

"Yeah. Okay. Dude, are you okay?"

I broke eye contact with Jen briefly to watch the crowd behind us in the mirror. In the sea of people, I could still see Ang, towering over everyone. I looked back at Jen.

"Yeah. I just need a few minutes." I handed her my shaker. "This is a Long Island. The rest of the order is already on the bar ready to go. My bartending guide is under the counter if someone orders something that you don't know how to make. You know where everything is and how to work the register."

Stepping back from Jen, I gave her a reassuring pat on the hip, and walked out of the half door at the end of the bar into a narrow service hallway that customers used to get to the bathroom and from the front bar to the back dance floor.

There was a long line for the women's restroom, which narrowed the dark hallway down to a one-way street. I squeezed through and made my way to the front room, wading through the crowd toward where I had last seen Ang.

I got stopped several times by customers and acquaintances giving me hugs and trying to make small talk. I smiled, hugged them back, and made excuses about being on the clock and continued on my way. I made it to the front windows and found Ang and Kate. Kate still appeared to be grumpy with Ang.

Just as the song ended, Tick blew the air raid siren, which resulted in the entire crowd letting out an excited whoop. Tick transitioned to "Hey Ya!", creating an audible reaction as throngs of people began heading to the back dance floor. Even some who had been waiting an eternity in line for drinks gave up and started pushing their way to the back room.

I took a peek at Jen, and she looked relieved that the line had thinned out.

"Hey," I said to Ang and Kate.

"Hey," they both said back, turning to me.

I slipped my hand into my pocket and rested it on the wine key that was stowed there. The handle was smooth and cool, and I nervously plucked with my thumbnail at the sharp tip of the corkscrew, which was folded flat against the handle like a Swiss Army knife.

I really had no desire to talk to either one of them but couldn't let Ang's behavior pass unchecked.

"So, Viv. This is Kate," Ang said.

I nodded to Kate, and she nodded back.

"Ang, do you really think that blindsiding me with this while I'm at work was such a good idea?"

Kate nodded, looked at me consolingly, and spoke up.

"If it makes you feel any better, I had no idea that we were going to meet tonight either. Not until we stepped up to the bar, and she started introducing us."

I frowned at them both.

"No, that does not make me feel any better."

"Oh," Kate said, disappointment thick in her throat. She broke eye contact with me.

"Hey, don't be a dick," Ang said and staggered a half step forward.

"The only one here who's being a dick is you. I think that's something Kate and I can agree on."

Kate gave a slight nod.

"Fine. We're leaving," Ang announced a little too loudly.

I rolled my eyes. I really despised being around drunk people.

The crowd was still thinned out, but people were trickling back into the front room since "Hey Ya!" had ended.

"Come on, Kate," Ang said and started to push past me.

"Hang on. Wait a minute. Ang, you're not driving, are you?"

"Yes, as a matter of fact, I am."

Kate gritted her teeth and looked at me, pleading for backup.

"No. Fucking. Way. Ang, you're a goddamn deputy. You know better than to drive drunk."

"I'm fine," she said, trying to push past me again. "It's only a few blocks."

I held my arm out in front of her, catching her across the gut and holding her there. I could feel how strong she was, and all the raw energy she had.

"No. Now, hold on a second. Just hang on, Ang. You're not driving anywhere. Let me call you guys a cab. Or can Kate drive your car back?"

"Yeah, hon, give me your keys, and I'll get you home safe and sound," Kate said soothingly.

My skin grew tight when I heard Kate call Ang "hon."

"Nah. Nah. Nope. I'm not some lightweight dickwad teen. I know my limits. I'm fine to drive."

"Ang, you know what? You're really obnoxious when you're drunk. You're like a sixteen-year-old boy right now. It's pretty lame." I knew I shouldn't be antagonizing her in that moment, but I couldn't help it. I was so pissed at her but also wanted her to get home safely.

"Give me your fucking keys. Now." I held my hand out to Ang, who swayed again. Kate steadied her with a hand around her waist.

Suddenly Buck was at my side, with her four-cell Maglite in hand. It worked great as a flashlight but also made a wonderful bludgeon. Buck cleared her throat.

Ang took us both in with bleary eyes, drew the keys from her pocket, and handed them to Kate. Kate blew out her breath in relief, and I let my hand drop to my side. I gave Kate a nod as she led Ang out of the bar with Buck in tow.

I shook it off and popped behind the bar to relieve Jen, who was looking stressed as she fumbled through my bartender's guide.

"I'll take it from here, Jen. Thanks."

Chapter Twenty-Two

I lay stretched out next to Ang on her bed, between her and the wall. The soft down mattress cover and duvet were trying really hard to draw me down into sleep. Just off work, I was still fully dressed, aside from my boots, which were neatly lined up next to the front door.

The smell of alcohol was wafting out of Ang's pores, and her breath stank of beer and whisky. She was talking indistinctly about nothing in particular and would occasionally fade into a light sleep, only to wake up again and start mumbling.

She had a nasty contusion on her right thigh. Apparently, Ang had walked into a newspaper box on the way to the parking lot. The bruise was swollen and turning from red to purple to black.

Kate walked back into the room carrying a fresh ice pack wrapped in a pale-blue kitchen towel. She placed it over the contusion on Ang's thigh and sat down on the edge of the bed.

Peering down at her watch, she groaned. "It's four a.m., and I have to be at work in three hours." She rubbed her eyes and then looked back at me. "Can we talk for a few before I go?"

I was so exhausted but was clear-headed enough to know that I was mad at Ang, not Kate.

"Sure." I sat up slowly, so as not to disturb Ang, who had fallen into a stupor.

I carefully slid down to the foot of the bed and padded into the living room. Kate closed the bedroom door lightly behind her and joined me on the mahogany-colored leather couch. Ang had good taste and a job that paid well, so her apartment was well appointed.

"So, tonight's been insane."

I nodded in agreement, picking at a hangnail.

Silence strung out between us.

"Vivian, do you know what a metamour is?"

"In theory, yes. I've never had one, but I've read enough about poly to know they exist."

"So, in relation, you and I are metamours to each other because we both have relationships with Ang. In the past, I have had some really amazing, fulfilling friendships with other metamours." Kate paused.

I gave up on picking at my hangnail and looked at her. Her expression was genuine. From what I had seen of her that night, she seemed to be a really nice person. And I figured she had never intentionally done anything to harm me.

It was Ang's responsibility to inform her of, and follow, our rules, which I didn't think she was fully doing. And Ang hadn't told me anything at all about what boundaries and rules they had agreed to, so I could have even inadvertently broken some of their rules at some point.

Fucking Ang.

I blew out a big breath.

"Okay, Kate. Let's get together soon, just us, and chat."

She flashed me a beautiful smile that carried into every line of her face. Her brown eyes beamed. I could see why Ang was drawn to her.

We exchanged phone numbers, and she headed for the door.

"Good luck getting through work today on no sleep," I said.

"Make sure she hydrates when she wakes up and keeps icing that leg throughout the day. Nurse's orders." I nodded as she closed the front door.

I sat on the couch for a while, scanning the room and letting my mind slow down so that I could eventually sleep. Ang had a nice big TV, a top of the line DVD player, a rich dark hardwood coffee table that matched her couch and end table. Accent pieces were perfectly placed here and there. The atmosphere was somewhat masculine, but also modern with clean lines and a few feminine touches.

On the wall, she had a framed picture of her class photo from the Sheriff's Training Academy. Proud new deputies lined up perfectly, their Class A uniforms flawless. Next to that she had a framed photo of herself from her time in the Navy. She had on a well-worn blue jumpsuit, eye protection, and red muffs on her ears. She was squatting down on the deck of an aircraft carrier looking like one tough-ass stud.

I grabbed a bucket from under her kitchen sink, crept quietly into her room, and placed the bucket next to the bed. If the booze was going to make her puke, better that she puke in the bucket rather than on the carpet.

I looked down at her as she slept and realized that I loved her deeply, but part of me also hated her. Her tendency to do insensitive things hurt me. Yet I kept going back for more.

Jesus.

*

I fell asleep the moment I laid down and slept most of the day. The sounds of Midtown during the day were mostly drowned out by my fish tank, and exhaustion helped keep me under long enough to get some decent sleep.

After a solid twelve hours of sleep, I shuffled around my studio, drank a glass of water, and got dressed in running gear. My cell phone pinged several times, indicating that I had text messages coming in. I finally grabbed it off my shitty salvaged coffee table and flipped it open.

Twelve texts from Ang, and one from Kate.

I opened Kate's first.

> *Hi Vivian, this is Kate. Heads up. Ang is having a bit of a meltdown. I'm just off work and exhausted. Need sleep. Can you check on her?*

Hmph. Combining forces with my new metamour to manage my...or rather, our girlfriend. *Ain't that some shit?* I drew in a breath, scratched the back of my neck, and considered my options.

> *Hi Kate. I'm headed out for a run. I'll check in with her when I get back.*

I did not read any of Ang's texts. But I did send her a text that simply said:

> *Hydrate*

Running in Midtown during rush hour usually wasn't the best plan, but I needed to move my body and needed to think. It turned out to be a decent run, and I eventually wove my way back through the blocks to my apartment building at a good clip, sweat dripping and mind calm.

I spotted my brother's truck parked haphazardly in front of the building. As I approached the lobby door, key in hand, I found him passed out halfway in the dirt breezeway between my apartment building and the house next door. His legs were splayed out on the sidewalk and his head in the dirt. Standing over him, I said his name tentatively.

"Joey." No response. A little louder. "Joey." Nothing.

I nudged him with my foot. He grunted but didn't wake. I bent over and rolled him onto his side so he wouldn't aspirate if he puked while passed out drunk. He reeked of urine, and I spotted a pool of piss under him. Straightening up, I shook my head and walked away.

In the lobby, I checked my mailbox. Empty. Taking the stairs two at a time, I moved quietly since Ang's apartment was directly over the lobby and stairs. I wanted to dodge her until I could get back to my studio, read her texts, and give them some thought.

As I crested the top step, Ang's apartment door opened. She stood in the threshold wearing black athletic shorts with the sheriff's department logo on the thigh and a white T-shirt. She appeared to have showered and had her hair done in the style of tight bun that she wore for work.

"Viv," she said, her voice tired.

"Hey, Ang." I stopped in the hallway, my shirt damp with sweat and my breath still shallow.

"You haven't responded to my texts."

"I haven't read them yet. I slept all day."

"Hm."

"How are you feeling? How's that bruise on your leg?"

"Hungover. Bruise hurts like a son of a bitch. Do I want to know how I got it?"

"Ask Kate. Have you been hydrating?"

"Yup."

"Good."

I shifted my weight from one foot to the other and clasped my hands together. In the distance, the clang of an alarm alerted that the light-rail crossing arms were going down across Twenty-fourth Street.

I looked up into Ang's eyes and saw sadness there. I had a decision to make. Treat her with kindness, even though she had hurt me again, or turn my back on her.

Stepping forward, I hugged her tightly around the waist and laid my head on her shoulder. She wrapped her arms around me and rested her chin on top of my head.

"Are you hungry?" I asked quietly.

"Yes, I probably need to eat before work," she said.

I stepped back out of the embrace.

"Come on down to my place. I'll cook us some dinner, and we can talk."

She nodded, stepped out of her apartment, and closed the door. I took her hand and we walked slowly down the stark corridor. She had a significant limp and was clearly in pain, so we took our time.

Once in my studio, I had her sit sideways on the futon, her long legs stretched out, and placed an ice pack on her thigh. I ran downstairs with a bottle of water for Joey. Pushing open the lobby door I saw that he, and his truck, were gone. I headed back upstairs hoping he was safe.

I took my time chopping and cooking chicken, broccoli, carrots, and mushrooms for a light chicken and vegetable stir fry, with brown rice, while Ang sat quietly watching my fish tank from across the room. I was careful not to overcook the vegetables and served up two plates. I sat across the coffee table from Ang, and we ate without speaking.

The fish tank filter burbled, cars passed by outside, my upstairs neighbor paced. Ang finished her food and drained her glass of water.

"Thanks, Viv, that was just what I needed."

I nodded at her and sat back in my folding chair, the old frame creaking.

"You're welcome. So, what's going on, Ang? You're not acting like yourself."

"That's fair." She paused. "I'm just trying to figure out how to best navigate all of this. Last night, it overwhelmed me, I drank too much, and I made a poor decision. I'll own up to that. I should not have shown up with Kate at your bar without talking to you, and her, first."

"Yeah."

She gave me a miserable grimace.

"And, Viv, I would like it if you would try dating some other people too. It'll take the pressure off me."

I tilted my head at Ang, not knowing where to start.

"Me date others...to make this whole thing easier for you? Wow, you really sound like a self-centered dick right now."

"Fuck, Viv. Okay, bad choice of words. I'm still working through this hangover. But seriously, if someone catches your eye, go for it! Go get some, have a good time, play safe, and then tell me all about it. I love that shit. Go have some banging hot sex and tell me every sweaty detail."

She grinned at me, her eyes shining. I gave her a grimace in return. I didn't really know how to respond, so I changed the topic.

"You should probably know that Kate and I are going to get together at some point...just to chat. She wants to get to know me better. A meeting of the metamours, so to speak."

"And you agreed to it?" Ang looked surprised.

"Yes."

"Oh, Viv, that's so fucking fantastic. You have no idea how happy that makes me." The pallor faded from Ang's face, and a huge smile spread across it. Even the crinkles on the sides of her nose made an appearance. I hadn't seen her smile like that in a while.

I can do this. Doom and hope mingled in my gut, which was something I was becoming accustomed to.

Chapter Twenty-Three

Kate usually worked days and I worked nights, so scheduling was not smooth. But the following Saturday she was off, so we decided to take a ride on my motorcycle. With her on the back, I rode out across the Yolo Causeway, through Davis and Winters, and up to the Monticello Dam at Lake Berryessa. She didn't squirm around or lean away from turns. She was a perfect passenger and had clearly spent a lot of time on a motorcycle.

We got off at the dam and stretched our legs. The air was much colder than it had been down in the valley. The water level at the lake was low, and the giant concrete glory hole was visible, sticking up several feet above the surface of the water. We didn't say much as we gazed through the old chain link fence at the dam. Tourists came and went, stopping to take pictures on their way to Napa.

Back on my bike, I rode back down the hill, parking at Lake Solano. We got a bench on the shoreline and looked out at the serene water, which wasn't a lake so much as a wide point in the creek.

Watching kayakers and ducks float by, we munched on grapes, almonds, and string cheese that I had brought along. Occasionally a turtle would pop its head up in the shallows, creating a small ripple.

"What a gorgeous day," I said, as I relaxed into the bench, the dappled sunlight warm on my skin despite the fact it was almost winter. There was a sense of calm in my core that had been missing for quite some time.

"Indeed," Kate said. Her voice came from far away, like she was caught up in the slow lazy current of the creek.

"So, are you a cyclist?"

"Yes. I race and do endurance rides. Double centuries and beyond."

"Jesus," I said.

"It's a major commitment. The training, I mean."

"I imagine so. Is that how you met Ang? Through cycling?"

"Yes. She joined one of my riding groups when she started training for her century ride."

"Ah, okay." I paused and pulled up the courage for my next question. "So, do you have a primary partner?"

"I do. Ang is my primary."

That took me off guard. All I could say was "Oh."

"You sound surprised. Is Ang your primary?"

"Yes." I had just drifted into uncharted waters.

"Hm. Yeah, poly is complex, isn't it?"

"Wait. So does Ang consider you her primary?"

"No. She has always been clear that you are her primary."

"Oh my God, this is hurting my brain. So, she and I are primaries, but she is your primary, even though you are not hers? And you're okay with that? That works for you?"

"Yes. I am. And yes, it does. I knew going into this that she already had a primary. And I have no intention of disrupting what you two have."

"Well, I have to say, I've learned more from you about my own relationship dynamic in the last thirty seconds than I have in months of feeling this out with Ang. She hasn't exactly been forthcoming about this stuff."

"You may not want to hear this, but she has talked to me about why that is. She tells me that every time she tries to talk to you about the relationship you get angry or hurt. So, she avoids the conversation completely, or when you do get upset, she says she shuts down."

"Oh, well that's lovely. I had no idea she was discussing the intricacies of our relationship with her other girlfriend. What you say is accurate though. Every time I need her to comfort me and help me through this stuff, she turns cold and withdraws instead. It's pretty terrible."

"Viv, have you ever considered that it's not Ang's job to help you through those tough situations? Perhaps that is a better topic for your therapist, or a friend, or perhaps join a poly support group? Whatever happens with all of this, Viv, you're going to be okay. I can feel that about you. You're a survivor."

Kate leaned her head on my shoulder, and we sat in silence again, watching dragonflies skim the water's surface.

Chapter Twenty-Four

A couple of weeks passed in a blur.

Rolling my bike into the parking spot in the underground garage, I shut the engine down and stayed in the saddle for a moment. Heat radiated off the engine as it pinged from the exertion of hours on the road.

I had taken a nice, long day trip out to the coast to clear my head, at my therapist's encouragement. I had zipped along the twisties on Skyline Boulevard, stopping for lunch at the iconic Alice's restaurant in Woodside. The parking lots at Alice's and the trading post across the street were packed and like a bike and car show. After lunch, I had strolled up and down the rows of bikes and classic cars, chatting up the owners and feeling a much-needed sense of peace.

The flat, straight ride home on I-80 was agonizingly boring after the adrenaline rush and release from the more challenging riding conditions earlier in the day.

As I slipped my helmet off, my cell phone pinged deep inside my tank bag. Balancing my helmet on the tank, I fished out my phone and saw there were missed calls and voice mails from multiple 530 numbers, as well as three texts from Kate. I started with the texts. All three said:

Vivian, call me. It's important.

My gut dropped. Immediately, I worried that Ang had been injured or killed while on duty. I clicked on the voice mails and listened to them each one at a time. Three were from Sergeant Brickhouse and all were identical.

"Vivian, this is Sergeant Brickhouse, please call me. It is urgent." His voice had a serious tone, the edge of joviality that was normally there absent.

I had an additional missed call and voice mail from a different 530 number. The voice mail was from a prerecorded female computer voice, and as I listened, I nearly dropped the phone.

"You have an incoming collect call from an inmate at the Diablo County Detention Center. Do you accept collect charges from inmate—" There was a pause, and then Ang's voice. "Angela Sorenson." The computer recording took over again. "If you accept the charges, please press one."

That was it. The recording ended there.

"What the fuck!" I shouted to the empty garage. I looked to my right and saw Ang's Subaru parked in her spot.

"What. The. Fuck."

I hopped off my bike and rushed upstairs with my heart in my throat. I dropped all the gear onto the futon and shed my riding jacket as sweat started to drip down my face and bloom under my shirt.

I dialed Sergeant Brickhouse's number from memory. It rang several times and went to voice mail.

"You have reached the desk of Sergeant Rodrick Brickhouse. Please leave a clear and concise message, including your name and telephone number. I will return your call at my earliest convenience."

As soon as his outgoing message ended and I heard the usual beep, I yanked my brain back, to stop from sounding like a blathering idiot on his voice mail.

"Hi, Sergeant. This is Vivian Chastain. I am returning your calls. Please call me back when you have a moment."

I hit the end button and scrolled through my contacts to Kate's number and hit dial. Kate immediately answered.

"Vivian?"

"Yes, hi, Kate. I got your texts. What's going on?" I could hear her footsteps moving hurriedly down a hallway, followed by the sound of a door closing.

"Oh, gosh. I am so glad you called me back. I am at work and kind of freaking out."

"How can I help? What's going on?"

Kate drew in a deep breath.

"I was at Ang's apartment today for brunch before work, and the sheriff's department came. They arrested her," she said in a hushed gush of frightened words. "They knocked on the door. She answered it, and they pushed their way in with their guns drawn! One of the officers looked at me and said, 'You don't want to be here. Leave.' So, I left. But I stood out front of the building to try and see what was happening."

Kate sniffled.

"Holy shit," I muttered.

"All of the cars out front were from Diablo County sheriff's office. They took her away in handcuffs."

"Did they tell you what she was charged with?"

"No, they wouldn't talk to me. And they wouldn't let her talk to me on the way out either. But I missed a call from her a little while later from the jail. I figured there wasn't anything I'd be able to do to help her right then, so I came in to work my shift as planned. I used to be a nurse at the main jail, and I know booking takes a while."

"I missed a call from her too. What. The. Fuck."

"Please don't use profanity, Vivian."

That took me by surprise.

"Okay, Kate. Sorry. So, I also missed a few calls from Sergeant Brickhouse. He was the lead investigator on a case I was involved with. I hope these two things aren't related. Shit...oh, sorry. I mean shoot."

"It's okay. Listen, I am at work and making my rounds. There's not a lot I can do right now. Is there any way you can call around and find out what's going on?"

"Yes, of course."

"Keep me posted please?"

"Yup. Will do. Jesus, what the fu—"

With that, Kate ended the call. I stared at the blank phone in my hand and sat down heavily on the futon, shoving aside my riding gear.

My helmet made the short drop onto the vaguely tan carpet and rolled to a halt on its side. I stared at it while my brain worked at high speed, flipping through all the possible scenarios.

Realizing that I was chewing on my fingernails, I yanked my fingers out of my mouth. An old habit from childhood that I had broken myself of when I was twelve. Wiping my wet fingers on my jeans in disgust, I jumped when my cell phone began ringing shrilly. The screen showed Sergeant Brickhouse's desk number. I flipped the phone open.

"Hi, Sarge. What's up?"

"A lot. Hey, Vivian. Is this an okay time to talk?"

"Yes, your voice mails freaked me out. What's going on?"

"We arrested your partner, Angela Sorenson." He paused, allowing me a moment to absorb.

"I've heard. But what I don't know is why."

"Do you remember who Johnny Long is?"

"Yea. He's the guy I found in the warehouse, right? The one with his hands lopped off?"

"Yes, that's him. Well, as you may recall, as soon as the hospital released him, we booked him in the main jail on existing warrants and to keep an eye on him. He has not been a happy camper in jail, given his reputation as a perv and all, and with no hands, life's been rough for him. He wants out. He contacted the DA to try and cut a deal, saying he had information to share in exchange for a no contest plea and a release with time served."

"So, the DA agreed and then what, you got involved somehow?"

"I got involved because the information he shared ties back to Crystal Wylie and her involvement with sex trafficking." He paused there, letting out a long sigh. I imagined his line of work exposed him to some pretty terrible stuff.

I sighed back at him as I put some of the pieces together.

"What I hear you saying is that Ang was arrested because you believe she has ties to Crystal's sex trafficking business? Is that...right?" I didn't want to hear his answer but had to know.

"Yes. That is what I am saying."

I stared out of the window at the canopy of green leaves across the street, and let it sink in.

"I assume that because you arrested her, you have some pretty solid evidence. More than just the word of some scared Chester trying to get out of lockup."

"Your assumption is correct. I can't give you the details but will say that the info we got from Mister Long led us to more concrete information that backed up his allegations. And Miss Sorenson used her badge and position to do it."

"Fuck."

"Yup."

A long pause spread out between us, and I realized I was chewing on my thumbnail again. Yanking my finger out of my mouth, I clenched my jaw instead.

"You're absolutely sure?"

"Yes, Vivian, I am sure. I wouldn't have arrested her if I wasn't. She's a fellow LEO. An arrest for something like that can destroy her career, even if a jury finds her not guilty later. I didn't make the decision lightly. And...we're going to need to interview you, too, since you're so familiar with her. I'll recuse myself and have my partner do it."

"Wait, you need to talk to me? Do you think Ang has been involved in sex trafficking during the time that she and I have been together?"

"Yes. I know for a fact she has."

"Oh. Shit." I was at a loss for any other words.

"Do you happen to know a woman named Katherine Castellucci?"

My brain stuttered as I refocused on Sarge's voice.

"Uh, Castellucci. Castellucci. Oh, yeah. That's Kate. I know her. Not well, but I know her."

"What's her relation to Miss Sorenson?"

"You'll have to ask her that."

"Hmph. Okay. Understood. Can you come in tomorrow to meet with my partner? She's going to run through some questions with you about Miss Sorenson. You remember my partner, don't you?"

"It's all a blur. She was in the room when questioned me that first day, right? The day I ran into Crystal at the warehouse? Detective...."

I dug deep into my memory but came up blank on the name. I only remembered blurs of her as being kinda dykey and watchful...quiet.

"Detective Rocha," he said.

"Yup, that's the one. Yes. I can come in tomorrow and talk to her. Do I need an attorney?"

"While I can't give you legal advice, I will say that you're not a person of interest. Deputy Rocha just wants to ask some questions in relation to Miss Sorenson."

"While I'm down there, can I visit Ang? How do I get on her visitor list?"

"I would advise against that, Vivian. For now."

We made arrangements for me to meet up with Deputy Rocha the next day and then ended our call.

I stared out of the window, considering what to do with what I had learned and wondered what Kate would make of it all. I flipped open my phone and dialed Kate's number, expecting to get her voice mail. She answered on the first ring, her voice anxious and hurried. I could hear quick footsteps and then a door close.

"Okay, have to make it quick. I'm hiding out in the copy room but won't have privacy for long."

I told Kate everything Sergeant Brickhouse had told me, including that he had asked about her. She took it all in quietly. When I finished, she grunted what sounded like *"thanks"* and then hung up.

I didn't blame her. The news had just completely turned upside down what we thought we knew about our primary partner. A person we both trusted and adored. Recalling that we were metamours and both impacted by the revelation, I recognized that if I could comfort and support her, I should. I sent Kate a text:

Kate, I'm here for you if you need anything. We don't have to go this alone. Let's get together soon. Like, really soon.

I was still getting used to having a metamour and what that all meant for the three of us. Or...two of us now. If what Sergeant Brickhouse and Johnny Long said about Ang was true, there was no way I could stand by Ang or stay involved with her.

Something my therapist, Alexia, once said surfaced in my mind. We had been talking about stuff that had happened in my family when I was kid, and how it tied into my relationship with Ang.

Alexia had said, "I know that you didn't, but some kids do experience unconditional love. Yet adults, adults don't get the luxury of unconditional love in relationships. Some things cross the point of no return."

For me, Ang being involved with trafficking and using her position as a deputy to assist someone with it was inexcusable. I trusted that Sergeant Brickhouse had been thorough and was certain before he went after her.

There was a pang in my chest as I considered the reality that I would have to walk away from Ang. That the person I thought I knew may not have the honor and integrity I thought she had.

I realized how hard I had fallen for her, how I had ignored all the relationship red flags. I had even pushed it aside when Crystal called Ang by her name at the cottage in Guerneville. Apparently, I was a fucking idiot. I was indeed getting soft. When I had been in the service, I wouldn't have allowed myself to put up with all of that. I would have walked away a long time ago. Woulda, shoulda, coulda...dammit.

My phone pinged. It was Kate.

Yes, please. Can I come by after my shift? You live up the hall from Ang's apartment, right?

I gave her a quick reply:

Yes, #106. Come on by. I have to work tonight, but not till 9. See you soon.

Chapter Twenty-Five

I showered and got dressed in work clothes. The usual black beater, black Dickies, wallet chain, and boots. My life depended on tip money, and this was the look that paid.

I had allowed my brain to flow through various thoughts about Ang. Anger and doubt flip-flopped. *How could Ang get mixed up in this? Is she really a horrible person and I just missed all the fucking signs? She didn't really do this, did she? Crystal is just setting her up to hurt me.*

I put a stop to the flow as I stepped into the kitchen and prepared a light dinner of vegetable stir fry. I figured after a twelve-hour shift on her feet at the hospital that Kate might be starved, and she was.

She arrived dressed in scrubs, a light cardigan, and those slip-on clogs nurses wear. She took her clogs off by the front door and sat cross-legged on the floor in the living room, her dinner plate on the coffee table. She packed away the rice and veggies in no time but managed to do it with grace. I got her a second helping, and she worked her way through that a bit more slowly. We rounded off the meal with some peppermint tea as the sky outside the window faded from dusk to dark. I popped in a Dido CD, but it brought back memories of Ang, so I switched it out for an Ani DiFranco album.

I sat down and looked up the ceiling, gathering my thoughts. "I can't help but wonder if Ang is being set up...maybe even by Crystal."

Kate nodded and then removed her cardigan and sat down on the floor. She started a stretching routine as she considered what I had said. She stretched her legs out in front of her and leaned forward, folding herself in half as she grasped her feet. When she spoke, her voice was muffled because her nose was pressed against her knees. "Ang being set up is possible, but I can't help but wonder if we both somehow missed critical signs that Ang is not actually a good person and maybe actually did what she is accused of."

I groaned. "I hope like hell that this whole thing is just a mix-up somehow."

Kate turned her head and looked at me. "Police don't arrest other police unless they are damn sure about the charges." She released her hold on her feet and sat up slowly, raising her arms above her head in a graceful arc, like a ballet dancer.

I thought my thoughts until Kate finished stretching and took a seat on the other end of the futon. I motioned for her to put her feet in my lap and, after a moment of hesitation, she did.

I knew all too well what it was like to be an athlete and work a job where you're on your feet your whole shift. I took her foot into my hand and began massaging it. She gave a grateful groan and then picked up on the topic of Ang again. I listened to her as she did a lot of thinking out loud, waffling back and forth on how she felt, what she would and wouldn't do.

"Now, hear me out on this one," she said with a sigh. I nodded for her to proceed. "If she actually did what they are accusing her of, I know for me, there's no way I could stand by her through this. None. I've seen way too much of the damage caused by sexual trauma in my time working at the hospital. If she had any part of something like that, done. I'm out." I nodded at her again as I continued rubbing her foot. Kate was right. If Ang really was involved, I couldn't stand by her either.

The skin of her feet was stretched tight over bone, with veins popping up all over. They were the feet of someone who worked hard and played hard. The Ani CD ended, and I checked my watch with a grimace.

"I need to roll out soon. Work beckons."

"Aw, yeah, that's right. I forgot that you work tonight. So, will you keep me posted if you find anything out from this Deputy Rocha?"

"Yup, of course. We have so little info right now. I will see what else I can get so we don't have to keep circling around all these what-ifs. And if you happen to talk to Ang can you let me know what she says?" I asked hesitantly, not knowing if that request crossed a boundary.

"Yes, I'll let you know."

We both stood up and stretched our legs as if we had been sitting in a car too long. I made a quick trip to the bathroom to pee, wash my hands, and slide on a black Dickies jacket from the closet. Kate had her cardigan and clogs on.

In the narrow entryway I gently pulled Kate into a hug. She hugged me back, sliding her hands around my waist, inside my jacket. She was so petite and lean, her embrace so different from Ang's. Different, but good. She had a nurturing warmth about her that Ang didn't.

Kate gently ended the hug and looked up at me.

"Go get 'em, Meta. I hope your shift is fruitful and fast. Maybe you'll even get lucky tonight. I saw how those girls were eyeing you at the bar," she said, giving my arm a mock punch.

"Nah, I don't mess around with customers. But thanks for the encouragement."

I gave her a wink and locked up. We walked down the corridor and paused in front of Ang's apartment door before heading down the lobby stairs. I had never had a friendship like the one forming with Kate. Most of my friends growing up and into adulthood were guys. So, having a friendship where we could be physically and emotionally close, yet have not expectation of anything more, was new.

Huh, Ang was right, having a metamour is pretty great.

*

The next day I rode out of Sacramento to the Diablo County sheriff's department. After waiting around in the lobby, enjoying some people-watching, I was eventually called back.

A small woman who didn't make eye contact ushered me to a sparsely furnished interview room. Noting the surveillance camera in the corner of the room, I took a seat in the only chair that faced the door. There I waited for over an hour, beginning to wonder if I was a subject, rather than a witness.

Either Deputy Rocha was fucking with my head, or she was just busy. At last, she entered the room with a swagger about her that caught my attention.

As she got settled in the chair across from me, just a narrow conference table between us, I measured her up and was astonished that I hadn't really noticed her the last time I was there being questioned. I lent that to the fact I was concussed at the time, and probably a little bit in shock, after my tussle with Crystal.

How had I not fully taken in the presence that was Deputy Rocha? Even with a concussion, I would have been internally drooling all over her. She was smoking hot. She had on black tactical pants, a black Sam Brown duty belt fully loaded, and black department polo shirt. Underneath her polo I could see the bulge of a bulletproof vest. All of it fit her snugly, her physique on display.

She must have been Sergeant Brickhouse's workout partner. She was solidly built. Even her hands were muscular, leading up to tan, ripped forearms and biceps and delts that popped under her polo. Her jawline was square, her skin tone landed somewhere between tan and olive. When we finally made eye contact, I held my breath and reminded myself to keep a straight face.

Her dark eyes locked on mine, and I gave her a nod. She straightened her stack of papers and clicked her pen open and shut a few times.

"Vivian Chastain, right?"

"Yes, ma'am, that's correct."

Deputy Rocha gave a lopsided grin when I called her ma'am.

"You can skip the ma'am, and just call me Deputy Rocha."

"Nice to meet you, Deputy Rocha."

"We've met before, but no harm if you don't remember. You were pretty beat up at the time, and Sarge was the one asking all of the questions that day."

A twinge of defensiveness popped up when she said I had been beat up. I recognized that my pride was trying to get in the way but defended myself anyway.

"Hey now," I said with a chuckle, "I may have looked beat up, but I kicked the crap out of that Crystal Wylie too."

"Fair enough. Fair enough," Deputy Rocha said, holding up her hands in mock surrender.

I saw calluses on her hands from lifting weights. She could probably break me like a twig, but I could outrun her any day.

"So, what can I do for you, Deputy Rocha?"

She gave me a flirty smirk and then cleared her throat, getting back to business.

"I have some questions for you about Angela Sorenson. It's my understanding that she is your partner. Is that correct?"

I nodded and leaned back in my chair. "Yes, that is correct."

"And when did your relationship with Miss Sorenson begin?"

"Not long after my run-in with Crystal Wylie. That's actually what brought us together."

"And were you aware that Miss Sorenson and Miss Wylie were associates?"

Initially the question made my brain stutter. *Of course, they're not associates!* But I gave it some thought and recalled the night we caught Crystal breaking into my cottage in Guerneville. Crystal, who should have been a stranger to Ang, had called her by her first name.

It had raised a red flag for me at the time, which I had dismissed. Under the circumstances it seemed naïve that I had let it slide. You do stupid shit when you love someone.

"No. I was shocked when Sergeant Brickhouse told me what the allegations were."

"How is it you caught Miss Wylie in Guerneville?"

"I had a feeling that I was being followed, even though I had left town to hide, per Sergeant Brickhouse's instructions. Anyway, I set a simple trap, kept the same routine each day to make it really easy for whoever was following me to make their move. And what do ya know, up popped Crystal."

"Do you know how she tracked you to Guerneville?"

"She claims that she happened to be watching my apartment building when she spotted me packing up my truck. So, she followed me to Guerneville. Seems a tad convenient, but who knows."

"Aside from Sergeant Brickhouse, who did you share your destination with?"

"Just Ang. Miss Sorenson, I mean." I shifted in my chair, already knowing where that line of questioning was headed and I didn't like what it implied, not one bit. My already tight abdomen was trying to tie itself into a knot.

Oh shit. Hold it together. Keep your cool, Chastain.

"Do you think Miss Sorenson tipped Miss Wylie off to your whereabouts in Guerneville?"

"I can't answer that. I have no idea."

I hated that Deputy Rocha was implying Ang sold me out to Crystal and put me in danger.

Why the hell would Ang do that?

And Deputy Rocha asking me that question was just her trying to fuck with my head. I steeled myself for her next question. I wouldn't allow her to get in my head.

Deputy Rocha shot a quick glance toward the camera in the corner, ran her hand through her short brown hair, and then focused back on me. She continued with her questions, trying several different angles and tactics to get me to turn on Ang.

But I truly knew nothing about Ang's involvement with Crystal, so I had nothing to share.

The conversation became tedious. I leaned farther back in the chair and looked down at my hands, trying to signal that I was done, but she carried on.

Deputy Rocha's good looks no longer had an effect on me. I was over the process and her, so I decided to ask some questions of my own.

"Deputy Rocha, what does this all mean for Crystal...Miss Wylie, I mean? Last I heard she cut a plea deal on her other charges."

"That's a good question. That plea deal was for what she did to Mister Long. The new information that has come forward will likely result in fresh charges against Miss Wylie."

"So, then could Miss Sorenson turn witness for the District Attorney and get a deal by being a witness? What I was told is that Ang...er, Miss Sorenson, was involved in some way with Miss Wylie's sex trafficking operation, but not how involved. Could she somehow become a witness instead of a defendant?"

I looked up at Deputy Rocha to gauge her response. She kept a straight face and answered without hesitation.

"While I am not in a position to make decisions like that, I understand where your questions are coming from. You're hoping that Miss Sorenson wasn't intentionally involved in trafficking, but she was. Very much so. We have dozens of young women we scooped up during a sting operation who all identified Miss Sorenson as a key player in their capture, transport, and at times even stood as a lookout and provided muscle while they were forced into sexual acts with a variety of men."

Her words hit me like a freight train. I'd managed to maintain my composure up until that point. But what Deputy Rocha had just said pushed me beyond my limit. The Ang I knew would be the one to stand up and protect innocent women and children and would certainly not be a party to their enslavement and rape.

I was disgusted, and I was done.

"Am I free to go?"

Deputy Rocha hesitated and looked up at the camera again. "Well, yes. You're not being detained."

"Okay, thank you."

I stood up, pushed my chair in, and strode to the door, which I discovered was locked from the outside.

Anxiety sparked as my mind slipped into two places at once. Back to being trapped by my brother while our mother was not home and being trapped in a tool shed by a grabby first sergeant.

My throat was starting to close up, but I managed to squeak out a request to Deputy Rocha.

"I'd like to leave now. Please open the door."

Her chair legs scraped along the linoleum floor. She stood right behind me, the heat from her body radiating into mine as she banged on the door.

Thump! Thump!

I flinched. The smell of her cologne was overwhelming.

She didn't move, but rather remained standing so close to me that her breath grazed the back of my neck. I heard footsteps outside and someone fumbling around with the door handle before the door opened.

A gust of fresh air mercifully hit me, and I drew in a huge lungful as I stepped past whoever had opened the door. I didn't look up to see who it was but saw black slacks and scuffed men's dress shoes. It wasn't Sergeant Brickhouse because his shoes were always polished to a high shine.

I hustled down the corridor, back through the lobby, and outside to my bike. I straddled the saddle and forced myself to breathe and reorient.

You're safe. You're not a little kid back home trapped by Joey, and you're not in North Carolina trapped by your first sergeant. You're safe. Now, breathe.

And so, I breathed.

Across the busy street was the main jail, and somewhere deep inside it, under lock and key and a no bail warrant, was Ang.

I still wasn't quite willing to believe that she was involved with sex trafficking, nor was I fully prepared to accept Deputy Rocha's idea that Ang told Crystal where to find me.

It was all just too much for my brain to absorb.

But...dozens of victims all pointed to Ang. How could I argue with that? My heart sank. I just didn't understand. Why? Why would Ang get on the wrong side of something like that?

I wondered if the jail admin had her segregated from the general population. Being charged with sex trafficking and also being a cop, even as big and strong as Ang was, she would be pounded to a pulp before her first court hearing.

Part of me wanted to walk across the street to ask if they would let me see her, but the other part of me knew it would be totally out of line right now.

A deep loneliness took over me as I rode home, and by the time I had made it back up to my studio, I was under the heavy yoke of despair.

I didn't have therapy until the following week, so, disregarding his request that I give him space, I called Jared and invited him to come stay with me. He readily agreed to come up the next day, which surprised me.

Next, I dialed Kate's number, and she answered on the fourth ring. Her voice surprised me, as I was expecting it to roll to voice mail.

"This is Kate."

"Hey, it's Viv."

"Oh, Viv, I am so glad to hear from you. You caught me on my break, so I can chat for a few. How'd it go?"

Through the phone I could hear the sound of street traffic and her clogs on the sidewalk. Her breathing was elevated. She must have been out on a walk.

"Not good. The deputy who questioned me got into my head a little bit. And she gave me more details about what Ang is charged with, and it's bad. I'm totally floored. I can't imagine Ang doing what they say she did, but they have tons of witnesses. It's so, so bad. Have you heard from Ang yet?"

"She's called a few times, but I've missed her calls. She must think we've totally bailed on her."

"Yeah. I can't imagine what's going through her mind right now. I am having such a hard time separating my feelings for her from what she is accused of."

I heard the swish of an automatic door and the sound of Kate's clogs on a tile floor.

"Hey, Viv, I have to get back to work."

"Okay, oh, hey. My best friend is coming up to visit tomorrow. He's going to stay with me for a couple of days. I'd love it if we could all hang out."

"Sure, that sounds great! Talk to you soon."

Chapter Twenty-Six

I was expecting Jared to be withdrawn and standoffish, but he arrived full of smiles and hugs. It was such a relief to have him with me in person.

We sat by the pool all afternoon, chatting about work and family, and reminisced about when we were stationed together. Having a chance to relax with him and talk was very much like how our friendship used to be, and it was exactly what I needed. It gave me hope that our friendship would survive me turning down his proposition and gave me a much-needed distraction from stressing about Ang. And we avoided talking about the elephant in the room, which was our own damaged relationship.

Eventually I got ready for work, and we met Kate at Zelda's for some pizza before my shift. Jared and Kate hit it off right away, and we had a great time over dinner and drinks before walking a couple of blocks to the club.

It was early enough that Kate and Jared were able to get stools at the bar at my station. They carried on an animated conversation full of chuckles and eye rolls while I got to work. I was so happy to see them happy.

While it wasn't packed, the club wasn't dead either. Mostly regulars that night, aside from a few small groups of people stopping by as they barhopped around Midtown.

I spotted a couple of straitlaced businessmen in suits stop at Buck's podium. As they pulled out their wallets to pay the cover charge, one took a moment to look around, and his eyes popped when he saw all the rainbow flags and queers. He elbowed his buddy, whispered in his ear, and they both turned tail and walked out, bumping into another man who was coming in. There was a bit of grumbling and jostling before the businessmen managed to get out of the door. The man on his way in stepped up to the podium, slapped down some cash, and turned to scan the room.

"Oh, fuck," I growled under my breath. Jared looked up and followed my line of sight.

"Is that Joey?" he said, incredulous.

"Who's Joey?" Kate asked, looking toward the door.

"Joey's my brother. And yes, that's him."

Joey's eyes met mine and a huge grin spread across his face. He was sunburned, his hair as shaggy as it always was, and he desperately needed a shave. His clothes were clean and looked new, so that was a change for the better.

He put his hands out in a friendly gesture and began walking toward my station. Jared and I exchanged a glance, and I knew he had my back no matter what happened.

Joey tried to hug me across the bar. I patted him on the shoulder.

"Little *sissy*-poo," he shouted, and I realized he was hammered. His breath reeked of stale beer and fresh whiskey.

"Hey, Joey. What brings you down to Lavender Heights? This isn't the neighborhood you usually spend time in."

"Lavender Heights? Pfft. Whatever. Just wanted to see my sissy-poo. And hey, I just got paid. You like my new outfit?"

He stood back from the bar so we could all see his new skate shoes, baggy jeans, and surfer shirt. His shoes were untied, as always. I also noted that he had the remnants of a shiner around his left eye. He stepped back up to the bar and leaned in toward me.

"Have you talked to Mom lately? Man, is she getting even bitchier with age."

I leaned back to try to escape his intoxicating breath.

"Hey, Joey, do you remember Jared? And this is my friend Kate."

I pointed to them and Joey gave Jared an animated handshake and big thumping pats on the back as he laughed heartily.

"Jared! What's up, bro? Long time, long time."

Then he leaned around Jared to Kate and gave her a quick smile.

"Hiya, Kate."

Kate and Jared greeted him back, and he settled onto a barstool next to Jared.

"Viviiiii, lemme have a double whiskey with a Guinness back."

Oh, Jesus, this is not going to end well.

I nodded at him and got to work pouring.

He turned in his seat and started chatting up Jared. I made solid eye contact with Buck over the beer tap. She gave me a nod and touched her nose, letting me know that she would keep an eye on Joey. I slid a pint glass of Guinness and a tumbler of whiskey across the bar to him.

"That'll be ten dollars," I said flatly.

"Damn, Viv, really?"

"Hey, you're a big boy and even just got paid. Ten bucks please."

Joey grumbled and slapped a ten-dollar bill on the bar from his sweat-stained wallet. He took the double whiskey down in one long pull and followed it with a large swig from his pint glass. There was beer foam on his scraggly mustache, which he wiped on the back of his hand.

A young guy, who I knew was a sex worker, sauntered up to Joey. He went by the name Sloan and normally did very good business in the bar. I groaned internally and tried to wave Sloan off, but he was focused on Joey.

"Hey, there. You're new," he said as he rubbed shoulders with Joey, his voice taking on a conspiratorial tone.

Joey leaned away from him and looked him up and down, taking in his snake print skinny jeans and baby-T. Joey grunted.

"I'm straight. Fuck off." Joey turned back to his beer.

Sloan leaned in a bit closer and spoke into Joey's ear.

"Straight is right. Straight to bed. Let's go."

Joey stood bolt upright, sending his barstool tumbling. Buck took long strides across the room to intervene, and Jared stood up, ready to help.

I knew I needed to distract Joey before he knocked Sloan out.

"Don't touch me, you fucking faggot! I'm going to kill you, cocksucker!"

Everyone in the front bar fell silent and turned in our direction. I saw so many frightened faces. People who had made this bar their safe space suddenly had their safety shattered.

"Joey! Joey!"

He turned to me. His face was red with rage, his eyes bulged, and his fists were balled up. I was all too familiar with that look from him, and I knew how dangerous he could be.

"Don't," I said, holding his gaze.

He broke eye contact with me, shot out a hand, and grabbed Sloan by the throat, who immediately yelped and began clawing at my brother's massive, calloused hand.

Jared was larger than my brother by a bit and slapped a hand firmly on Joey's shoulder. He spoke into Joey's ear.

"Hey, Joey. Come on. Let's go for a walk."

Joey ignored Jared, and his face got even more red as veins began to pop along his throat and temples. Buck took her huge Maglite flashlight out of its holster as she closed the gap between them. She swung back and brought the Maglite down on the back of Joey's knee in one massive blow. His leg buckled and he howled, releasing Sloan as he tried not to lose his balance. Sloan bolted away, and Jared grabbed Joey in a half nelson.

"Jesus Christ, Joey. You're eighty-sixed. Get the *fuck* out of my bar, and don't come back," I shouted at him with disdain.

"What about my beer?" he said through clenched teeth.

I grabbed his pint of Guinness, leaned across the bar, and dumped it over his head, taking great satisfaction in ruining his new clothes. With how angry I was, he was lucky I didn't smash the glass against his skull.

"Now get the fuck out," I said through gritted teeth.

Jared and Buck perp walked him across the room and out of the door. Through the front windows, I saw Joey stumble drunkenly down the front steps and regain his balance on the sidewalk.

Several customers who had been standing out front smoking hustled inside to avoid him as he paced back and forth in a rage. One thing I knew for certain about my brother was that he had a horrible temper, a penchant for violence, and he didn't let things go easily.

Kate and I made eye contact as I drew in a long, shuddering breath, trying to bring my nerves down. She seemed unfazed. She probably saw a lot of crazy shit go down at the hospital.

Jared sauntered back up, straightening his clothes out before he sat back down on his barstool.

"Thanks, Jared. You handled that well."

I gave him a nod and slid a bottle of water to him. He twisted the cap off and took a mighty swig. Afterward he gave me a nod back, a twinkle in his eyes. He liked the occasional dustup.

"No worries. It's certainly not the first time I've had to deal with your brother when he was hammered."

"Hopefully, it'll be the last," I said sardonically. "Sooo, Kate, that was my brother. Lucky you. You're meeting all kinds of people from my life tonight. At least Jared is a gentleman, unlike my big brother."

"There's never a dull moment with you, Vivian," Kate said with a smirk. Jared gave a knowing nod and raised his eyebrows at me.

"Hey, punk," I said and flicked Jared with my bar towel.

We all had a good laugh as I watched my brother storm off down the sidewalk.

Chapter Twenty-Seven

The next morning, I woke up to sun streaming through the window as Jared threw open the blinds. He had slept on a foam mat on the floor and was up and moving around, already in his running gear. He had never needed much sleep to get by.

"Come on, Vivi. Up. Let's go for a run."

I chucked my pillow at him, which he caught and chucked right back at me. I put it over my head and took a moment to scan. I was bone tired, and the inside of my mouth was all chewed up. I must have had another night of bad dreams, although since I had gotten into a groove with my therapist those rough nights were becoming less frequent. I removed the pillow from my head.

"Fuck it. Let's go."

As I got dressed, I took a peek at my cell phone and saw that I had missed calls and accompanying voice mails from my mom and from the jail where Ang was lodged.

Not yet.

I left my phone on the kitchen counter.

Jared and I took a nice long run in a big loop around the Midtown grid. Some people were rushing off to work, while others were still fast asleep in doorways and alleys, surrounded by what few possessions they had. The stench of urine, car exhaust, and grass clippings mingled in the air.

It was hard for us to get into our usual rhythm because of all the intersections and people. We decided to sprint every other block, which made for a fun game. I had gotten to be faster than Jared, which was a surprise, as he could always outrun me in the past. We jogged the last few blocks home to cool down.

"You're getting slow, old man," I said, taunting him.

"You wish. Just been busy with work. I'll get back into my old form soon enough."

As we crested the lobby stairs, I gave a quick glance at the door to Ang's apartment out of habit. Back inside my studio we stretched and then gulped down big glasses of cool water. I was ready to face my phone and dialed up my voice mail.

First up was my mom.

"Vivian. This is your mother. Why aren't you answering? People with real jobs and responsibilities are awake by now. But I suppose you are asleep." She let out a huge sigh. "I am calling because your brother got arrested again last night. I'm not bailing him out this time. They'll probably release him once he sobers up anyway. But I do want to see about getting him into rehab. So, he's going to need your support..."

I snorted and hit delete before she could finish.

The next message was the same recording I had gotten before from the jail. It was Ang trying to get hold of me. I hung up and leaned against the kitchen counter.

I wanted to scream with frustration but held it in because Jared was watching me intently from where he sat on the living room floor. I crossed my arms, hiding my hand under one arm, and pinched my side through my shirt as hard as could I stand. I clenched my jaw and kept pinching until I had had enough, and then released it. The burn and sting that followed rushed through me and I was ready to rejoin Jared.

I slipped off my running shoes and sat on the floor next to him.

"I wish I had gotten a picture of Joey all red faced and with beer all over him for my eighty-six photo album. Oh well."

"I know I'm being nosy, but who called?"

"My mom and my girlfriend. Or is it ex-girlfriend?"

"Anything you want to talk about?"

"My mom said Joey got arrested last night. God, I hope he didn't hurt anyone else after we kicked him out. Anyway, she's sending him to rehab, and wants my support." I paused, picking at my cuticle. "Ever since high school I have been expecting the call that they found him dead in a ditch somewhere. Or that they've arrested him for killing someone while drunk. That's a shitty thing for a little sister to have to go through, and a shitty way for him to live his life. He contributes nothing positive to this community. All he does is lie, hurt people, and take, take, take."

I couldn't make eye contact with Jared, so I focused on the slight stubble lining his jaw. He pursed his lips as he worked through what I had said.

"You know what, Vivian? I think you should help him. I think you should give him the support he's never gotten before. Your mom is an empty well, so you know he's not going to get what he needs from her. What if it were me? I know you would show compassion if I needed help."

At first, I had no idea how to respond. I was initially angry at Jared for taking my brother's side, but also angry because he was right...*right?* My brother had no support from anyone. He had burned all his bridges a long time ago and was adrift in a personal sea of misery that he had made himself. *But wait, no, fuck that.*

"Here's the thing, Jared. If it was you, of course, I would be the first one in line to help you. You've always done right by me, and we've always had each other's backs. But Joey? He's abused me since we were toddlers. He tormented me until I was old enough to buy my own car and run away. Just because he is my blood doesn't mean I am obligated to help him.

"This is our mom forcing him into rehab. It's not gonna stick, just like it didn't stick last time. I'll tell you what, when Joey is ready to help himself, I promise I will be there for him. But until then, I'm not getting involved."

Jared looked down at the floor, an air of disappointment about him.

I picked at my cuticle, enjoying the sting where I had pinched my side, and listened to the fish tank burble away. Minutes passed as we both spent time in our own thoughts. Finally, Jared broke the silence.

"I think that's where we have a fundamental difference. I am Christian and was raised to always give a person a hand up when I can."

"Christian or not, you were also raised in a family with two nurturing parents who gave a shit, and you didn't have siblings abusing you every chance they got. Every single person has a different upbringing and family and experiences.

"You and I are coming at this from very different perspectives. My blood family did nothing to protect me as a kid, so I joined the military and gained a chosen family, which you are part of."

Jared scrunched up his eyebrows and bit his thumbnail. His hazel eyes cast down. He drew in a breath and began to speak.

"But...what if you are what he needs right now?"

I had no response to that, so we sat on the floor of my studio, at an impasse, a light-rail train whooshing by down below.

*

High winds rustled the dry boughs of the redwood trees around the park. The massive wooden structure of "Big People's Park" swayed and creaked. Russell and I had climbed up to the very top of the structure, which was dangerously high off the ground. We had snuck out of our houses in the middle of the night and met up at the park. Anything to get away from the pressure cooker of living with Bernadette and Joey. The chance to get some freedom, some sense of self, out in the quiet of the night.

Russell was my best friend at the time. He sported the typical early '90s long shaggy hair, jeans, flannel shirt, and leather jacket. The cold from the wooden floor seeped into my haunches through my thin jeans and I shivered, wrapping my jacket more tightly around me. Russell saw my discomfort and pulled me toward him. He leaned his back against a post, and I leaned my back against him. He wrapped me up in his jacket and took my frozen hands into his, which were warm. My hands instantly began to thaw out, and I was grateful for the comfort Russell saw I needed, and that he so willingly gave to me.

We sat like that for hours, looking up at the stars while the structure swayed and creaked beneath us. We chatted intermittently, but mostly just sat there in silence absorbing what we could from each other. Both the product of divorce, growing up as latchkey kids in homes with absentee working moms, we were able to understand and recognize the void in each other. There wasn't much to say, but we both needed that silent connection so badly.

Chapter Twenty-Eight

Jared had to get back to work, so left the next morning. We had agreed to disagree, but it was clear he thought a bit less of me, because I wouldn't help my brother.

I didn't like that the year had placed two wedges between us and our friendship, but I was still confident that our friendship would recover, even though I knew it would take some time. And in the meantime, I had some other shit to handle.

I picked up my cell phone and opened the contacts folder. I scrolled down to an entry labelled "Bernadette." I never could bring myself to title the entry "Mom."

I hit the dial button and sat down on my futon, gazing out of the window at the trees across Twenty-fourth Street. The leaves rustled impatiently as I waited for my mother to answer.

"This is Bernadette," she said, the usual sharp edge to her tone.

"Hi, Mom. I'm returning your call from the other day."

The sound of a door closing and a seat squeaking came to me through the phone.

"Vivian. It's about time. I'm at *work*," she said with a huff.

I could read right between those lines. It was a well-known fact that she would prefer it if I had a desk job like her. She sighed and continued.

"So, your brother was released from the jail. I took him straight to that rehab place out in the East Bay. You know the one. Anyhow, I insisted he sign himself in, and he did. I called his boss, to try and negotiate a leave of absence, but they wouldn't talk to me about it. All they said was they had fired him for job abandonment. Unbelievable."

"Well, while that sucks, there are plenty of demolition jobs out there. He'll get another one. And most don't care if you're a slovenly drunken mess as long as you show up and can break shit and don't get hurt on the job."

She huffed again. "Language, Vivian."

I rolled my eyes and pursed my lips tightly shut to keep from talking back to her like a petulant teenager.

"Anyhow, I want you to go visit your brother. He needs some cheering up."

"Mom, is he in rehab because you pushed him into it, or did he ask to go?"

"He did not ask to go, but I certainly didn't push him into it."

"When he got into your car at the jail, would you have dropped him off anywhere other than rehab?"

"No."

"I've got to go, Mom."

"Viviannnn," she hissed at me as a warning. A sound I was all too familiar with from childhood.

"Yes?"

"I am at *work*, so I can't get into a conflict with you. Your brother needs your support right now."

"Do you know what he did the night he got arrested, Mother? Your precious son came into my bar, assaulted one of my customers, yelled homophobic slurs, and would have done far more harm had others not intervened. I have no idea what he did afterward that got him arrested. Also, he's an asshole. I will help him when he is ready to help himself."

Bernadette sighed heavily. I slid the phone closed, ending the call.

I rested the small cell phone on my leg and sat back, staring at the ceiling as the sound of my upstairs neighbor's incessant pacing filtered down to me. I imagined my mother sitting at her desk, all high strung and miffed at me.

I imagined my upstairs neighbor frantically chewing his fingernails and chain-smoking cigarettes with the window closed as he paced his studio.

I heaved a big sigh and wasn't surprised in the least when my cell phone began to ring. I looked at the screen and found that it was the Diablo County Jail.

Sure, why the hell not. What's a little bit more stress?

I slid the phone open and pressed it to my ear. "Hello."

The standard recording began, explaining that an inmate from the jail was calling me, followed by Ang stating her name. I accepted the call.

"Hello? Ang?"

"Oh my God, Vivian! It's so amazing to hear your voice," Ang gushed and drew in a long breath.

"Ang, wow. Sorry, I've missed all of your calls."

"Yeah, I've had a hell of time reaching anybody. But...Hi, oh my gosh. Hi, hi, hi. I miss you so much!"

Guilt popped up as I recognized that my enthusiasm didn't match hers. I wondered why I had the urge to mirror Ang's feeling, under the circumstances. *I'll just blame that on my fucked-up childhood. The root is probably in there somewhere. Holy shit, I have a lot to talk to my therapist about next time.* I ran my hand over my face and took a breath before responding.

"I've been worried about you," I said, and it wasn't a lie.

"I'm okay. They've got me segregated, so it's been really lonely mostly. And the food is all mystery meat, starches, and canned veggies. Not doing my fitness any favors."

I snorted. "Sounds like chow hall food in the Army back in the day. I'm glad you're not in with the general population. That makes me feel better. Have you gotten a chance to talk to Kate yet?"

"No. Haven't reached her." Disappointment hung heavy in Ang's tone.

"Well, she's doing okay. She's just been working a lot, as usual."

"You guys are still in contact?"

"Yes, of course. Isn't that what you wanted? Your metamours to have a fulfilling meta relationship and all that?"

"Well, yeah. I guess I just feel really isolated in here."

"You were right. She is a pretty cool chick. We get along well."

Ang didn't have a response to this, which seemed backward to how she was prior to her arrest. I guess I couldn't blame her. She was locked up and cut off from those closest to her.

I cleared my throat.

"So, any word yet on what the DA is planning? Do you have a private attorney or a public defender? What do I need to know?"

"What do you know already?" Her tone had an edge to it.

"All I know is what Sergeant Brickhouse and Deputy Rocha have told me. But I'd really love to hear your side of things."

"I can't get into it over the phone. They listen in and record our calls. Hi, Deputy Florence, I hope this call is entertaining for you. Anyway, I've asked to have you cleared for my visitor list, but they said since you were a witness to Crystal's past shenanigans and they still consider you a potential witness to this new bullshit, you can't visit me. But they will allow Kate to visit. Just wish I could get a hold of her to let her know. And of course, I can't write you a letter about my side of things because they read our mail."

"So, basically you're saying there's no way for you to tell me your side of the story right now?"

"Pretty much."

I grunted sardonically. "Hey, Deputy Florence, out there in space with your headphones on listening in, I want it noted for the record that this is bullshit."

There was silence, but I assumed that Deputy Florence was rolling his eyes.

"So, Ang, what now?"

"Without getting into detail, just take everything they tell you with a grain of salt. Remember who I am and what my morals are. Then consider Crystal and Johnny, and what their morals are."

"Of course. I give no credence to what Johnny and Crystal have to say. But, Ang, what about all the women who were rescued? What about what they are all saying about you?"

"Wait, what? What are they saying about me?" Ang raised her voice with a level of ferocity I had never heard her take on before.

In that moment, I heard a click, and a man's voice cut in.

"Time's up, inmate."

The connection went dead.

I stared down at my phone.

"What the fuck?" I said to my empty studio. I looked up at the ceiling. "What the fuck?" I growled to my upstairs neighbor since he was the only human nearby. He continued to pace, undeterred.

Kate, Kate, Kate. I need to talk to Kate.

Chapter Twenty-Nine

I had managed to get hold of Kate and thankfully our schedules lined up so that we could get together for a motorcycle ride. We bombed out the back roads to Monticello Dam and then back down to Lake Solano, just like we had before.

The park was deserted, so we snagged the same bench as the last time, right near the water's edge. The air was much cooler than before, so we both kept our jackets on. I offered up some snacks and we sat side by side quietly gazing out at the calm water and nibbling on protein bars, almonds, and bananas. We passed a thermos of peppermint tea back and forth. A group of ducks drifted by on the lazy current. The reeds rustled and a car rumbled over the small bridge nearby. I hated to break the peaceful moment but couldn't hold it in anymore.

"I spoke with Ang," I said, keeping my voice calm and low.

"Oh?"

"There's not much to report. She couldn't say much over the phone. I'm not allowed to visit her, but you are. If you want."

Kate didn't respond right away. She kept her gaze on the far bank, her eyes following the travels of one very agitated squirrel.

"Maybe," she said vaguely before abruptly changing the topic. "So, your brother. Wow."

"Yeah, wow is right."

"I am so glad your friend Jared was there. And of course, Buck and her trusty Maglite."

"Yup, Jared's a good guy. And Buck never shies away from kicking a hater out of the bar, family or not. They've both dealt with my brother plenty of times."

"Hmm," she said, tilting her head, eyes still on the far bank.

"So, about Ang. What should we do?"

Kate turned in her spot on the bench to face me and I met her brown eyes. She brushed a wisp of hair off her forehead. "There's not much to be done at this point. The DA has the burden of proof. So, we wait and let this thing run its course."

I drew in a breath and considered what she had said. "But what do we do about Ang right now? Just abandon her in jail until her trial if that's where this thing goes?"

"I don't have an answer to that, Viv," she said and turned back to face the small lake.

I didn't know what to say, so I said nothing. Kate shifted in her seat, and I realized she also had something to share.

"I didn't tell you this when we talked in your studio before, because I hadn't put two and two together yet, but I saw them. The girls the police freed during the sting operation. They were brought into my hospital. I saw them. I triaged some of them. A couple were in very dire straits. The others were pretty malnourished and traumatized. What do I do with that? Knowing that my primary partner, who I trust and love deeply, may have been very much responsible for their trauma and injuries? What do I do with that?" she asked.

Shocked by that news, I put my arm around her and pulled her close to me. She rested her head on my shoulder. I drew in the smell of leather from our jackets as I considered what to say, but I was too gobsmacked to come up with something comforting to say. The last time we had sat on that bench together, she had shared some words with me, and it was time for me to return them.

"For what it's worth, whatever happens with all of this, Kate, you're going to be okay."

We sat in silence again, under the canopy of an ancient oak tree, watching turtles sunning on a log while uncertainties flitted around in our heads.

*

The cold evening air crept into the gaps of my riding jacket as I throttled my motorcycle across the Yolo Causeway, heading back to Sacramento. Kate was so petite I barely noticed her on the back seat of the bike, but I did notice when she went limp behind me. Her full body weight suddenly pressed against my back and her hand hung next to my thigh. I pulled out of traffic onto the shoulder near the Harbor Boulevard exit and popped the kickstand down. I reached my hand back and grabbed a fistful of her leather jacket to steady her as I slid off the bike. My adrenaline surged as I flipped open the visor of my helmet and turned to face her. Her chin slumped down to her chest and her foot slid off the peg.

"Kate," I shouted at her over the rush of cars flying by on the freeway.

Her head lolled slightly and then slumped back down.

"Hey! Kate," I shouted again, this time grasping her chin under the helmet and raising her head up. Her eyes fluttered open and she gave me a confused frown as her hands flapped up weakly to my hand where it held the front of her jacket.

"Whoa. Are you okay?" I asked as she looked around, getting her bearings. Her brown eyes blinked heavily behind her visor.

"Uh. Yeah. I'm fine. I just...I think I fell asleep." Her voice was thick with sleep and muffled inside the helmet.

"Fell asleep? On the back of a speeding motorcycle?" I said. A big rig pulling two massive trailers rumbled by, whipping us with a bitter cold blast of air. I let go of the front of her jacket and, thankfully, she stayed upright, propping her foot back up on the peg.

"Yeah. Sorry. I used to fall asleep on the back of my dad's bike all the time when I was a teenager. He would tether me to him with an old belt. I probably should have warned you about that."

Pursing my lips, I shook my head in wonder at her, not really knowing what to say.

She raised her hand up to tuck her hair behind her ear but dropped it quickly as she realized she still had a helmet on. "I am sleep deprived from long shifts at the hospital, and with everything that's been going on with Ang, I guess I'm just worn out."

"I totally understand. You're burning the candle at both ends. But hey, we aren't stopped in the safest spot. Are you okay to ride the rest of the way to my place?" She nodded in the affirmative and shook her arms in front of her to get the blood pumping. I hopped back on my bike, gravel crunching under my boot.

We made the short ride back to my studio. I pulled into the underground garage and my assigned spot. The subterranean garage was freezing, and Kate's breath misted in the air as she pulled off her helmet and handed it to me.

"Thanks for the ride and chat, Viv. I appreciate you."

"Do you want to come upstairs and thaw out for a little bit?"

"No, thanks. I think I just want to head home and take a nice hot bath and crash." She slipped out of the jacket I had lent her and handed it over. She reached across the bike saddle and hugged me. I wasn't able to hug her back since I was juggling two helmets and a jacket but pressed my cheek against hers to make up for it.

Kate headed out of the pedestrian gate that led to Twenty-fourth Street, and I headed for the lobby door. I stopped at the door and turned to look at Ang's car. A Subaru that was normally out on adventures instead sat there parked and sad, covered in dust. Another reminder of Ang's absence.

Once inside, I bounded up the lobby stairs two at a time. I paused momentarily in front of Ang's door. The black numbers stared back at me vacantly.

"Dammit, Ang," I said to the dingy-white door, and strode away.

My studio greeted me with a hollow sterility that was usually comforting, but on that day, I could have used something a bit warmer and more welcoming.

While putting away all the riding gear, I listened to the symphony of my studio; the fish tank filter burbling away, the light-rail alarm clanging outside, and my upstairs neighbor pacing relentlessly.

I stripped out of my clothes and filled the tub. As I slid down into the hot water, my cold feet burned with the abrupt temperature change. Being that it was a small apartment tub, I couldn't exactly submerge myself all the way, but I was grateful for it and watched the steam rise from the surface of the water.

*

My face, throat, and lungs burned with an intensity I hadn't felt before in my home state of California. Sucking in the bitter cold air in the darkness of a winter morning in South Carolina was a painful relief as I ran in Group A with my platoon. Group A was designated for the fast runners, and for the first time, I cursed myself for pushing so hard during fitness testing and landing myself in that running group.

Snow drifted lazily down around and on top of us. I was the third runner in the second column. Steam streamed off the heads and shoulders of the soldiers running in front of me. Their foggy breath, visible each time they exhaled, flowed back to me. The pace was difficult to maintain on the slippery road, and I couldn't quite catch my breath. Each inhale sliced at my throat and lungs but brought the relief of oxygen with it that my body needed. Fuck, I muttered to myself. The soldier in front of me grunted his agreement.

Running in the dark and snow, wearing our shitty light-gray PT sweats, black beanies, and black leather gloves was a lesson in itself. Not one article of clothing we had been issued was appropriate for weather that cold. But I took solace in the anonymity of running in the middle of a formation in the dark. The drill sergeants were barking at us, but by being buried in the orderly heap of bodies running down the road I had the luxury of letting my mind drift a bit.

I snapped back when the soldier to my left let out a yelp and immediately slowed, causing a log jam of people behind her. She hobbled out of the formation and the runners behind her filled the gap, swallowing up the hole she had left behind. Ah hell, *I thought to myself, knowing she was in my squad and I couldn't leave her behind. I tapped the soldier to my left to let him know I wanted out and did a quick do-si-do with him without losing our stride. I was spit out of the formation and spotted the soldier who had fallen out. She was attempting to jog solo. Group A pulled unceasingly away ahead of us. Behind her I could see Group B turning the corner onto the main road.*

She caught up to me and I grabbed her arm and draped it across my shoulders so I could carry the weight on her injured side. She nodded and we began shuffling up the road.

"Thanks, Chastain," she said, strain in her voice.

"No worries. What's hurt, Tucci?" I asked her, coughing as the cold air hit my throat. I spat and saliva flooded my mouth.

"My fuckin' knee. Dunno what happened. I was trucking along just fine and pow, something in the back of my knee exploded."

"Damn, that doesn't sound good. You okay to keep on going till we get to the barracks?"

"No other choice," she said through gritted teeth.

"Too easy," I replied, using the now familiar term. I heard a solo set of footsteps fast approaching behind us and knew it had to be Cadre, and unfortunately, I was correct. Right on cue, the shouting began.

"Sweet baby Jesus, what in the hell is this! Isn't this a cute little cuddle session! Taking a nice stroll in the park, eh? Do you two females want some lemonade and cookies when you're done with your walk?"

I knew the voice. He pulled up level with us and slowed his pace so he could yell at us up close and personal. I spoke up to draw attention away from Tucci.

"No, First Sergeant," I said back as loudly as I dared. There is a fine line between insubordinate shouting and actually calling out as loud as they expected you to.

"Well. Two fallouts from third platoon, is it? Lovely. Freakin' lovely!"

Neither of us spoke. Tucci and I continued jogging as fast as Tucci could manage. I gripped her arm tighter and picked up more of her weight to help her along.

"Soldiers, remove your tags and hand them over!" What he hadn't said was to stop moving, so we awkwardly pulled our dog tags out from under our sweatshirts, up over our heads, and handed them over to him while still on the move. First Sergeant swiped the dog tags out of our hands and picked his pace back up, leaving us in his wake.

We were passed up by Group B and the drill sergeant who was running with them. They didn't even acknowledge us. As Tucci and I jogged up to the barracks we were greeted by the first sergeant, dangling our dog tags from his fingertip. The rest of our company was already going through the cool down and stretching routine. I released Tucci's hand and let her stand on her own. We plucked our dog tags off First Sergeant's finger. I placed mine over my head and dropped the tag under my shirt. The metal was icy cold and burned as it hit my hot skin.

"Enjoy your walk?" he shouted, even though we were standing directly in front of him. I hesitated to answer, as questions like that from Cadre were always a trick. No matter what you said you would be punished. I was still panting from my exertions. Before either Tucci or I could blurt out a reply, First Sergeant got the jump on us.

"Front leaning rest position. Move." I bit back a groan that nearly escaped me, and immediately got down into front leaning rest position. Tucci complied as well, but much more slowly, and was favoring her injured leg. First Sergeant proceeded to smoke us so hard I had snot dripping down my lip and sweat blossoming all over my face despite the cold. I coughed until I gagged. Push-ups, side straddle hops, burpees. Up and down, up and down. Over and over again until Tucci couldn't take the pain anymore and melted into a sobbing pile on the concrete.

"All right, Chastain. Take Tucci to sick call," he said and strode off toward the chow hall. The smell of bacon was in the air now, and despite overwhelming nausea from the exertion, my appetite was ravenous. One thing about basic training...I was always starving. Every minute of every day.

"Come on, Tucci. Let's get you to sick call," I said as gently as I could and placed a hand under her shoulder to help her stand. She struggled up, stifling a whimper. The sun had begun to rise, and the clouds had cleared. Steam was rising off a wooden bench where the sunlight hit it. A wooden bench no basic training soldier would ever actually be allowed to sit on.

*

The water in my bathtub had long gone cold, and I shivered as the memory faded. I drained the tub and stood up, turned on the shower as hot as I could manage, and stood under the water until my skin was red and I was warm to my core again.

Chapter Thirty

After a few hours of restless sleep, I was up with the sun, muscles tight and sore. I spent some time stretching and getting warmed up and then went into the bathroom where I peed and got into some running gear. On my way out, I tapped a few flakes into the fish tank. The communal corridor outside my studio was freezing cold. As I locked the door my landlord walked out of his apartment, looking like he'd been on a week-long meth bender, which was probably accurate. His skin was waxy, his clothes were stained and wrinkled, and his beard was more askew than normal.

"Hiya, Vivian," he said as he walked by. I turned to face him.

"Good morning, Paul. It's mighty cold out here in the hallway."

"Welp, it's an old building. They didn't install central HVAC."

"Okay, see ya," I said, not wanting to make small talk with him. He stank worse than he looked. Heading for the stairs, I heard him over my shoulder.

"Hey, uh, Vivian? You're friends with the woman from unit one-oh-one, right? I've seen her going into your studio."

"Yes, I know Ang," I replied, not caring to share any more than that.

"I haven't seen her in a long time. Her rent is on auto-bill so that hasn't been an issue. Just worried about her is all."

Hmph, I doubted he ever worried about any of his tenants so long as they paid rent and didn't burn the place down.

I continued walking toward the stairs, considering how much I should share with him. Not much, I decided, and patted door #101 as I started going down the stairs.

"She's out of town," I said over my shoulder and took the stairs two at a time. Technically it wasn't a lie. She was in fact out of town. There were things he didn't need to know, like she was my girlfriend and she was in jail, accused of a litany of charges related to running a sex trafficking ring.

I shoved open the lobby door, hopped up the steps to the sidewalk, and started to jog. It had often proven difficult to go for a run during morning rush hour in Midtown, but my body needed to move. I ran up *Q* Street and hooked a left on Alhambra. All the stop lights frustrated me, but I eventually made my way to McKinley Park and was much happier once I hit the path at the park. Out of the crush of cars, crosswalks, and tempers my thoughts were free to roam.

Oh, Ang. She had pushed my boundaries at every turn. So much so, that I knew deep down I should have ended the relationship early on.

I turned the corner on the running path and jogged past the dormant rose garden. When those rosebushes bloomed it was mighty impressive. Kate and I had run that path together a number of times. She and I were both in a tough spot, wondering what to do about Ang. We both were absolutely shocked by her arrest and what she was accused of. And the question of "now what?" loomed large, as we both waffled back and forth on whether to stand by Ang through her trial or break it off.

I turned the corner and ran along the edge of the pond and past the library. After a few more laps I wove my way back through Midtown, relieved that rush hour traffic had dissipated.

Back at my studio, I found I had a text from Kate:

> Good Morning. On my way over with tea and muffins.

I hit the reply button and began typing a response when my apartment phone rang. It was Kate at the lobby door. I buzzed her in and waited in my doorway for her. The icy air in the hallway gave me chills as my sweaty body cooled down.

"Good morning," Kate said cheerily, her hands full.

"Great timing, I'm just back from a run. Here, let me help you with that." I took the cups of tea and a reusable fabric shopping bag from her. "I'd hug you, but I am totally gross right now." She nodded and kissed my cheek as she passed through the door and made herself at home, slipping off her hospital clogs and her jacket. She had on some snug black scrubs, with a gray cotton long-sleeve shirt underneath. Being an endurance and racing cyclist, she had practically no body fat, which forced her to dress in many layers for work.

We sat down on my futon and sipped on the hot herbal tea she had brought.

"Thank you," I said, incredibly grateful for how thoughtful she was.

"You're welcome. I also brought some muffins, from New Helvetia," she said as she pulled them out of the bag.

"You're a saint. How was work? Looks like you were on last night."

"Yes, I got called in to cover last night. I have a couple of hours off and then have to go back in."

I shook my head but knew she didn't mind it. She was a workaholic and had student loans she'd been dead set on paying off.

We fell into a comfortable silence. Wind whistled outside and I got another chill, goose bumps popping up on my quads and arms. I got up and swapped out my sweaty wet shirt for a fresh dry one and pulled on sweatpants over my shorts. As I came out of the bathroom Kate fixed me with a sharp look. I sat back down on the futon and tilted my head to the side, wondering what was on her mind.

"I'm going to go visit Ang, probably tomorrow," she said as she massaged the back of her neck.

I turned my body so that I was facing her and patted my lap. She knew the drill and put her feet in my lap. I pulled off her socks and went to work massaging her foot.

"That's great! I am sure she will be really happy to see you. When I talked to her, they still had her separated from the general population. She must be lonely."

"Yea, maybe. I just need to know her side. I can't carry on not knowing what she has to say about all of this. I just...I can't in good conscience stay involved with her if there's a chance she actually did what they say she did."

I nodded and switched over to massaging her other foot. She gave a grateful groan and sipped her tea.

"Agreed. They still won't let me visit her. She won't put anything in writing in a letter because they screen her mail and won't tell me anything on the phone because they monitor her calls. I'm in the dark."

"I just need to know," Kate said, flapping her hand sharply to emphasize her point. Clearly Ang's situation was cracking Kate's normally calm disposition. "I just keep thinking back to the night the police freed all of the women Crystal had kept captive and forced into sex work. We blocked off a whole section of the ER for them so they could all be evaluated and treated. The looks on those young women's faces. That night will forever be burned on my brain. And if Ang had anything to do with it...I just can't even imagine it. I never thought Ang would be capable of something like that. In the time I've known her, her ethics and morals always seemed steadfast and unflappable. She's a cop, for heck's sake."

Kate pounded her fist into her hand, the sound startling me. She shook her head and drew in a deep breath, held it, and blew it out. Then nodded. With that cleansing breath Kate's face went from angry and exhausted to calm and clear.

"Not all cops are good people. Just look at Jon Burge and Joseph Miedzianowski from Chicago PD. Fuck those guys—"

"Please don't use profanity, Viv."

"Okay. Sorry. I mean, I agree with you that Ang seemed to be above board, seemed to share the same ethics as me. I never doubted her, never thought her capable of something like this. But here we are." I finished up massaging Kate's feet and slipped her socks back on.

Midmorning light filtered in through the window, landing on Kate, ten years my senior. Delicate crow's feet huddled at the corners of her eyes. More wrinkles clung to her forehead and cheeks. Being a cyclist meant she spent a lot of time out in full sun, and her lack of body fat added to it, causing her skin to stretch tightly over her cheekbones. Her bun had started to come loose, and a few strands of her hair hung against her cheek. She swiped absently at it and hooked the lock of hair behind her ear as she considered what I had said.

"I'm going to head home and take a quick nap before my next shift," she said as she got up from the futon and gathered her things.

"Okay. Hey, thanks, Kate. I appreciate you stopping by. If appropriate, will you let me know how it goes with Ang tomorrow?" I followed Kate to the door and opened it for her. She gave me a smile and a hug.

"Of course. Be well, Vivian."

*

The week passed by in a flash as I went through my usual routine. Run, work, sleep, repeat. I had a day off midweek and took a long motorcycle ride along Lake Berryessa to Napa and the coast. The ride was frigid and uncomfortable, but I needed to be on the move. I ate my lunch while sitting on the deserted wet sand of Goat Rock Beach, the ice-cold wind whipping around me. Thankfully, my riding gear was relatively wind and damp proof. I watched the waves, fought off pushy seagulls vying for my sandwich, and sipped on lukewarm tea from my thermos. After lunch, I brushed the wet sand from my ass and headed back to Sacramento, grateful for the heated grips on my bike and wishing for a heated seat.

Kate and Ang were on my mind much of that week as I waited to hear from Kate on how their visit went. By Friday, word hadn't come, but I didn't want to press her for an update. *She's probably just busy with work*, was what I told myself whenever I checked my phone and found no messages. I couldn't help but have a twinge of upset that a person I had grown close to potentially had big news that impacted us both and hadn't reached out.

Saturday, I woke up to a massive rainstorm. Wind gusts drummed the rain against my window and brought down what was left of the leaves on the trees on Twenty-fourth Street. My mouth was mossy and the insides of my cheeks burned. I had chewed them to a pulp in my sleep. I untangled from the blankets and went into the bathroom to swish and spit mouthfuls of water in the bathroom sink. Each had less and less blood until the water I spit out was clear. I ran my tongue over the grooves I chewed into my cheeks and tried to remember the last time I had had such a rough night's sleep.

I grabbed a yogurt and my cell phone before bundling back up in my blankets on the futon. As I flipped the phone open, I was surprised to see what time it was—already after 2:00 p.m. I'd slept ten hours, which was nearly double what I normally got. The surprise was immediately pushed aside by relief when I saw that I had a text from Kate. I sat with a spoonful of vanilla yogurt suspended midway between my mouth and the yogurt cup as I read her text.

Hiya Vivian. Busy week. Let me know when you're up. I'd like to call you during my afternoon break to talk about Ang.

I shoved the spoon into my mouth to free up my hand and hurriedly texted Kate that I was up and available to talk.

I finished breakfast, did some stretching and a core workout, and then puttered around washing dishes and dusting. I kept the cell phone in the pocket of my sweatpants so I wouldn't miss Kate's call. And sure enough, my phone began to ring late in the afternoon.

"This is Vivian."

"Hey, Vivian. I'm on break so don't have too much time to chat, but really wanted to touch base with you." I could hear announcements over the hospital's intercom system in the background.

"Of course, thanks for calling. What's up?"

"I made it out to Diablo County Jail to visit Ang. It's taken me this long just to process it all." She took in a breath and I heard a chair creak through the phone. I knew my job right then was to shut up and listen, and that's what I did. She spoke when she was ready.

"She looked good. Though being indoors around the clock and not being able to work out the way she likes has had an impact on her overall appearance. She's sort of deflated, folding in on herself." Kate paused before pushing on, "We had some small talk and got caught up on current events in our lives. Near the end, she finally broached the subject of the charges against her. She firmly denied all of it. And she made a good point. She pointed out that Crystal's operation was run out of an entirely different county and region. Crystal was based in Diablo County. How the hell could Ang have had the time or access to work for Crystal between working twelve-hour shifts at the sheriff's department here, training for the century ride, and two girlfriends? And why would she get involved in something like that in the first place?" Kate stopped there, which gave me a moment to absorb and consider what she had said. I heard footsteps on tile pass by her and more announcements on the hospital's intercom system. Her chair squeaked again.

"May I ask a question?"

"Of course."

"What about all of the women freed from Crystal? Sergeant Brickhouse said they all ID-ed Ang as having been involved in their capture and confinement."

"Yea. I wondered about that, too, and she addressed it. She is emphatic that she is being set up, but she wouldn't go into details about it."

"Okay. And after spending time with her in person you feel like that's the case? That she didn't do it and is being set up?"

"Yes. No doubt about it."

I rolled that around in my brain for a moment. "Welp, I'll trust your intuition and her word on it. I guess I'm still on Team Ang. I should probably write to her."

"Yes, she would like that. She asked about you."

"Thanks for the update, Kate. Let's get together soon."

"You're welcome, Viv. Yup, see you soon."

She hung up just as I heard a code being called over the intercom. I was certain she was already running off to go help. *I fucking love nurses.*

And there it was. Kate trusted Ang's side of the story. While I had told Kate I was on Team Ang, doubts still lingered. I hadn't been in the room. Hadn't had a chance to see Ang's body language as she spoke or hear how her voice fluctuated. What if she was a really skilled liar and was conning Kate? I figured I had those doubts because Ang hadn't always been exactly forthright and trustworthy in our own relationship. I would support Kate in her belief that Ang was innocent, but I wasn't convinced.

*

Chores and phone call finished, I checked outside and saw that the rain had let up, though angry rainclouds huddled to the west. I got dressed and was on the way out of the door when my cell phone rang again. The screen showed that it was my mother. I let out a groan.

"Yes, Mother?"

"Hello, Vivian."

"I am headed out. What's up?"

"What's up?" She drew out the words as though they tasted disgusting. Truly unpalatable to her. "I am calling to ask if you have gone to visit your brother at his rehabilitation facility?"

"No, Mother, I have not gone to visit Joey. And I will not. We have already been through this."

Bernadette huffed angrily into the phone, pushing her frustration and disappointment through the cell phone signal to me. I rolled my eyes and my body grew cold as the frigid air from the corridor outside my studio flooded into my studio and right through my clothes.

"Mom, I am on the way out. I need to go."

"Vivian. You've got to go visit your brother. It is your duty as his sister to support him."

"No, it is not. Not when he has been my lifelong abuser."

She scoffed loudly at that.

"Not when you forced him into rehab. I will support him when he decides, on his own, that it's something he actually wants to do for himself. How many times have you forced him into rehab only for him to be a drunken pile within twenty-four hours of being released? Never mind, don't answer that. We both know the answer. I'm going now. Goodbye." I disconnected the call, jammed the cell phone into my pocket, and headed out to my truck.

The streets were wide open, and for good reason. As soon as I buckled my seat belt the clouds opened up with a massive downpour and the wind came back full force. I changed my mind about going out and dashed back to the building, getting completely soaked in the process.

The ice-cold air in the corridor outside my apartment hit my drenched clothes and pushed me into instant and brutal full-body shivers. As soon as I entered my studio I stripped down and got into a hot shower.

Jared came to mind. Jared, who I hadn't heard from in a while. Jared, who had been my best friend for many years, but things had become awkward. I decided to call him as soon as I got out of the shower. Shutting off the tap, I took pause because I still heard the sound of running water. Sliding open the glass shower door, I saw water pouring from the light fixture and exhaust fan, and pooling on the floor.

"God damn it! Come on! Really?"

I shouted so loudly that my throat was instantly raw. I yanked a towel off the towel rod and wrapped it around my waist. I didn't even bother covering my top half, since my hair was long enough to reach my nipples. I heard hurried footsteps upstairs as my neighbor rushed to shut off his overflowing bathtub.

I stormed out into the corridor and down to the manager's apartment. I pounded on his door relentlessly, to no avail. The icy air nipped at my body, but I was too irate to care. I continued my rampage up the stairs to the second floor and began pounding on my upstairs neighbor's door.

He opened the door sheepishly and his mouth dropped open as he saw me. Naked, wearing only a towel around my waist, black hair dripping and askew, tattoos everywhere, and no doubt my face was curled into some kind of horror show of anger. He began to close the door, clearly assuming I was a maniac. I jammed my bare foot into the door. The smell of pot and overflowing ashtrays wafting out from his studio.

"Dude. How many fucking times are you going to overflow your fucking bathtub before you start paying attention to it? *Enough*! I have had *enough*! *No* more! I'm *done*. Never again, do you hear me?"

He nodded and scrubbed at his unshaven chin with nicotine-stained fingers. I tried not to place judgment on his sallow skin and greasy, unkempt hair. He certainly needed the bath he was running. I heard several doors up and down the hallway open, and saw people popping their heads out to see what was going on. Letting them all get a look at me, I stormed back down to my own studio to clean up the deluge in my bathroom and get dressed for work.

I'd lost all the warmth in my body from the hot shower and shivered as I got into my work clothes. It took me far longer than usual to calm down. I had been working on my temper with Alexia and hadn't popped off like that in quite some time. *What is going on with you, Vivi?*

Once dressed, I forced myself to sit down on the futon and dial up Jared. His phone went straight to voice mail, but it wasn't his usual recording in his familiar deep voice. Rather it was the generic robot stating that the number dialed couldn't answer and to leave a message. I didn't leave a message.

Work was the usual controlled chaos, the place packed despite the rainstorm. Sheila had set up a coat check station in the closet under the stairs, complete with a cute little baby dyke working it. I could tell she was nervous, probably her first time working in a club. She had gone all out, wearing a dress shirt and tie, her short hair slicked back. I smirked as I thought how the cougars would eat her alive. *Good luck, kid.*

Even though the club was a lesbian space, a few gay men were regulars. They preferred the energy in our club to what some of the other gay clubs in town had to offer. And we had Sloan.

There was a new guy hanging around that night. He didn't seem to be with Sloan or any of the male regulars and didn't appear to be a guest of any of the women in the club. He was sitting by himself at a table near my station, nursing a bottle of water he hadn't bought from me. He was gangly, with long skinny arms and legs. He sported some shaggy carrot-colored hair and had freckles and a sad attempt at a goatee on his pale face. I always felt bad for redheaded guys who had that particular hair color. I had seen boys with orange hair get teased and bullied relentlessly in grade school. And this guy had an air about him of defeat and lack of confidence to match his slumped posture. His clothes were simple. Well-worn jeans, a ratty checked flannel shirt, and tired old sneakers. His attire didn't match the clubbing outfits most everybody else was wearing, so he truly stuck out. Hypervigilance was one thing that lingered from my time in the military, and I couldn't help but keep an eye on the guy.

He didn't mingle or talk to anyone. He even brushed off Sloan when Sloan attempted to chat him up. It soon became apparent that he was attempting to eavesdrop...on me. He was trying to look at me without my seeing, but I saw. It was pretty pathetic, actually. Every time the music stopped and someone talked to me he leaned in, but did his best to act like he wasn't listening.

At one point, Jen came bebopping behind the bar, swinging her wallet chain around her finger, all sass and good vibes, doing a hoppy little dance move. She slapped my ass as she passed behind me and hollered "Vivviannnnn! Whoop!" before she got busy stacking fresh glasses on the shelves for me. I happened to be watching my watcher when that happened, and his eyes lit up when Jen hollered my name. My guess was he was trying to get a clear ID on me, because after he had heard my name he stood up and wove his way through the crowd to the exit. I engraved his face, posture, and stature in my mind because I figured I would be seeing him again. And I wasn't wrong.

After work, I drove home but ended up having to park farther than usual, which I didn't like since it was damn near 4:00 a.m. and dark. My tip money was tucked away in my boot. I pulled my stun gun out of my tip bucket, turned off the safety with my thumb, and tucked it discreetly into my hand.

The street was mostly deserted, but I saw a man standing in the middle of the sidewalk between me and the entrance to my building, right under the streetlight. He stared at me, not moving. I automatically thought it was one of the unhoused guys who slept in the alley, but a moment later, it registered that the person on the path was the weaselly-looking guy who had been watching me at work earlier. *What the fuck*? was my first thought, and then that old, deep-seated rage rose up in me. Whatever that guy wanted from me, I didn't care. In that moment, I was dead set on harming him before he could harm me. Adrenaline dumped into my system and my chest exploded with crackling electricity. I was trained for that shit, and an old part of me enjoyed it.

I held eye contact with him and found he did not look very sure of himself. Like maybe he was expecting me stop since he was barring my way. But since he was blocking the sidewalk and not moving, I assumed ill intent and acted accordingly.

The cool plastic of the stun gun felt good in my hand. Rather than stop or slow down, I began sprinting toward him. As I closed the gap, staring him right in the eyes, he got a sudden look of panic. His pale face drained of color. Clearly my behavior wasn't what he had anticipated. I smiled at him, and in response he gave me a confused look, his poor excuse for a goatee framing his thin frowning lips.

Pacing it out in my head, I leaped up just as I reached him, and shot my left hand out as I blew past him. I pressed the button on the stun gun and zapped him right in the throat, smack dab on his big bobbing Adam's apple. The satisfying crackle of the stun gun made me smile. I didn't even lose a step as I landed on the concrete. He let out a short squeal and I heard him hit the ground. I carried on down the steps to the lobby and unlocked the door.

I flipped the safety back on with my thumb and put the stun gun back in my tip bucket. My building was exceptionally secure, so I wasn't concerned about him making an attempt to come inside and accost me that night.

Chapter Thirty-One

The next morning, I was up, excited despite only having about three hours of sleep. I was keen to get out on the trails. I slid open the blinds and was glad to find the sky was blue and cloudless. Touching the window glass, I found it was icy cold, which told me I needed to dress in layers. I packed a lunch in my small cooler, shoved the usual gear and snacks in my day pack, filled up a couple of bottles of water, fed the fish, dressed myself and clipped the stun gun and my folding knife to the waistband of my trusty hiking pants. The same knife Crystal had jacked from me and slashed my truck tire with. I smirked because she was in prison and I was going for a hike. Last, I slid a trail map in my back pocket. I had set a goal for myself to hike every single trail at Briones, so each time I hiked there I used a highlighter to mark off the trail I had hiked. It helped to have the marked map in my pocket so while out on the trails I knew which trails I still needed to explore.

It was smooth going on the freeways. I jumped off at Pinole and wove my way out the back roads to Briones. After parking, I hopped out of my truck and stretched, and then pulled my hiking boots out and sat on my truck's tailgate to change into hiking socks and boots. I slid on my day pack and locked up the truck. There was only one other car in the lot. An orange Subaru with a roof rack. I saw that car almost every time I went to the Bear Creek

Staging area. The man was methodically going through safety checks on his mountain bike, as I had seen him do before. He was a super fit, super handsome African American man with a shaved head and dressed in spandex cycling gear. While we had never spoken to each other, he always gave me a nod in passing. Otherwise the lot was empty, though I saw plenty of cars in the other lots at the trail heads farther down Briones Valley Road.

I used an outhouse on my way to the Abrigo Valley trail head and then crossed through the gate and hit the trail. The trails were muddy from the rainstorm over the weekend, and I loved it. Briones was truly my happy place.

Abrigo Valley Trail was designated by East Bay Regional Park District as an "easy hiking option." It was a wide, well graded track with very mild inclines. It led to harder trails I had not hiked yet, so I had just shy of a one-mile warm-up on that trail before shit got real. There were plenty of prints on the muddy track: dogs, kid's shoes, adult-sized sneakers and hiking boots, cow and horse hooves, mountain bike tires. I heard a jangling dog collar ahead and spotted a filthy, joyous Irish Setter come bounding around the corner of the trail. He gave me a quick sniff as he ran by, but didn't stop, continuing on the way I had just come. I rounded the corner and saw his owner jogging along. We crossed paths, exchanging a friendly "Good morning." I carried on until I got to sign marker #8. I stopped and had a few sips of water, checking the map. Motts Peak Trail. One thing I had learned about the hiking trail naming conventions at that park...any trails with the words Peak, Ridge, or Crest in their names were guaranteed to have some brutal inclines. But the reward for all that hard work was always the view. Briones never failed to reward me with spectacular views.

I stowed my water, snapped the chest strap on my pack, and turned on to Mott Peak Trail, which immediately switched from a nice, wide, well graded trail to a narrow uneven track. A narrow uneven track that climbed a steep hillside. *Fuck yes. Here we go!* I grit my teeth and got going.

Mott Peak proved to be a worthy opponent that had me gasping for air with shaky burning legs. Eventually I reached sign marker #39 and turned onto Briones Crest Trail, which eventually gave me the reward I was looking for—wide-open views of Mount Diablo, the Carquinez Straight, and the lush green hillsides of the bluffs. I trudged along for quite some time, huge piles of mud caked to my boots, eventually peeling off at sign marker #70 to Seaborg trail. By that point, my legs and feet were feeling the miles and all the elevation I had climbed over the last couple of hours. I stretched out my legs and acknowledged that I was incredibly at peace. Every time I hiked there, no matter if it was the dead of winter or luscious springtime or dusty summer, I felt so connected to the hills and trails. It centered me. It calmed me. It challenged me.

I peeled off my long-sleeve shirt and jammed it into the crisscrossing bungee cord on the outside of the pack and headed down some super steep declines back into the valley.

Eventually the trail spit me out in another parking lot. It felt weird to have concrete under my boots again. My legs had an incredibly satisfying looseness to them that I always got after a challenging hike or run. The looseness would turn into some serious muscle soreness the next day if I wasn't careful. I stomped my boots, dislodging big clumps of mud.

A massive hunger took over me, and I was shaky. I picked up the pace as I walked across Briones Valley Road and closed in on my truck, which had my lunch in it.

And there, leaning against my back bumper, was the weaselly little shit I'd stun gunned in the throat less than twelve hours earlier. I was still a good fifty yards away, walking up the narrow spur road that led to the parking lot. He stood up as he saw me approaching, his eyes wide. I stopped when I was about twenty feet away and scanned the area. There were several people in the parking lot either getting ready to hit the trails or just getting back and going through the ritual of changing shoes, shedding layers, drinking water, or stretching.

"Over here," I called out to him, establishing command presence in my tone and posture.

He hesitated and then walked toward me. I scanned him as he approached. I didn't see any signs of weapons, and he didn't appear to be a physical threat to me, but I remained alert. He stopped just out of my reach.

Maybe he isn't as much of an idiot as I thought.

I was angry because he had invaded this sacred space and ruined the peace I had gained on my hike.

"What. The. Fuck. Do. You. Want?"

He stammered.

"You, you fucking twit. Everywhere I go, there you are. What the fuck do you want?" I hissed at him through clenched teeth.

He shifted his stance and stammered again. The kid looked frightened.

Good.

His wispy poor excuse for a goatee shook in the breeze.

My temper flared again. I clenched my fists, restraining the urge to pummel his stupid ass.

"What. The. Fuck. Do. You. Want?" I demanded again, spitting the words at him like nails.

"I-I'm supposed to bring you a message," he said, sounding unsure of himself.

I glanced over my shoulder quickly and scanned the area around us again. It felt like a set-up.

"And?" I shouted, glaring at him impatiently.

A family walked past us, heading for the open field near the picnic area. Their two dogs were off leash and making a mad dash for the grassy area. Two small children lagged behind, dragging toys. We waited until they were out of earshot.

He drew in a breath. I exhaled loudly. The man with the orange Subaru rolled past us lightning fast on his mountain bike, covered in mud, just back from his ride. He paused at his car to watch our exchange, making eye contact with me to check in that I was okay. I nodded at him, and his posture softened. Nice to know that someone else from the trails had my back.

Patience gone, I stepped toward the kid. I was a ball of violence ready to explode.

"*What do—?*"

He sniffled and closed his eyes, raising his hands, readying himself for my fist in his face. He sputtered, gathered himself, and shouted. "*Jared sent me!* He's in trouble."

Acknowledgements

This book began my journey as an author, and I could not have completed it without the support of many people, including my mentor Pat Henshaw, my tireless cheerleader J. Scott Coatsworth, the staff of the Lavender Library & Cultural Exchange, and the members of both the Queer Sacramento Authors Collective and the Bay Area Queer Writers Association.

Closer to home, I thank my son, my friends, and the rest of my family for their patience with me as I have chased this story down and wrestled it on to paper.

I would be remiss if I didn't thank my editor, Elizabeth Coldwell, for her thoughtful handling of this novel, and M.D. Neu for giving one last push that made a huge difference.

I'd also like to thank the East Bay Regional Parks District for being such good stewards of our public lands. Can I also thank a place? If so, I thank Briones Regional Park, whose trails have proven to be some of my biggest challenges, while also being my place of inspiration, and my soft place to land. I have literally shed blood, sweat, and tears at Briones, and I am all the better for it.

About the Author

Liz is a recovering workaholic who has mastered multitasking, including balancing a day job, solo parenting, writing, and finding some semblance of a social life. In past lives she has been a soldier, a bartender, a shoe salesperson, an assistant museum curator, and even a driving instructor.

Liz lives in the East Bay Area of California and enjoys exploring nature with her son.

Email: liz.faraim@gmail.com

Facebook: www.facebook.com/liz.faraim.9

Twitter: @FaraimLiz

Website: www.lizfaraim.com

Coming Soon from Liz Faraim

Stitches and Sepsis

"What. The. Fuck. Do. You. Want?"

The weaselly man, who looked like a damn scarecrow, stammered but didn't answer my question.

I hissed at him through clenched teeth. "You! You fucking twit. Everywhere I go, there you are. What the fuck do you want?"

He shifted his stance and stammered again. The crease between his eyebrows told me he was frightened.

Good.

His wispy, poor excuse for a goatee shook in the breeze. I clenched my fists, restraining the urge to pummel his stupid ass.

"Last chance," I said, spitting the words at him like nails.

"I-I'm supposed to bring you a message?" He sounded unsure of himself and I halfway hoped he pissed his pants a little.

"*And?*" I shouted, glaring at him impatiently.

He drew in a shaky breath. I exhaled loudly; my patience gone. A ball of violence, I stepped toward him. He sniffled and closed his eyes, raising his hands, readying himself for my fist in his face.

"*Jared sent me!* He's in trouble."

"Oh, really." I sneered at him, skeptical. "Jared sent the worst tracker ever to bring me a message? I doubt that very much."

"He told me you wouldn't believe me. He also told me you might kick my ass." He paused, rubbing two red marks on his throat where I had hit him with a stun gun the night before. "He told me to tell you you'd believe me if I said the words lemon tree."

I squinted at him, considering the phrase "lemon tree," and let out a bark of laughter. Embarrassed, he lowered his chin. I mulled the news over and watched the guy, making him wait while I took my time drinking water and eating some dried apricots from my hiking bag, trying to cover up the fact that my hands were shaking from low blood sugar.

He adjusted his weight from one foot, clad in a grubby worn-down shoe, to the other, and he rubbed his hands together as if he was washing them in a sink. The raspy sound of his skin annoyed me.

"Okay, fine. Lemon tree. That'll do. Who the fuck are you, and what's the message?"

"I'm nobody. What matters is that Jared got mixed up in a relationship with some whacked-out woman, and she won't let him have contact with anyone. Not friends. Not family." He started speaking faster. The floodgates had opened. "She only lets him go to work. He has to spend all of his time off with her. Like, he's practically her prisoner."

"I'm not a fan of the 'crazy girlfriend' misogynistic bullshit. What's really going on? I need details."

"She's fucking nuts, man."

I raised an eyebrow at him, and he cowed down a bit.

"Okay. Okay. Here's the deal. Right after they started dating last year she moved into his house. She is trying to get him to quit his job and work with her. And she is a drunk. She gets blackout drunk most nights. She pukes in the bed and on the floor on purpose...and she makes him clean it up every single time." He rumpled his shaggy hair and tugged at his baggy pants. "She won't let him out of her sight except for work or when he goes running. She won't even let him shower alone. Can you believe that shit?" His eyes flicked up to mine and spittle at the corners of his mouth glinted in the sun. "She has a rule that he can't jack off, and she thought he would do it in the shower since that was the only privacy he has left. So, they have to shower together now. It's beyond fucking insane."

Also Available from NineStar Press

Connect with NineStar Press

www.ninestarpress.com

www.facebook.com/ninestarpress

www.facebook.com/groups/NineStarNiche

www.twitter.com/ninestarpress

Made in the USA
Las Vegas, NV
15 August 2021